Hope you enjoy the book
Fenella! Helen x

Thirty Seconds
Before Midnight

By Helen J Beal

Published by Carapace 2012

Carapace
Acre House
11-15 William Road
London
NW1 3ER

www.carapacebooks.com

PART ONE
Chapter One

Digby clattered his little red hook of a beak on my shell the morning that I first saw the dominoes of my life topple. Over one went, tipping into another, knocking it onto the next. Several had gone already, escaping my notice, and though I was unable to see where they led, my instincts told me that at the end of them there was something thrilling; a climax of sorts, fireworks, perhaps.

The Source, She who sparks all life, had been up and shining for a while. She had gone to bed late the evening before, leaving me to wander the lazy heat She left behind, browsing and grazing. I'd fallen asleep in a long grassy clump, letting its cool fronds drape over my tucked up self.

I stuck my neck out and opened my dew-glazed eyes. I was rather chilly since, although the air was warming, the clump had kept me in the shade. Ambling out into the rays I rolled my eyes at Digby, who now bounced about in front of me, hopping from foot to foot.

'Herbert!' he squawked. He did have a terrible habit of squawking. It was most noticeable when he was a tad overexcited. I had a feeling he'd been at it for a while. He was sounding rather hoarse. 'Phew! You're awake.'

Digby was a parakeet, he would inform me. Incessantly. Very proud he was, too. And ever so exotic, apparently. His feathers were the colour of the newest, tastiest grass, although, in fact, they had very little flavour themselves and did tend to stick to my tongue. Digby did not like me nibbling on him but since he used to stand a bit too close he really only had himself to blame. He did like to perch on my shell, and he did like talking. He was a veritable stream of consciousness, Digby was.

'Digby… you weren't being sort of… hmm… hysterical again, were you?' Digby regularly thought that I had passed away in the night and would spin into panic. It was because I am a cold thing and all of my breathing gear's tucked neatly inside out of sight. All quite unnecessary but he was not the brightest of buttons, my little Digby. Still, it was sort of nice to know he cared.

One of my favourite games when I was bored and I hadn't seen him for ages, because he was, no doubt, off doing something far more interesting far, far away, was to wander over to the Wall and crawl up it just enough to tip myself backwards and land upside down on my back on the grass. I'd wiggle my legs around for a bit and then, when that became tedious, I'd fall asleep with all four of them and my neck splayed out. I have no idea how long it took him to find me; I just used to snooze. But when he did find me, he created the most dreadful palaver, flapping about, screeching and tugging at his plumage. I just lay there, chuckling to myself silently. He'd usually attract the attention of the zookeeper or the zookeeper's daughter and they'd come and flip me.

'No, no. No, absolutely not. Not at all! Not even a tiny teeny bit!' A kind of mania was enveloping dear Digby. 'But, please, get moving now! Something strange and very exciting is happening. You must see it! Now, or you could miss it!'

At this point ennui and anticipation-disappointed washed over me. Digby had only hatched the last but one Awakening so had only lived through a single Hibernation. I, on the other hand, had seen (well, slept through) a grand total of thirteen Hibernations by this point in time. Digby tells me they are super cold and sometimes white and he becomes quite hungry, so I am glad that I tuck up, unnatural as it might be for my particular species, who evolved in the tropics.

Apparently I am likely to have another hundred and twelve Awakenings to come, a fact which some days delights me and on others sends me directly to the doldrums. I have been told that Captain Cook gifted the Tongans a tortoise that lived for one hundred and eighty eight Hibernations. Poor soul. Although it's possible that Tonga was somewhat more interesting than Bestwood, where we live and breathe.

Regardless, this made me a baker's dozen times older and generally better than Digby and that's not even taking into account the millennia of memory and knowledge passed on to me by my ancestors in my carapace, something that Digby sadly lacks. He has no encyclopaedic exterior packed to the brim with history. History admittedly limited to the direct experience of my bloodline, therefore mainly that of a small crop of volcanic islands cluttered around the equator. Nonetheless, we are hatched with an education, of sorts. Some creatures are and some aren't. Some, like bats, need their mothers to teach them to fly. Woe betide them should they fall as babies whilst clinging to their mater's wing. Most beasts instinctively know their predators and food sources, but no creature, I believe, is born or dies wiser than the tortoise, no matter how much cramming they might do.

So, having foolishly fallen prey to Digby's enthusiasms on previous occasions only to discover that his heightened state of vitality was attributable to something as starkly unmomentous as the popping out of yet another meerkat kitten or the sight of a newly sheared alpaca, I think I can be forgiven for not immediately jumping to attention.

'Quick! Quick!' He fluttered round my head leaping about in the air, frantic. 'Hurry! Please, Herbert! You might miss it and you won't see any of it from here!' He flapped up the Hill and landed on a clump, his twitching head beckoning me to follow. 'Come ON!' he clamoured.

Two thoughts rumbled through my brain at this point. One was what precisely did he mean by "Quick"? And the other was actually less of a thought and more a pervading sense of suspicion since Digby had his own games he liked to play with me. One of which was to inform me I was not witness to something utterly thrilling. He would then lure me up the Hill a bit in order to view said extraordinary spectacle, and then up a bit further and then tell me to come up the Hill a little bit more and again and again until I finally reached the very top, entirely breathless. Then, barely able to speak such was the extent of his humour, he would gasp that it had now gone. And hilarious Digby would laugh so hard that he would fall backwards off the Wall in a guff of down. I am ashamed to admit that I had been a dupe for this gag more than several times during our acquaintance, mainly as a result of there not being a lot going on.

However, on this particular morning, suffering twinges of overnight cramps and also spotting a rather glorious pool of Sourceshine just yonder, I decided a stretch and pre-prandial stroll were in order, so I put suspicion aside and I played along with Digby.

My Family and me lived on the Hill within the Wall. The Wall was thigh-high to a grown human and made of flint. None of us really knew how far the Wall rounded although we did conduct several measuring experiments over the Baskings, mainly on my say-so since the others seemed so unutterably content with lying about generally, but I think it was about three hundred and twenty nine Gramps (he's the biggest in the Family). The others tended to become distracted or fall asleep during the experiment so we never fully completed it. They say that it is my youthfulness that imbues me with heightened activity and improved wakefulness. I just think I am different. I do not anticipate my curiosity to decline as my age soldiers on.

Gramps is, I was told (although I have to say, having seen the Family's antics post-Awakening, it's anybody's guess), the sire of my sire. Apparently I am expected to sire one day. This task does not appeal. I feel none of the required attraction to the ladies in the Family. Perhaps this is a fault of a lackadaisical adolescence or maybe it's attributable to my never having met my mother. Was she supposed to enlighten me as to communications with the females of the species? I am not sure since my relations with all of my relatives are strained at the best of times, irrespective of their gender.

My mother failed to survive the Hibernation during which I hatched. She laid me late in the summer, her clock befuddled by the weather of this small island, so unlike the steamy consistency of the archipelago of our evolution, where the easiness of our being allowed us to develop gigantism.

Now that I think about it though, it's not unusual for tortoises not to know our mothers. I have met all of my Family but that's because of the restrictions of the Wall. Were that not the case, we might have chosen to roam free of each other. We are not pack animals, after all. And our mothers do not wean us as babes. We are weaned inside our eggs, our shells forming within a shell. We break ourselves out, taking responsibility for our own delivery. Our close cousins, the sea turtles, lay their eggs in nests dug into the sand. Once these young are deposited, off the mothers swim, not interested in being party to the self-extraction of their young from their soft, leathery cases. They provide no protection against the predators on the beach, the birds and crustaceans that do not see a newly formed creature on the threshold of their life but, rather, a tasty snack.

The Family told me that food had rotted inside my mother and poisoned her blood as she slept. My predominant emotional response to this was disgust, but of course I was never attached to her. I never had the opportunity. Not like Stella, the zookeeper's daughter, and her mother were. They had seven Hibernations and Awakenings together where I had none with my mother. I was born alone.

Anyhow, the Hill looked out to many more hills that rolled over one another. Sometimes they were deep green covered with thick, wet grey but more often they danced a chaos of bright yellow splashes and dustiness striped with many verdant hues. At their horizon was a sea, to me the most glorious Glittering that reflected the colour of that day's sky. The hills and the Glittering were connected by a strip of sand, a beach, which shrank twice a day to a sliver then stretched far with the outward-bound tide.

Stella informed me that the rolling hills were the Downs (but they looked more like Ups to me) and that the Glittering was a part of a sea that they, the humans, called the Solent. I found the word quite ugly, when what it described was very much the opposite and so I renamed it for my own entertainment. For me it was the Glittering and the pinnacle of my visual pleasure.

There was also an enormous grey Spike poking up through the treetops, soaring towards the sky, which Stella called the Cathedral. She described the building to me, and its functions, but I could not comprehend any sense in them (religion consistently baffles me) and besides, from my viewpoint I could only spy the Spike. I could not see any of the vestries and chambers she described. Digby said that the Peregrines inhabited the Spike. Sometimes he tried to point them out, suspended on the air, but they vanished in a blink. He was very much in awe of them and would bleat on and on about how they were the very fastest things on Earth and ate at least a pigeon a day. Monstrous carnivores. I, myself, had reservations as to how and why such a record breaker would choose to inhabit a place of such little consequence.

As I turned towards where the Source rose each day, I was faced with a big bush shaped like a cockerel. Once, I imagined, it might have been neatly trimmed. Today its feathers were ruffled. Beyond the cockerel there was a bronze statue of Atlas, unclothed, his rippling muscles buffed by the elements and heaving the celestial sphere upon his broad shoulders. Then, majestic, was the Big House. It was flanked to its left by the fishing lake, which was fringed by willows weeping into its water and prim silver birches, fettered with catkins at Awakening. A decrepit rowing boat was moored against a rickety pontoon.

The Big House was white with a porch that was itself the size of the whole Gate House where Bob the Zookeeper and Stella lived. A drive lined with sea-worn pebbles ran between them. At the highest curve of the Wall, where the honeysuckle rambled and scented, I could survey all of this and, if the air were clear, the wind would bring me sound, clear as a bell, too.

The Big House was three windows tall and nine wide and had a copper roof that was a weathered green patina. Just after Awakening, the vine that clad the porch dripped pale purple flowers whose sweet fragrance clambered up the Hill and played in my nostrils. On the side that faced the Glittering leaned a glass orangery, its doors opening wide to a large patio; squirts of weeds spurted out of the cracks in the square paving slabs. Behind it I had a glimpse of a stagnant swimming pool that swam, out of my sight, around the back of the Big House.

Behind me was the forest, a rustling thicket of oak, beech and hazel, a feast of nuttiness as the Baskings played themselves out, surrendering to the incoming cold.

The Arnolds inhabited the Big House and it was their bloodline that was responsible for its construction hundreds of Hibernations before. They were a vision of tweed and shotguns, rusty and rosy and rarely seen. We, the menagerie, were the brainchild of a different generation and our continued existence was the product of sloth and inattention rather than solid intention or ambition. It is also possible that nobody wanted to upset Bob the Zookeeper. He was a man defined by a sporadically boisterous temper and extensive tattoos. He had been in the Navy since boyhood, until he'd married Beryl and Stella had made her appearance, at which point he'd come to Bestwood as Groundskeeper. As the grounds diminished, sold piece by piece to the encroaching farms, the estate shrinking ever closer to the walls of the Big House, the menagerie became Bob's domain. When he wasn't here, he was on the Glittering or in The Ship.

As I valiantly scaled the Hill, there was no evidence of tweed. There was, instead, a vast cacophony that seemed to eclipse even Digby.

It was rambunctious, a seething mass of shouts and swearing and music. Its loudness was such that the leaves on the Oak visibly vibrated. There was a bass note of machinery; the steady low thumps of powerful beasts beating their metal hearts.

Looking down the Hill, I saw what Stella later told me was a limousine, slick and long, and four very startling human beings stood around it. Excitement indeed - the parakeet was right. We didn't have many visitors other than Bob and Stella and her own Digby, an overly plump girl we had nicknamed Fat Hannah. Apart from the odd school trip in the Baskings, the Hill was mind-numbingly quiet.

'SEE!' Digby very nearly took an eardrum out.

'Digby, please… turn it down a bit,' I firmly instructed.

'What are they?' he whispered, gratifyingly. He had his limitations, Digby, but I will say this about him: he was obedient.

'They are, humans, you numpty,' I replied, superciliously.

'But where are the Arnolds?' he goggled at me.

'They've gone,' I said with an air of absolute certainty.

'Are you sure? But the Arnolds have been here for, like, forever!' His volume increased with his incredulity. I wasn't completely sure, actually, since I had no evidence to support my hypothesis. However, what intuition told me was that the likelihood of these two sets of humans inhabiting the same space in any kind of harmony was considerably less than slim-to-none. Plus, elusive as the Arnolds had always been, I racked my brains and couldn't really remember when I had last seen them.

What I could see now was a man wearing what looked like white pyjamas rather late on in the day. His head hair ran down his back to his waist, streaky like Roger the gregarious badger's fur. His face was rubbery and lined. It had a fuzziness crawling upon it like Bob's when, after a three-day stint in The Ship, he reappeared all fumy. Shouting at him was a phenomenally tall woman who was all limbs, and the colour of the beech leaves as they fall before Hibernation. Her hair was a buzz of white. She was carrying a creature in the crook of her arm, whose size approximated that of a rat but it was fluffy and white like her hair and it appeared to be wearing jewellery. There were couple more of these yapping around her teetering ankles.

Nearby there was a pair of most intriguing young men, smoking and leaning against what I recognised as a VW camper van, because Stella had one too. She had painted hers a pale rosy pink, reminiscent of the flamingos, but this one was a deep metallic purple and had the word 'Throbbing' stencilled down the side in luminous green.

What was most fascinating about these two young men was that they were the spit of each other. I blinked a few times but there were definitely two of them. Twins, comparatively scarce in the human world. They were the same height, the same weight and had the same hairless heads. Their shoulders were the same breadth and their bottoms equally perky. They were both dressed in black and wearing shades lodged on their shaven pates. They watched the argument between the tall woman and the man with the long hair with matching wry smiles on their identical faces.

The man with the long hair took a step towards the tall woman, his palms outstretched to the sky as her mouth alternately stretched and puckered. I caught a few of her words that won the war over the musical din emanating from the camper van and the limousine. Amongst them were, 'Dave, you are a useless knob-head,' and, 'pair of wasters,' and, 'where are the fucking keys, then?'

Digby and I looked at each other sideways. It would have been fair to say that she was a touch livid. She was using language that previously I had only heard spill from Bob's mouth, although I had been told that fish wives and harlots were fond of tasting these sounds too, and it wasn't a dialect unique to our keeper.

I felt the start of a rumble through my claws and, soon enough, five large lorries, each with 'Bust A Move' printed on their sides, began popping up at the bottom of the Hill. One by one they turned in, passed by the Gate House and made their way up the pebbly drive. The man with long hair crossed his arms in a manner that closed the subject under discussion, smiled serenely and nodded knowingly at the tall, foul-mouthed woman. The two young men laughed and she stomped a foot, turned on her heel and swallowed herself into the limousine in an evident hump.

When the first lorry pulled to a stop in a burst of dust, the matching young men opened its back doors. A tiny woman with dark blonde hair curled up into a tight chignon, wearing a black trouser suit and crisp white shirt, jumped out. She had a clipboard clutched to her chest and a phone glued like a wart to her left ear. She landed her kitten heels perfectly.

Out of the cabs of each the lorries piled three burly men in orange boiler suits and a procession of objects streamed into the house, carried by the Burlies. Chignon directed the procession with much waving of arms and reference to clipboard. The whole thing reminded me of the leaf cutter ants. I wondered where they had gone. For a time they had been spotted crawling all over the Hill, after Bob had left the lid of their vivarium off one day and never replaced it. I had not spotted one passing by in a long time, now that I considered it.

We saw: a sofa sporting a hide just like that of one of our pair of aging zebra sisters (Daisy and Dolly), a massive silver sleigh bed, and a total of twenty-three guitars. There was one of every colour in a rainbow, and one of them was all of them at once. There was a stuffed grizzly bear, the appearance of which triggered a further tantrum from the tall woman. There were chairs that looked like eggs and a huge piece of glass that may have been a table. And there were boxes, so many boxes.

Digby was, refreshingly but a little disturbingly, struck dumb. Actually, while we were watching this I was mildly concerned that he might inadvertently eject his eyeballs as a result of over goggling.

There was a mannequin bent like 'The Thinker' made of tiny square mirrors, a cerise-felted snooker table, and more brown boxes, with room names scribed on them in perfect capitals that could only have been Chignon's; KITCHEN, BEDROOM (one to eight thereof), BATHROOM (one to nine), DINING and, bizarrely, SNUG, CINEMA, RECORDING STUDIO and BAR. And POOL ROOM. I was sure the Arnolds never had those rooms. All I remembered was a mention of a ballroom and a drawing room.

There was a white lacquered grand piano, an ebony harp at least the height of the tall woman, and five keyboards, followed immediately by a four-foot white china poodle, a totem pole and a leopard skin loo seat. Every now and again, one of the mirror image young men, I couldn't tell which, would appear with a tray carrying fifteen mugs of steaming milky tea and the orange Burlies would take time out, slumped against the wheels of their lorries slurping so hard that even Digby and I could hear it.

When this spectacle ended, Chignon had checked her last box and the lorries crawled back down the driveway, the Source was dipping and Her rays were easing off.

The smell of sweating onions was in the air and then the piquance of tomatoes blubbed with an overcoat of garlic; for a while, all was still. The Family had somehow slept through all of this. As the Source made Her bed, one-by-one the windows in the Big House began to glow. A quiet, gentle music squeezed out and up the Hill. A voice like vanilla caramel swang with it, wafting through the now abuzz menagerie.

I could see Dolly and Daisy and the Alpaca tribe hanging their necks over their fence, peering, having spent the Arrival nonchalantly grazing and taking surreptitious glances over at the Big House. The flamingos were a juddering pink blancmange of feathers, quivering with questions as to the meaning of it all. The mob of meerkats, all forty-two of them (I liked to keep count), were stood in a line from biggest to smallest, facing forwards but occasionally turning their heads to consult with one another. Their noses twitched. Digby was in the Oak, preparing to roost with the flock of parakeets, who had swept in during the course of the afternoon, called to return to base camp by their unique messaging system. Brian the Gibbon, silvery grey, was hooting and swinging from his ropes, trying to gain enough momentum to launch himself over his moat, and the giraffes were flashing their lashes. Roger the gregarious badger pottered out of the forest, flanked by a team of loose deer. Rabbits were scrambling everywhere and the pipistrelle bats were sonically swooping over the roof.

But Bob the Zookeeper was nowhere to be seen.

Chapter Two

I was up with the Source the next morning, before Digby had so much as stretched his wings. I could detect no movement in the Big House. My sleep had been ridden with dreams of thunderclaps and bolts of lightning, but there was no sign that a storm had passed through; just gentle damp clinging to the grace of a web woven overnight on a bramble and forming tender tears on the points of grass. There was a high haze in the sky that would burn off before long.

I heard the latch of the Gate House door click shut and watched the speckle of Bob the Zookeeper grow as he strolled the curve of the pebbly drive, past the silent Big House and alongside the fishing lake. He plucked one of the many stray sprouts from the bush shaped like a cockerel and dropped it into his bucket. He nodded at Atlas. He arrived at the bottom curve of the Wall just as the main door to the Big House flew open with an almighty smash, and the man with the stripy hair stood proud on the step, naked as a nectarine. With his hands on his hips, he screamed as though his toenails were being extracted.

Bob dropped the bucket. It tumbled down the Hill, emptying its contents - a delicious assortment of lettuce ends and cucumber starts - in its wake. First his face, weathered like one of Stella's vintage handbags, went a chalky white. Then, as the Naked Man, his hair swinging against his gluteus maximus, posed in prayer and then like a standing star and then low down like a wheelbarrow, so low that I was sure that the tip of his genitalia must have been scraping on the gravel, Bob turned puce. And then he stomped off to the feed shed.

As Bob clattered about in the shed, I watched the creatures began to wake and listened to their chatter about the night before. The naked man with the stripy hair continued to pose, balancing on one leg, crouching with his arms bent in front, bending and stretching and generally waving his thing about, apparently oblivious to the literally hundreds of eyes upon him. He was clearly a complete exhibitionist.

Bob pointedly ignored him. But when the stretching was finished and a curt bow to the Source was done, Naked Man sprang up the Hill to where I could see Bob bending over, pouring kibble into the meerkats' bowls, and he caught him from behind, unawares.

'Peace!' the naked man exclaimed.

Bob stood up and turned around. The meerkats' chain-link fence separated them but left nothing to Bob's imagination. He looked to be at the tipping brink of boisterousness.

'What?' Bob barked.

I observed the naked man's bottom, which was the same shade of golden brown as the rest of him. He jiggled it, just a little bit. It was evident that he spent a lot of time unclothed and soaking up the rays of the Source. A wise man, I thought.

'I said 'peace', dude. As in, 'peace on earth', 'I come in peace', 'let there be peace.' Yeah, man…' the naked man stopped speaking as Bob took a step towards him, his booted foot landing squarely on the tail of meerkat number thirteen, who yelped. Always having accidents, was number thirteen – getting its head stuck in the fence, eating the wrong thing, falling off the top of the tall mud towers Bob had built them; that sort of thing. It looked accusingly up at Bob, who gently shifted it to one side with the toe of his steel-capped boot, whilst very deliberately not taking his eyes from the naked man's face, who took a step back and held his arms out, palms up, supplicant, '… man, it's peaceful here.' The bells in the Spire pealed a couple of miles away. 'Isn't it?'

'It was,' Bob snapped, opening the gate, exiting the meerkats' enclosure and striding straight past him.

'So, er, I thought I would introduce myself,' said the naked man, turning around to be faced with Bob's retreating back.

'Put some fucking clothes on first.' Bob threw the words over his shoulder and kept walking.

The naked man stood and glanced down at his tackle, shrugged and wandered into the Big House. Before long the whiff of fried pork haunch sizzling from their kitchen was making me nauseous, me being a vegetarian. Most of us were, apart from the obvious exception of the mob of forty-two meerkats. There was also a possible aberration on the part of the flamingos, who were rumoured to eat bacteria and algae or shellfish in the wild by swinging their heads upside down and filtering, but nobody seemed entirely sure. Here, they had mysterious pellets of unknown origin that they claimed were foul tasting but had the desired effect of dying their feathers rosy-rose. They were narcissistic, those flamingos. They were always preening and posing, admiring their own reflections in the grot of their greasy pond. I thought they looked like they had their knees on backwards.

After the burning pig stink had dissipated and we were all able to breathe again, the tall woman, with her constantly circulating white pet creatures, and the naked man appeared. He was no longer naked, but wearing a long, orange wrap-over skirt, co-ordinating vest and turquoise beaded flip-flops. His hair had been woven into a thick plait that whipped down his back like a hooked fish. They departed in the limousine. Not long after that, the purple camper van sped off, helmed by one of the identical boys. The camper van spat out harsh rhymes that stamped along to a surly beat from its windows.

All was then tediously serene. I sighed and tutted for a bit. Digby woke up, flew down, was updated, sighed and tutted a bit himself, then flew off, leaving me to my exquisite boredom.

More fool he.

As the Source reached Her absolute zenith and I was thinking I might even, possibly, maybe be a little bit too hot, perhaps, an astonishing, grating zing zung. It startled us all from our noontime slumbers and galloped over the Ups. The mob of forty-two meerkats clucked in unison and I am sure a giraffe farted.

Brian the Gibbon was swinging from one hand, rocking himself to and fro and talking a million miles a minute.

'I can see him; it's the other twin lad. He's awake and wearing shorts like the flag they pull up on the Spike sometimes – you know, the red, white and blue one and his chest is almost entirely smooth but he has quite hairy legs and very ugly toes and he's wearing one of those guitars – you remember the dark red, shiny one and he's stroking it! And the windows are open, that's why it's so loud and it's chained to a box by a big snaky thing, and it's the box making that noise.' Brian was barely stopping for breath.

Every creature faced him, listening intently, as another huge melodic whine span out from the house. This time, it was higher with a hockey stick end that rang out all across the Ups and made all of the hairy animals' hair stand right on end. Brian was so shocked he let go of his rope and plummeted onto the grass, landing with a flump. He stood on all fours, looked right and left, shook himself out a bit and wandered over to the edge of the moat, where he sat down, picked a dandelion clock and blew it, dispersing umbrellas.

I looked at the Big House; the French windows on the balcony were wide open. The Source glinted off their panes, Her shafts glancing down onto the roof of the porch. He was silhouetted in the window. I watched his arm stretch out and he picked up an item that he placed on his head. It was a top hat. The Source hugged the edge of it and made it look like a super-sophisticated halo.

The vanilla caramel voice we had heard late last night was back. The words it sang were round and gentle and deep and sent a bolt of white-hot energy through my shell. As the bolt subsided, it left me with a profound and pure happiness. It emanated from my very core and spilled through my internal organs to the tips of my claws, rather like the ripples on the fishing lake when the pike leapt and landed in spawning. I couldn't move any more than a slight sway this way and that, as the molecules in the air transmitted the vibrations of the music into my ears, onto my scales, through my blood. My heart pumped at the same rate that the music beat. Its pitch was true with a life force that rang inside me, like an ancient music bowl having its rim skimmed. My every electron weaved around its nucleus in perfect time. I was part of the grass. I was the grass, the soil that nourished it, the stone strata below, the molten core of the planet and every single living thing. I was elemental to the universal soul.

Then there was silence, and I was just Herbert again. No more, no less. I was mortal, reptilian and utterly insignificant in the grand scheme of things. And ever so slightly depressed now, actually. Although, despite myself, I now found myself stretching my neck out and up as far as it could go and hopping, albeit very slow hopping, from foot to foot and making a noise that sounded much like my Family when they were boshing each others' shells just after the Awakenings.

The Hill was alive with the sound of creatures; the Family uttering the same guttural groans as me, the flamingos quacking wildly, the meerkat mob trilling away, the alpacas humming and warking and the Zebras were barking. Most astonishingly, the giraffes, who we all thought were mute, were making a curious fluting whistle. Brian was hooting, Roger churred and the deer snorted and scraped their hooves on the moss at the edge of the forest. The pipistrelles pipped.

I could have sworn I even heard an outrageously loud purr, as if there was a very big cat nearby, although there hadn't been one of them here since The Mauling of Beryl by Gavin the Tigress the day before I hatched. I had heard it said before, however, that not everyone was convinced that Bob the Zookeeper had actually shot and killed Gavin, and her stripes had been spotted slinking through the trunks of the forest since she was purported to have passed.

Beryl had been his wife, of course, but he had raised Gavin the Tigress from a cub. Rear-Admiral Williams (Gavin Joseph), an old friend of Bob's from the Navy, whose chronic asthma had forced him out of service, ran customs at a nearby port. He had found a tiger cub smuggled as a stowaway, destined to perform in a circus. The Rear Admiral brought the little big cat to Bob (Captain Trimble, Robert James) immediately upon discovery, knowing that the Captain would provide sanctuary. Although Captain Bob could be brutish with his own kind, he was legendary for his tenderness with creatures outside of the human race. Despite the feline's obvious femininity, Bob insisted on naming her in honour of her saviour, the Rear-Admiral Gavin Joseph Williams, and proceeded to bottle feed and molly coddle her. Many people said that Gavin's crime was one of passion and, not so far away, not so long ago, would have been a valid defence against a death sentence.

And then suddenly he, the twin, was here. He'd run up the Hill and leaped right over the Wall. He was taking a bow; where the Naked Man's had been punchy, his was wide, generous and all-inclusive.

'Hello!' he yelled. 'I'm Ollie! Ollie Palmer. And it's my absolute pleasure to meet you all!'

Chapter Three

Ha-ha! I loved to have one up on the parakeet and Digby was fair fuming on his return from his jaunt when he learned of the goings on. I displayed my smugness exuberantly, which ruffled his feathers most satisfyingly. I did, however, very nearly overcook it, as I had not realised his expedition had been a constructive one and mainly in my interest. Thankfully, Digby was not one to sulk. His predilection for gossip eclipsed all else.

'I've been over at Fat Hannah's house,' he informed me.

Hannah was actually not fat. Not any more, anyway - she was leaner than svelte, more than skinny. This was a relatively recent metamorphosis. When I last went into Hibernation, she was well and truly wide, maybe three times more so than Stella. Her periwinkle eyes were lost in her sponge of a face. When she reached up to sweep her hand across her sweaty hairline, a roll of fat immersed her belly button and wobbled over the top of her too-tight hand-me-down jeans.

But when she had first visited this Awakening, I had not initially recognised her. I had thought that Stella had found a new friend. It was only when she spoke that I saw that Hannah was there, her icy eyes now huge in her face, glancing off hollowed cheeks. Her head looked a little large for a body that now, when she stretched, displayed a rib cage like a xylophone through her flimsy, clingy t-shirt dress. Her hair was different too; it was lighter, bouncing about in shiny corkscrews, when once it had been a muddy fuzz.

'Oh?' I said. 'Do you think we should call her Fat Hannah still?' I asked, almost as an aside.

'Doesn't matter,' dismissed Digby. 'I have news.'

Ooh, I thought, news!

'Fat Hannah has gone to the airport,' Digby announced. This sent me wild. This was the very news for which I had been longing: Stella was on her way back.

I had seen Stella only once since this Awakening and that had been fleetingly, as she had delivered a plate of chopped cucumber heart, tickled me under the chin and basked alongside me in the Sourceshine.

'I'm off on an adventure!' she had told me. 'Off to visit your homelands, Herbs, just for a few weeks. It's a field trip. There are twelve of us going, and a lecturer. We'll be living on a boat - for a month! There will be five crew, and one of them's a full time naturalist guide. What a job to have - imagine it!'

It felt as if she had been gone forever. In the past, I had seen her every day, that I was awake, for a chat. Well, she chatted. I delivered sage and insightful advice to which her ears were unfortunately impervious. She seemed to manage well enough without it, though, or maybe it kind of osmosed itself into her subconscious. Who knew?

I saw her father every day still, but it was not quite the same, frankly. He fed and tidied. Sometimes a little erratically, admittedly, but ultimately we could always rely on him to keep us clean and our hunger at bay. But he never talked, not to me, anyway, although he did have a bit of a thing going on with Brian the Gibbon. I think they found much of themselves in each other.

Brian was the last of his clan. Like me, he had been born here. In fact, his great-great grandfather, Boris, had been the original menagerie resident. He was fifth generation Bestwood, if you like. Boris had been removed as a baby from his dead mother's back in the jungles of Burma; poachers had shot her and abandoned them both, and Boris was rescued by the then Earl, Lawrence Arnold, explorer, and soon-to-be animal collector.

Lawrence was extremely fond of Boris and had built him a magnificent moated island. The island itself was a charming copse of beech trees for Boris to climb and hang upon. But Boris was a piner. He pined for the tropics. He pined for the heat and, bizarrely, he pined for the rain. I was of the firm opinion that there was quite enough of that here, thank you very much. But most of all, Boris pined for the primate touch. He missed his clutch on his mother's fur. He yearned for the methodical searches through his pelt for naughty hidey creatures and in the empty dark of the night his pain peaked.

Despite having been provided with a spectacular tree house, envied and invaded by many Arnold boys, he could not appreciate its space and light, since all he wanted it filled with was the beating of other gibbons' hearts. He embarked upon a hunger strike. The Earl consulted his animal collector colleagues and, without exception, companionship was advised.

Back to Burma Lawrence went. He returned with an embryonic gibbon family - a mother and her daughter and the mother's sister. A period of what humans might term 'incest' passed, and a colony was born. My Family told me how the colony hooted high in the beeches at night, keeping them awake but amused with their handed-down anecdotes of life in the lofty teak forests of their homelands.

I wondered about my homelands. My mind wandered around the landscape of memories passed on to me. As I said, in actuality, my homeland was Bestwood. The cells that made me up had never been where Stella had gone. I had hatched at Bestwood, just like Digby, who had fallen out of his nest in the Oak moments after hacking through his shell, to land right in front of me on a soft, freshly formed molehill. We were both Bestwoodians with foreign heritage.

Digby had been a grotesque baby, scraggy and entirely unkempt. I was the very first thing that his bulbous, new eyes had perceived and, as a result, he had mistaken me for his mother. Although she had never sought to correct him (so busy was she with the rest of her brood), I had attempted to put him straight. He said he understood the impossibility of his suggestion, but his early misapprehension left him unusually pliant to my whims - something I did not complain about, since it was this that made him an ally in my quests and operations.

Bob had discovered him on his rounds, featherless and helpless, and had whipped him off to the Gate House, nursing him until he was big enough to fly on his own and re-join his roost. But it was always me he wanted to share his news with first. And what news!

When Stella had told me about her adventure, she had meant the homeland of my ancestors. Even some of the Family here, my immediate relatives around me, had known the feel of their four feet on that land, a place where lizards swam in the sea and birds with blue feet dived amongst huge flat fish with eyes on their skin, and sleek furry creatures with huge, brown eyes, rather like Stella's. Their pups rolled cutely on the beaches and their fathers battled and waddled and yelled. Some of the Family, if they could be bothered, would point out that, in fact, this still was not the spot of our original origination. They would cite the relative newness of the volcanically created lands, would reference floatings and returns to the water, but our mass memories became lost in the primordial soup.

Once she had delivered her news, Stella had stood up and said, 'Gotta go, Herbs!' and she was gone in a swish of her shiny hair. She skipped down the

Hill, twirled on her way past the bush shaped like a cockerel, and kissed the cold lips of Atlas. She jumped into her pink camper van and whizzed off through the gates. She abandoned me to the inane chatter of the parakeets, breeding in the Oak rustling above my head and the buzz of a bumblebee buffeting about on the breeze.

Stella was the first thing that I had seen when I had hatched, the day after the Beryl and Gavin incident. Unlike Digby, I had not mistaken her for my mother; we tortoises are not daft. But her treatment of me then and over the subsequent years had resulted in my unparalleled affection for her. When I first hatched, I fitted in the palm of her hand, even though she too was a lot smaller then. She was in a whole world of pain, having just lost her mother and she made me the centre of her universe, something I challenge any creature's ego to resist. For a long time, she took me everywhere with her. I had a special box in her bedroom and she would carry me in a bag out into the Ups and let me mooch around and explore. When she and I became too big for this, she returned me to my Family, who were, by then, entirely alien to me.

Digby scratched about in the dirt as the Source rumbled to an apparent halt above the Big House, huge and flamy, just hanging there, bearing down.

'Digby? Are you saying Stella is back? Back from her adventure?' I asked.

'Yes, Herbert. That I am,' Digby clearly enunciated. I slowly expelled all of the air in my lungs. I wanted to scrub my toes, rinse my eyes until they were bright and polish my shell to a gleam. I was very excited at the prospect of seeing her.

Digby had a dust bath.

The door of the Big House slammed and startled us from our ablutions as the twins piled out of the house and into the purple camper van, and scooted down the drive. At the gate there was a kerfuffle of brakes and mildly abusive language as Stella's pink camper van swang around the corner and in, very nearly coming to blows with the purple one on its way out.

Stella parked at a jaunty angle in front of the Gate House and she and Hannah leapt out, all legs and scant triangles of clothing, hair showering over their shoulders. They ran up the Hill and scrambled over the Wall straight to me. Yes, to me! Digby hid in the Oak, overcome with shyness all of a sudden.

'Herbs, my darling, favourite, best thing!' Stella cooed and tickled me under my leathery chin. I stretched my neck out as far and high as it would go, so as to show my appreciation. She sat cross-legged on the grass. 'Oh Herbs, I've missed you! I've had such an awesome time. I met so many of your cousins, they reminded me so much of you. I want to give you a cuddle but you're not really made for that!' She tried anyway, enveloping me in a lengthy hug throughout which I felt her heart beat through my shell. Then she lay back on the grass with her arms stretched wide. 'Ooh it's nice to be home,' she sighed.

Hannah was still standing, towering over me, putting me in her shadow, fidgeting. I chewed a buttercup stem distractedly, trying to pull the shiny flower down to my mouth. A brimstone butterfly fluttered past, its yellow wings glowing sulphurously against the pale blue of the sky.

Hannah pulled a fat, hand-rolled cigarette from the pocket of her tiny denim skirt and lay down next to Stella, leaning on an elbow. She lit the cigarette with a heavy, rectangular metal lighter enamelled with the flag that had been on Ollie's underpants. Its smoke was sweet.

'My, my,' said Hannah, 'those guys were buff.' She lustfully heaved smoke into her lungs, holding it and then letting it drift slothfully from her lips. 'Spliff?' She proffered the smoking joint to Stella. Fat Hannah's now long, slim fingers were clustered in piles of silver rings. This smoking of spliffs had begun in the previous Awakening and I loved the way it made Stella laugh, the way her joyful energy spilled out of her lungs and scampered about the Ups.

But increasingly I had found myself concerned. Although she seemed to have fun, she also seemed distracted. Her formidable brain was dampened. Stella was studying nearby, a BSc she told me, in Zoology, naturally. When she wasn't in lectures, she and her books would be here with me. But since the spliffs had made an entrance, her studies included increasing bouts of general gazing about and lousy laziness. It worried me, frankly.

These humans, from what I can see, have a relatively difficult life. They have to find their own food, for starters. Mine arrived with a monotonous, yet welcome, regularity, and if supplies were short from Bob, there were plenty of tasty morsels simply growing around me. They, however, the humans, have to produce or procure the essentials for themselves. I suppose they could forage and hunt, but it might take an unfeasibly long time given all the other things that they like to do - building, drinking, making music, reading, talking, cooking, playing – that sort of thing in endless variations. Hobbies, I think they call it. Also, they have no inbuilt, or out-built, perhaps, shell and have, therefore, to find their own shelter. They cannot afford to be cold since there's not a useful hair on them and their metabolisms aren't, like ours, kick-started by a few choice beams from the Source.

On the plus side, they have no need to worry about predators as far as I can tell, with their wealth of weaponry and opposable thumbs; apart, of course, from each other. And they appear to have disease generally under control, or at least a systematic way of dealing with it. We in the menagerie benefitted from their disease control systems. Although infrequent, the visit from the 'vet' was a welcome little drama with mostly positive results, despite reports of unwelcome intrusions and painful little pricks.

However, ultimately, they only have themselves to rely on for survival. Stella had serious potential to survive super-successfully, anyone could see that. She hadn't had the easiest of starts in life, what with the Beryl and Gavin incident and a difficult, booze-fuelled father. She deserved the best of everything, I felt. More fun would be good, yes, but debilitating distractions, no.

'Thanks.' Stella took the spliff from Hannah. 'Yeah, they were fit. But could work on their manners. Daddy said we had new neighbours. Guess that's them, then.' She took a small toke on the spliff. Stella still wore her mother's plain gold wedding band on her right hand. The Source burnished it. I saw she still had her there with her every day.

'I thought I recognised them,' said Hannah.

'I didn't really see them' replied Stella.

'Maybe we went to school with them?'

'You are joking? Living in that house? Like anyone we know could afford to live there! The Arnolds were some sort of aristocracy - royalty even, remember.' She inhaled and exhaled. 'It's weird them not being here anymore. They were practically an institution.'

'Where did they go anyway?' Hannah leaned on an elbow, cradling her chin in her hand.

Digby flashed low over the top of us, squawking something about a commotion in the kitchen that he was going to inspect. The girls watched him without comment. Ha! Not so exotic after all, I thought, rather meanly.

'All corners of the earth, apparently. Dad says they finally ran out of money. As you know, they ran out of women long ago. The oldest one, with the pipe – Tom - well his wife ran off with that gardener…'

'Ooh, yes I remember him,' Hannah licked her lips. Stella laughed.

'Okay, I'll give you that; he was quite yummy. Not much between the ears, though…'

'Like that matters!' Hannah giggled. Stella rolled her eyes.

'Tom's brother, Charlie, well his wife was responsible for the gin bottles littered around the back of the fishing lake. Don't know how many more have sunk from view. Hope no-one dredges it.'

'I remember her. She went yellow didn't she?'

'That she did. And let that be a warning to you and your liver!' Stella pointed at Hannah.

'Oh, I hardly think I've reached that scale yet.' Hannah rolled onto her back. 'And the young one? The one that looked like he had his ears on upside down? The one with the stammer and the weird hair that started half way up his forehead?'

'Timothy. Poor Timothy. Now there was a child who was not his father's son. Poor Tom, he must have been cuckolded many times before his wife finally ran off with that gardener. I always thought that Timothy bore an uncanny resemblance to Dad's old ship mate, Gavin.'

'Ooh, the scandal!'

'Anyway, must be a decade since there were any women in that house. Tom lost a stack of money on the stock markets and most of the remainder in the casinos in Mayfair, so Dad says. Charlie apparently was a sucker for get-rich-quick schemes that did nothing but get him poor in double time. And Timothy, well he was shipped off to boarding school for most of his life.

And he's now at agricultural college in Somerset, apparently. Should suit him I would think. Charlie's gone to Goa on the last few pennies they have. And Tom, well, Tom's a bit of a mystery. Dad says he headed down to the marina and took off in his yacht. Not a word to anyone about where he was going. The Arnolds gave up. Or were beaten, I suppose,' Stella sighed.

'Wow. How the mighty fall. They were royalty weren't they? You said they were?'

'Earls; bastard descendants of Charles 3rd. Major landowners in the county - they built Bestwood.'

'Imagine having all that and losing it...' Hannah and Stella lay in silence, watching small puffs of cloud stretch and turn overhead. They started to play one of their oldest games, telling each other what they could see in the clouds; a marijuana leaf, a duck, the face of Eliza, the lady behind the counter in the Post Office, and me, a giant land tortoise. I tipped my head so I could look up, but I couldn't see it myself.

The remainder of the afternoon passed in a hot flash. The Source was at Her strongest so far. She had burned all the clouds away until not a single one could be seen. The Glittering was chock full of boats bobbing about with blowsy sails of all sorts of colours and the beach was teeming with picnics and kites. A grass snake snuck by with a rustle and curled up on a flat stone, his scales flashing the Sourcelight. His name was Colin. He was not terrifically friendly and actually a bit thick. I was not keen on his habit of gobbling mice; I liked the mice. Stella and Hannah did not notice him. I pretended he was not there.

The Baskings were reaching their peak and the countryside was high with plants and swarming with insects, busily mating and pollinating and setting up the seeding and fruiting that would keep everyone going through our Hibernation and begin the cycle again next Awakening.

The girls lay in the grass, stoned, flapping away the odd fly or wasp. Digby returned and sat on the Wall.

'It's all happening in the Big House!' said Digby.

'Oh, really?' I said. 'What's occurring?'

'Well,' Digby said. 'Apparently the Arnolds left some of their things behind. The tall angry woman is unimpressed; she's throwing them at Chignon and shouting, 'Why is all this crap still here?' Naked man with the badger hair was grabbing her and being swatted away. She seems much stronger than him. She is tempestuous.'

'They almost look like they are having a chat, don't they?' laughed Hannah, waving a hand in our direction.

'They probably are, babe. Why shouldn't they be? I don't imagine we have exclusive rights on communication, despite our elevated notions of superiority.'

'What are they talking about, then?'

'I have absolutely not a flipping clue!' answered Stella, looking at us inquiringly.

Digby laughed at them and flew off into the fields to play in the ears of corn.

Eventually, as the shadow of the Oak leaned into its longest, the girls lifted themselves up, Stella patted me on my head and they went on a tour of re-acquaintance around the menagerie. Stella said hello again to each one of the mob of forty-two meerkats, then the flamingos and the alpacas and they patted the giraffes' long necks and snuggled stripy Daisy and Dolly. They found Brian the Gibbon a banana from the feed shed, lowered the drawbridge across his moat and skipped across. He wolfed the banana while hanging around Stella's neck. I was quite jealous.

The smell of hot cheese buffeted about in the air.

'I'm starving. Aren't you?' Hannah asked Stella.

'Ravenous. I've got a major case of the munchies coming on!' Stella said, and I heard her tummy rumble. 'Let's go and make some supper. Don't know what's in the fridge; Dad's probably down the pub. I suppose we'll see him after closing - or in the morning. We can help him feed the animals.'

'If we must,' sighed Hannah, inspecting the chips on her nails. 'I might just lie-in.'

Stella laughed, ever patient. 'You've changed! You used to love feeding time!'

'I have different interests now!' claimed Hannah.

'Like what?'

'Like sex and drugs and generally having an absolutely fucking wild old time!' Hannah grabbed Stella's hand and dragged her off, running down the Hill at full pelt like little girls again, their laughter pealing up behind them.

Hannah shouted, 'Look at the size of that cock!' as they passed the big bush shaped like a fowl. They stopped at Atlas, and Hannah peered at his groin and then had his bronze dangly thing (which, incidentally, compared very favourably to that of the new resident who had been exercising naked in the driveway that very morning) in her hand, then bent over and put it in her mouth. Stella was doubled over with laughter and making gestures like she was taking pictures. I was mildly entertained, but found it more than a little unseemly.

Neither of the girls had noticed that the new resident, returned and still in his orange skirt outfit, was framed in the open doorway of the Big House, his arms crossed as he smiled with amusement at the girls' antics. I didn't like the way he was looking at them. Like he wanted to mate with them.

Hannah, tiring of performing lewd acts upon Atlas, glanced up at the doorway to the Big House. She squinted hard and shielded her eyes from the last of the Source, who hovered low in the sky. Her jaw dropped. Stella turned to see what it was that Hannah was gawking at, then turned back and mouthed, 'Oh. My. God.' Hannah was standing straight now, apparently gobsmacked.

'Jesus, fuck,' she said, looking at the man in orange. 'You're Dave Palmer.'

'That I am,' Dave said, nodding knowingly like a sage. I hadn't the foggiest who he was.

'But you're an absolute legend,' said Stella breathily and yet not breathing.

Dave laughed. 'That I am,' he concurred, with supreme self-confidence.

'But...' Stella started, confusion written all over her stunning stunned face. 'What on earth are you doing here?' I'd never seen her so flustered. She was blushing. A faint line of perspiration beaded on her upper lip.

'Well, I live here,' he replied. 'Perhaps we should introduce ourselves properly, since I was wondering the very same about you.' Dave didn't move. His dark green eyes ran over the girls, whose nipples were nubby in the cooling of the day. I wanted to punch him. Difficult for a tortoise, but he inspired violence in my veins. Stella stumbled over to him, gangly and nervous. She proffered a hand.

'Stella Trimble.' She stared at him. 'I live in the Gate House. With my father. Bob. The zookeeper. He said he didn't know who...' Dave took her hand and kissed her fingers, giving her mother's ring a twist as he let go.

'Ah, yes. Well, it was a bit of a secret. And this is...?' he asked, looking straight into Hannah's wide, aquamarine eyes. She looked a little unsteady on her feet and she was not attempting to move nor speak.

'This is Hannah,' volunteered Stella. 'My best friend. We went to school together. She lives in the village, just up the road...' She petered out.

'Well, I think I should welcome my new neighbours with a drink!' Dave waved them round to the patio that ran down the left hand side of the house with a view over the fishing lake. I craned my neck to see. There was a wooden table and eight chairs with square cushions covered in cream. A hammock had been hung between a pair of silver birch trees.

On the fishing lake, lilies laid their glossy pads along the meniscus and cheekily petalled bursts of cerise and buttery yellow. A damp frog sat on a pad and chirped and dived with a little splashy splosh. Colin the grass snake rustled through the rushes at the edge and I gulped, hoping the frog would swim fast. I hadn't even noticed Colin leave his slab of Sourceshine.

The hammock was lined with purple and pink cloths embroidered with stars in silver thread along the trims. It was full of the long-limbed beech coloured woman with the buzz of white hair; her head lay on an emerald velvet cushion. She was yawning and looking at them, like a lioness. I thought I heard Gavin growling beside me but saw nothing. Maybe Gavin had a ghost, I thought.

'What is this?' Hannah exhaled, apparently in some sort of state of wonderment.

'This,' Dave gestured at the woman in the hammock, 'is my new wife, Issa. Darling Issy, would you be a sweetheart and crack open a bottle of pop?' Issa stared at Dave and did not move a single, slender muscle. I admired her poise.

Hannah rushed over to her and shook her hand furiously. Issa, the likeness of a lioness, let slip a hint of a smile whilst otherwise continuing to appear entirely motionless.

'This is awesome!' exclaimed Hannah. Issa smiled and sat up, swinging her legs over the side of the hammock and leaned on her pointed, painted toes. A ball of fluff emerged from under her white, sequinned kaftan and yapped at Hannah.

'Shush, Tinky Winky!' The tall woman pushed it off the edge of the hammock. It landed in a squirm. The other two yappers appeared from the shadows and the three of them dervished. Hannah blanked them, blinkered. Colin slid back out from the fishing lake, flicking his tongue and looking hungry. The white yappers set off in my direction. I braced myself. They were like dogs. But like opposites of the Arnolds' gun dogs. Fearsome, slavering black Labradors, they had been. These were tiny, silly, things - doglets.

'Like we don't know exactly who you are!' Hannah gushed. 'Twice as many covers as any other model, every top designer's favourite muse; one of the most photographed women in the world - the pride of Brazil.' She paused. 'And you... you are even more amazing in real life. Fuck me sideways, you're even more famous than he is! I didn't even know you were together.' Issa smiled her wide, full mouth and crinkled her nose. Her eyes were warm as she soaked up the compliments; they seemed to be the force that fed her.

'Well, I suppose it depends in which circles you circulate,' Dave sourly sniffed. 'We got married last week. In Hawaii. A whirlwind romance, some might say - we met five weeks ago today when Issa turned up to star in the video for my new single. I thought she was going to be something special – I handpicked her for the job! Well, as they say, when you know, you know.'

35

The girls beamed at the romance. He brightened and said, 'I'll go and hunt down the pop.'

He returned moments later, followed by Chignon, now in a simple, white dress and carrying a silver ice bucket under one arm. It was wrapped in a white napkin and she had four long and dazzling glasses dangling from her other hand. She put the bucket on the table and set the glasses down one by one. She pulled a bottle out of the bucket, dripping in icy water and popped the cork. She poured liquid bubbles into each glass, tipping them gently and letting them settle until they were full.

She walked a pair of glasses over to Hannah and Issa and then another pair to Dave and Stella. Issa arched a manicured eyebrow at Dave.

'It's a special occasion,' he replied to the eyebrow, and raised his glass. 'To our new home and our very sexy new neighbours.' He grinned at the girls. I scowled at him. Not that he saw. The doglets had reached the zebra and alpaca field and were doing their best to worry them. Daisy and Dolly seemed to be trying to stamp on them. They whizzed around their legs and then back under the fence and down the Hill in a line back to the patio.

Issa laughed and scratched Tinky Winky behind an ear. 'There is always a special occasion with you, Dave, despite your resolutions!' She stood up with her glass. She was staggeringly high, even barefoot. Her legs were endless and her thighs taut and concave. The dips of her collarbone were pronounced and her shoulder blades were razors. Her body was proportionally shorter, almost caricature, and her breasts were more womanly and curvaceous than either Stella's or Hannah's. Actually, Fat Hannah's had been excessive, bounding around, but now there was barely anything left.

'And don't be a letch, Dave,' Issa admonished. 'Yes, they are gorgeous girls.' Stella and Hannah blushed and held onto one another. 'But they're young enough to be your daughters. They are younger than your boys, I'm sure!' This confused me slightly, since she too was obviously many, many years younger than he. In fact, I don't think that she can really have been much that much older than Hannah and Stella, twenty Hibernations each, by my reckoning and yet she was his wife. Her forehead was taut and wrinkle free and her lips plump and glossy like the girls'. But she carried herself differently, was worldly-wise, perhaps even a little world-weary.

'My groovy sons,' Dave said thoughtfully, as he took a sip of his champagne. 'There are two of them. Identical twins. A right pair of opposites, although they look the same. Like yin and yang. Twenty-six years old now. Far out! I still think I'm twenty-four!' Issa sniggered unkindly. He continued, unbothered. 'They are from my second marriage to the uber-groupie, Marianne. She called them Oliver and Sidney. Solid names. I was on tour in Berlin and missed the birth. Anyway, I was so fucked up at the time I wanted to call them Funky Moonbug and Dizzy Munchkin. Thankfully, Marianne was having none of it; pregnancy sent her sober and sensible.' He paused. 'Issa, though, is my third and my very favourite wife so far.' Dave smiled at his Brazilian trophy, who rolled her eyes at him and picked up a different one of her matching trio of doglets and let it lick her nose, cooing over it, calling it 'Po'.

They all sipped on their bubbles as Chignon emerged again from the house, this time carrying a thick wooden board with a gargantuan pizza resplendent upon it. It was sprinkled with slices of mushrooms and fat black olives and glistened with oil. A vine of tomatoes reclined beside. Garlic and oregano frittered in the air. The girls burped gently under their hands and smiled at each other, like geishas. They sat down at the table, curling their legs underneath themselves. Issa brought them each a silk scarf and wrapped them around their shoulders, murmuring something about the chill of this miserable country's paltry attempt at a summer. I agreed.

'Eat!' she commanded as Chignon melted away and the girls, needing no further encouragement, grabbed a slice each and managed the mozzarella strings, licking tomato sauce off their fingers. They ate and, as the alcohol took the edge off their stonedness, the girls relaxed. Dave continued to pour glass after glass of champagne, bottles replenished with a click to Chignon, and deliberately failed to answer his wife's eyebrow.

Issa drank a single glass of champagne and picked the olives and mushrooms off a single slice of pizza.

Dave sat back and said, 'Sid, the eldest of my two sons by less than five minutes, is the party animal. He's on the dark side of the moon. I tried to give him the best of the best for his education, but he was having none of it. Got himself chucked out of everywhere - almost made a career of it in itself. He blames it on me, naturally. Says he had no father figure, I was never around. Tells me that I was a bad example, not what a parent should be. Sun shines out of his mother's arsehole, of course.' He paused again and slugged back his half glass before refilling it. 'Now, of course, his career is shagging his way around the totty in London and being papped. Still behaving badly and is a sucker for a bird in a short dress. Much like his old Dad. Was.' He squeezed Issa's hand.

Stella and Hannah laughed and confirmed that there was rarely a week without a report of Sid's latest conquest – a litany of actresses and popstrels.

'Yeah, he's cool,' said Dave. 'I mean, he's only young, sowing his oats, having a ball and I did plenty of that myself. But, you know, all these girls, I think they are just after their five minutes in the limelight. Using him, really. He's a rung on their ladder to fame and fortune. Of course, he thinks he's the big man, in control. But really, how bleeding dull to be famous for being someone's son,' Dave sighed. 'He would be better off in life if he found his talent. He's gifted but he's a squanderer. He's a good musician, of course - not exceptional, not like Ollie. Ollie's something else entirely... his polar opposite. Thoughtful, creative, dedicated.' A pair of bats jaggedly swirled over the surface of the fishing lake, peeping, picking off gnats.

'What do you think Sid's talent might be?' asked Stella. 'Is it true that everyone has a talent?'

'Haha!' exclaimed Dave, thumping the table and sending the doglets into a flurry. 'Talent or luck? Hard work or being in the right place at the right time? Do I deserve my success - do I really deserve all of this?' He wafted his hand about at the Big House, at Issa, over the champagne. 'Was it really me, or was it the team behind me? I may have been the lead, and sure, I wrote some lyrics somewhere along the way, I think. It's been a bit of a blur. But I was merely the spokesman - the mouthpiece, if you will - and I couldn't have done anything without the manager, the musicians, the support – sound technicians, artists for the covers. So many people at the top of the game and virtually invisible. Me, I was fucked off my face most of the time. I used to think I was all that, but now I have found humility.' The girls looked at him, agape. 'And let's take Issa as another example. Other than looking pretty - hey okay, way more than pretty - and keeping herself thin, does she have any talent? Does she work that hard? Is it her or is it her army of make-up artists, stylists, hairdressers, marketers who are the true success of the beautiful brand that they create, how they all pay themselves?'

'Dave, you're ranting nonsense.' Issa was irked. I found myself wondering what my talent might be. No-one seemed interested in photographing me. I couldn't play a musical instrument, I couldn't write - I couldn't even run very fast. I felt frustrated. Suddenly I saw how the rest of the Family had resigned themselves to their fate of eating, sleeping, mating, hibernating and waking and I felt devastated. What could I do with my life?

'But Issa, everything has changed for me,' Dave took her hand.

'This I know,' she replied. 'You're not the man I thought I was marrying!'

'No.' Dave stood up. 'I am a better man. I eschew all groupies and casual carnal encounters. I am a paragon of virtue and empathy. Issa, you are the only woman for me – for ever and all of eternity. Even though that is a very long time, particularly towards the end.' Issa had the grace to smile at this. I wondered why humans tried so hard to mate for life when it seems monogamy is so unnatural to them. It worked well for some creatures, such as doves for example, but not for others such as tortoises, gibbons, meerkats - most, in fact. I felt monogamy was probably over-rated from what I had observed. I failed to see the point.

'I have seen, nay, I have discovered the light,' Dave rambled on. 'I am in tune with myself. Issa, I know that you laugh at me, that you find my meditations silly, but I am achieving a state of calm and understanding. My life was utter chaos; I'm on the path to harmony.'

'I know, darling.' Issa seemed to soften. 'But life is now so very dull. Only a few weeks ago, when you were wooing me, we were at the best parties, in the best company, living the life in the world's most luxurious hotels, fifty-metre yachts, flying in first class or preferably private jets. Now the honeymoon's over, you've moved us out to this big country pile so that - what…?' She fiddled with a plump black pearl earring, dangling on a string of diamonds. 'So we can think away the rest of our lives?'

'Oh, Issa. You know I have big plans - huge plans, massive plans for this place.'

'What sort of plans?' Stella sat up abruptly.

'I'm going to breathe life back into Bestwood, Stella.' He leaned forward, spilling champagne from his flute as he tipped towards her. She looked at him sternly but I saw a kind of fear flicker across her face. 'Bestwood is going to become a destination. Some people may even find their destiny here, tucked away within themselves, released by retreat. I'm going to create a mega-escape, a home for enlightenment and spiritual freedom. I'll build an environment where people will breed epiphanies and dreams, where I can teach the masses the lessons that I have learned. A place where people will expand their minds, let loose their creativity and discover purity and the sanctity of love.' Stella looked aghast. Issa looked sort of disgusted.

'You know, Dave,' Stella said, 'there's a whole lot of history with this house.'

'History! Exactly, adorable Stella - we cannot live in the past. It is our job to create the future. This place is decrepit, neglected, unexploited. I'm going to change all of that. The house is structurally sound, yes, but it's going to take some time just getting the thing clean. It'll be months before Issa considers it properly habitable. She'll be zipping off to Claridge's for a quick bath every five minutes, no doubt.' Dave winked at his wife.

'It's nearly three hundred years old, Dave, parts of it even older than that,' said Stella.

'And now it has promise. Courtesy of yours truly, this place is no longer going to rack and ruin. I'm going to diversify. All this beautiful land - I'm going to share my bounty. I'm going to do what those chinless wonders the Arnolds should have done years ago.'

'I think they tried,' said Stella.

"Tried' as in 'invited their mates around for a bit of shooting'? Did a bit of travelling and collected a few bits of art and a couple of animals? They didn't apply themselves, Stella. They got left behind. But Bestwood's going to catch up now. It'll be the best of the best. It'll be the global centre for serenity, peace and purity.'

'What happened to the man who bit the head off bats and snorted his father's ashes?' laughed Hannah.

'That man is gone, Hannah. This is a reincarnation you see before you - a new spiritual leader.'

'Men and their fucking egos,' growled Issa. 'They always need to be centre of attention.'

Digby returned and sat quietly in the Oak behind me. 'What's occurring?' he asked.

I told him I had seen Colin the grass snake earlier. He said he wished he would just stay in the lake.

'Anyway, what are they doing?' he enquired, peering over at the little group of humans down on the patio.

I told him they'd just been chatting.

'What about?' he dug.

'Change, Digby.'

'Oh,' he said. 'What sort of change?'

'I'm not sure, exactly. It appears we are going to be the centre of something.'

'That sounds exciting!' Digby said, turning his attention to them.

Dave was smiling beatifically at Hannah and then turned to Issa. 'My darling wife, most beautiful woman in all of the history of all the world.' Issa looked a little mollified in the light of the candles that Chignon had lit on the table. 'You think you are going to be bored here, don't you?' Dave grinned at his third wife.

'I'm already bored and we have been here all of five minutes,' she replied. 'No offence,' she nodded at Stella and Hannah.

'It's been a marvellous evening!' Dave mouthed 'sorry' at the girls. 'It's your birthday tomorrow, Issa.'

'I know,' she snarled, very like a caged wild beast. 'A whole heap of fun that will be. Us and a stinking zoo - yippee.'

'It was going to be a surprise, babe.' Dave's eyes glinted with excitement.

'I hate surprises.' Issa sat with her arms crossed and her forehead furrowed.

Dave chuckled. 'Woman, you are so contrary.' I could feel a deep calm emanating from him. He was sort of hypnotic, like the music that his son Ollie had unfurled.

'Well, we are having a party - tomorrow. There is so much for us to celebrate. Marvellous you, our wonderful new home, and we will launch my plans to the unsuspecting masses.' Issa sat up and a smile started. 'Anyone who's anyone is coming. It starts at eight and it finishes when it finishes. Stella and Hannah, you must join us. You will meet my sons.'

Chapter Four

The next morning, I spotted Bob and Stella over at the feed shed. She was huskily hung-over and Hannah was absent. Bob held onto his head as he bent over to pick up a bucket.

'Were you in the pub again all day yesterday?' Stella asked him.

'You're not looking on top form yourself, love,' he replied with a sheepish smile and a small scowl. 'What's your excuse?'

'Too much champagne.' Stella took a deep breath as she stood up and held onto her stomach.

'Champagne? Where have you been learning these high-faluting tastes?'

'I met our new neighbours last night. You didn't tell me, Dad.'

'Tell you what?'

'Well, who they are, for starters.'

'Who are they? All I know is that the Arnolds finally threw the towel in.'

'They are like, totally famous. Beyond!'

'Really? For what?'

'Oh my God! Where have you been? Actually, don't answer that - the Ship, of course.'

'It's the centre of the universe, Stella, you know that. Anyway, famous for what?'

'He's one of the greatest musicians ever, Dad.'

'Better than Elvis?'

'OK, maybe not better than Elvis.' Stella smiled a wide one.

'Well it was a big secret I think, Stella. Besides, you weren't actually here. You were off gallivanting! There was quite a stir in The Ship yesterday. I was bought many a pint to spill celebrity gossip, as I think it is known.'

'What did you tell them?' Stella laughed.

'Well, regaling them with the tale of Palmer Senior screaming in his birthday suit kept the grog flowing! I'll be drinking out on that for years to come.'

'So you know his name, then.'

'Only since I was told it by the barman; news travels fast round these parts! Although, from what I gather, there may have been some kind of press release. It was on the front page of yesterday's Observer.'

'Do you know what they are doing here, Dad?'

'What do you mean, sweetheart?'

'I mean, what they are planning to do to the place?'

'Nothing, I should think. They'll be bored soon enough and bugger off back to the city. They'll just come down for the odd weekend when they think they might need some fresh air.' Stella frowned at him. 'What is it, love?'

'Dave Palmer says he's going to change it here.'

Bob looked at his daughter, evenly. 'Does he now? Well, my favourite girl, we'll see about that.' He crossed his arms and set his jaw. 'Now, enough of this idle chit chat; take these to Herbert and the rest of his crew,' he commanded.

'Aye, aye Captain,' Stella said and put a brisk hand to her head, jerking it outwards and upwards.

She advanced up the Hill towards me. I had been studying a blotch of limey lichen creeping about on the Wall but I looked up and saw that she had two huge heads of frilly lettuce, peaty soil still clinging to their stems and roots, hanging from her hands. I could tell that they had been yanked from Bob's vegetable patch mere minutes earlier and just knew, without a shadow

45

of a doubt, that they were sumptuously delicious. She lobbed them over the Wall and then followed them, scrambling over. I trundled across and started to munch one. Yup, leafy ambrosia. She picked the other one up, pulled it apart and scattered the leaves at the Family, who were mooching about.

She sat down with a big, harrumphing sigh, her back against the Wall and drew her knees up against her chest. She was wearing a grey t-shirt that hung loose and half way down her thighs. It had a very large, glossy red mouth printed on its front. The mouth's enormous tongue stuck out lasciviously. Her graceful calves were clad in sand-coloured sheepskin boots and there was a glimpse of her lace-trimmed pink satin knickers. She was wearing a cream wool hat, a beanie, knitted in cables that had bits that hung off the sides and dangled around her ears, tufted at their ends. Her hair straggled out from beneath it.

Bob continued with his daily chores around the menagerie. The mob of forty-two meerkats had a bucket of kibble, carrot and mealworm mix. They'd been standing in a row, as they did, worshipping the generous Source, warm things becoming ever warmer. I wondered how they did not spontaneously combust. Their fur must have been mega toasty. I fantasised that they would all leap over the Wall and pile on to me, the whole mob's heat enveloping my shell to its total peak of hotness, my body becoming astonishingly alive, and then I would see myself haring around the Hill, scooting over clumps and hopping like I was on springs up at the tight juicy leaves of the big bush shaped like a cockerel.

As always, my fantasy remained just that, and Bob gave the giraffes, alpacas and zebras their daily bales of hay. Brian the Gibbon had a hemp sack full of fruits slung his way for him to unpick like a picnic. Something was poured into the flamingos' pond. They were all asleep, one-legged and neck-less.

Stella sat thoughtful and dozy. Bob, with everyone now fed, pottered off to the Gate House. Stella stretched out in the Sourcelight, flat on her back. The Palmer's limousine swept out of the drive, through the gate and off up into the Ups. Stella snorted a great snuff of a snore and woke herself up. She twisted onto her side and the t-shirt rucked up above her belly button, which sparkled in the sun. She had a jewel there, piercing a loop through the skin around her pucker of a navel. The pink knickers stretched tight across her buttocks. She kicked her boots off. Her toenails were like mother-of-pearl.

The front door to the Big House opened and one of the green-eyed twins emerged, in black and shades, barefoot with a steel-strung wooden guitar slung across his back. He lit a cigarette and headed towards us. On the bicep of the arm of the hand that smoked was the Source, indelibly inked, Her rays flaming out. I was sure that this one, this twin, was Ollie, the musician. He nodded at Atlas and winked at the bush shaped like a cockerel. He sat, legs akimbo, at the point where the zebras' and alpacas' fence met the Wall. He strummed and hummed, and gazed upon Stella's prone form on the grass. I felt Bliss.

As he began to sing, Stella's left hand slid over her hip and up across her flat tummy, resting itself with its heel under the swell of her right breast, the top of her palm brushing against its sensitive centre.

Ollie stopped playing and adjusted his position. A crow took off from the top of the Oak with a loud raspy caw. Stella woke with a start, her eyes opening straight onto Ollie, who was staring right at her, his irises full of pupil.

'You filthy, bloody perv!' Stella sat up and yanked her t-shirt down. Her beanie leaned crookedly to one side. A lock of hair stuck to a small drool on her cheek.

'Hey, lady, I'm not the one touching myself up in broad daylight.' Ollie laughed at her. Possibly not a good move. I held my breath. I was good at that.

Stella jumped to her feet, deeply riled. 'In the privacy of my own home!' She glared at him. 'You - you… intruder!'

'My home too, now. In fact, more mine than yours, honey.' He smiled like he'd played a winning hand. Yikes! I thought.

'Get your tank off my lawn!' Stella shouted at him, flushing wildly.

'Er, that would be my lawn, sweetheart,' he said. 'But you are very welcome to rest your tank upon it, if you like.' The apples of Stella's cheeks continued to burn with her blush.

'It's your father's bloody lawn, not yours,' she hissed at him. 'I was born right here, I'll have you know. In that house - that one there.' She jabbed her finger at the Gate House. 'I was born in the bedroom that I sleep in every single night!' She pointed at the Gate House, leaning towards him, baring her teeth like Brian the Gibbon when Colin dared slide across the moat onto his island.

'Ah yes,' Ollie said. 'My new recording studio.'

'What?'

'Well, we own that outbuilding now. We can, you know, do what we want with it.'

Stella wavered on her feet. 'Outbuilding? That's my home. It's not a frigging shed. My Dad's the zookeeper,' she said.

'Yes.' He paused. 'But there won't be a zoo, not anymore. Not that this is much of a zoo anyway, for fuck's sake. It's a mediocre bunch of past-it misfits, if you ask me.'

How rude, I thought.

'I wasn't asking you.'

'Whatever. I am telling you anyway. We won't be needing a zookeeper anymore.' He crossed his arms and stood back from the fireworks.

'Are you telling me I'm homeless?'

'I didn't think this would be news to you. I heard you got cosy last night drinking my father's cellar. I assumed he had appraised you of his plans.'

'He wasn't quite this specific. This will destroy my Dad. This place, these animals are his life. And I have plans too! Where the hell do you expect us to go?'

'I don't think that's our problem, petal.'

'And the menagerie… what are you going to do with the menagerie?'

'Er, let me think. Get rid of it?'

'But, how? Where? What are we supposed to do?'

'That'll be your conundrum, honey,' He fiddled with a loose thread on his shorts. She had no colour left in her face.

'You wanker,' she said and she properly flounced off. Understandably, I thought.

Ollie stood for some time. He watched as she went and then stood and watched where she had gone. Expressions scudded fast across his face and I could not interpret them all, but I thought that I saw superiority slide into admiration, some lust bundled with amusement and all of this then swamped with a deeply seated perturbation.

Finally, he fled into the guts of the Big House. You are a coward, I thought.

His departure was immediately marked by the comings and goings of many vans, all of them different colours and sizes and each of them spewing something: zillions of bunches of creamy white flowers, lights and candles, chinking boxes, tray upon foil covered tray. From one emerged a huge castle-shaped brown cake. Even Chignon looked impressed with this.

Digby fluttered down beside me. 'What's been going on then?' he inquired.

'Oh, preparations,' I replied, distracted. Ollie's news on top of last night's… I could barely take it all in. All my life I had yearned to see beyond the Wall but now it seemed as if I might be taken somewhere unknown, somewhere not of my choosing. And, even more disconcertingly, there seemed no guarantee that my future would include Stella - or Digby, for that matter.

'What's up, Herbert? Aren't you excited about the change any more?'

'No, not really.'

'Why not?'

'Apparently the change does not include the menagerie, Digby. I mean, it does. Just not in a very good way.'

'I don't understand. Please explain.'

'It seems we are not up to scratch. And we are going to be disposed of.'

'Disposed of?' he gasped.

'We are like an old hat. Not worth keeping. We'll be shipped out somewhere. Or worse.'

'Well, this is awful news, Herbert. What can we do about it? Can we fight it?'

'Fight it? How on earth would you propose that we do that, Digby? I'm stuck in here. At the mercy of what the humans decide. My only hope would be escape…'

Digby pondered this as the limousine swept back up the drive to be greeted by Chignon and a yawning, dishevelled Ollie. Then there was a steady whumping of air.

The whumping reached fever pitch and a helicopter popped up above the forest, whipping its millions of leaves into a collective shriek. 'Choppers' Stella called them. We were familiar with these, as we often watched the coastguard's on blustery days saving silly sailors on the Glittering. However, the coastguard's chopper had never been this close. Daisy and Dolly and the alpacas were hoofing it around their field, swishing their tails. Digby was blown right over and when he flew up into the Oak he was knocked into a branch, but managed to grab hold of another with a clawed foot on his way down. The forty-two meerkats dived into their burrows. Brian the Gibbon was strung out on a steady right angle to his rope. He clung to it by a single one of his hands.

The chopper landed in the space between the Big House and the Gate House, the long grass there flattening radially. I was perturbed as to the effect this would have on Bob's vegetable patch and did indeed see several apples fly off the Braeburn tree and bounce juicily over the ground. The ripples on the swimming pool waved all the way along to the far end that poked out from the other side of the Big House.

The whumping slowed to a whirr and then a stop. The door swung open and a bunch of pearlescent balloons emerged, bopping in the currents left by the gently wibbling blades. A well worn but expensive tan loafer appeared and a long leg of smartly distressed denim followed it, along with more balloons. I tried to count them as they bobbed about. One caught on the door handle and snapped off its string and lifted off, bumping into a blade and then flying high, melding into the neutrality of the late afternoon sky.

It was Sid, the first twin, dressed all dapper, in a pressed pale grey shirt and a charcoal jacket with his jeans. As he handed the balloons to a delighted looking Issa, who kissed him on his cheeks, his smile was Dave's. He was just like Ollie but lying somehow. He wore mirrored sunglasses. Issa took the balloons from him, thirty in total I think, including the one that got away, and passed them to Chignon, who fastened them in bunches to the bushes on either side of the porch. Sid turned to take a large domed object covered in a white silk cloth, encircled by a wide pink ribbon tied in a bow, being passed to him by the chopper pilot.

The dome unmistakably said, 'Flattery will go far tonight.' Sid passed it to Dave and winked at him. Issa looked from one to the other, the eyebrow quizzical. The doglets sat in a row, wagging their little tails, their ears curious.

'Happy birthday, my love,' Dave said as he placed the dome on the pebbly drive.

'For me?' Issa giggled. 'Is it a massive, talking diamond?'

'Open it,' grinned Dave. He stood back, and rocked on his heels. Ollie shuffled over in his slippers, his interest piqued, as indeed, was mine.

Issa pinched the top of the silky cloth between her thumb and forefinger and whipped it off as if she were a conjuror. She gasped. Inside an ornate golden cage was a big blue bird. He or she, I could not tell which, was not as big as a flamingo and had much shorter legs. Actually, the more I looked at him or her, the more he or she looked like an over big Digby.

'Oh Dave!' Issa put her hands to her face. 'A parrot! A talking parrot!' Issa gave Dave a generous, wet kiss on his rubbery mouth and he took the opportunity to give her bottom a hefty squeeze. Digby and the other parakeets racketed above my head, shuddering the branch upon which they were congregated.

Issa swatted Dave away impatiently and stuck her fingers through the wires of the cage, wiggling them at the macaw, who responded by saying, 'Love begets love.'

'Oh, it's adorable,' she said as the macaw nipped at her perfectly manicured nails, which she withdrew sharply as she took a quick step back.

'He's a Hyacinth Macaw,' Sid said, opening the door to the cage.

'Only the best for you, my brandy snap!' cooed Dave into Issa's ear as the blue bird hopped up the arm of Sid's jacket. It tugged on his shoulder seam with its grey beak and deposited chalky liquid from its back end onto the cuff of his shirt.

'Eugh!' squealed Issa. 'It shit on you! But I will call him Hyacinth.' She dared to tickle its head and it looked up at her with an eye ringed in bright yellow. Dave held out his arm and Hyacinth traversed up to his arm as the chopper pilot threw out a leather bag that landed on the pebbly drive with a smack. Sid picked it up and they all made their way back to the Big House as the chopper began to whump again and we all braced ourselves as its hurricane blew, carried away by it.

No sooner had the front door shut behind them, and been reopened so that a trailing Po could catch up with the other doglets, did a stream of vehicles begin flooding up the drive, each parking half on the grass. As the Source was settling Herself down behind the forest, more and more cars appeared. They parked on the drive until there were so many that some were parking outside the gates. People swarmed up to the Big House.

Digby was keeping up a running commentary on the outfits and haircuts and looks of the people as they all piled into the house and reappeared in the orangery, spilling out onto the patio and around the pool.

I was starting to feel a little dizzy with the onslaught of information and activity. For many years not very much had happened at all and, to be frank, I am not sure I had seen so many humans in one place all at once before. I couldn't keep up.

There was a small commotion at the bottom end of the Wall. Stella and Hannah were clambering over. Digby took off, landing on the peak of the roof of the Big House, silhouetted against the sinking Source.

Over the hubbub and chinking of glass coming from the patio and the orangery, the girls began to talk. They each wore a dress that was tight around their torso and that flounced out to stop, in Stella's case, since she was taller, just above her knees. Hannah's was just below. Stella's was a pale shimmery gold and she had gold painted around her eyes. Hannah's dress was a cobalt blue, like the Glittering at the very end of a long, clear day.

'Let's be having some wine then, Stellamouche.' Hannah leaned over to Stella, who unscrewed a bottle and poured a glass of velvety red liquid into Hannah's outstretched mug. I smelled blackcurrants. Hannah lit another of her fat, sweet cigarettes and lay back with a jangle. Both of the girls were wearing an astonishing array of jewellery and scraps of additional fabric hanging off their ears and wrists and waists, even wound into their hair. Hannah's eyes were circled in a smoky black that made the blue of her irises pop. They were both barefoot, although on the top of the Wall I saw two pairs of short lace-up boots, neatly lined up.

'So,' said Hannah, blowing a smoke ring. 'What's the plan of attack tonight?'

'In what respect?' asked Stella.

'The boys, Stellamouche. You want a blow-back?' Hannah cocked her head at Stella. She sipped her wine.

'Go on, then. I don't know about the boys, Hans. You haven't stopped yattering about Sid all afternoon. I was about to scream if you made me check another magazine for pictures of him. Anyone would think you were in love.'

'Love, shmuv!' Hannah said and turned the spliff around and put it backwards between her open lips, the burning hot ember end inside the small cavern of her mouth. She leaned over to Stella and cupped her hands around Stella's mouth and a tube of smoke streamed tightly between them. Triumphantly, Hannah took the spliff from her mouth, a ring of shiny pink around its middle and passed it to Stella. 'I do want to fuck him absolutely senseless, though.'

Stella spluttered, her eyes watering and then guffawed. 'Hans, you've changed! Do you have absolutely no shame?'

'Nope! None whatsoever!' Hannah winked. 'I got bored of being boring. I have reinvented myself as a wanton harlot!' They both cackled then and swigged mouthfuls of wine. Hannah stood up and went to sit on the bottom curve of the Wall, her bony back to us.

'I recommend we divide and conquer,' she said over her shoulder.

'I divide and you conquer?' replied Stella. 'I'm not sure I fancy being with a bunch of strangers all night, Hans. I might just go home if you manage to bugger off with him.'

'Why don't you try your luck with Ollie, then?'

'Because, Hannah, I think he is a total tosser.'

'He's very sexy though, don't you think?'

'You haven't even met him.'

'But he looks just like his brother, right? And his brother is hot.'

'Looks aren't everything. I told you what he said to me. He's such an arsehole. He's making us homeless so he can have a new playroom. They are going to destroy Dad. How can they take his menagerie away? It's everything to him.'

'All the more reason for you to make friends with him, then, surely? If you could get into his pants you might be able to stop all of this. Imagine what you could achieve if you could make him fall in love with you. He wouldn't want to kick you out then, would he? You know, if you played your cards right, you could even have all of this!' Hannah spread her arms wide.

'Make him fall in love with me?' Stella laughed, mirthlessly. 'And, pray tell, my ugly-duckling-turned-slapper-swan best friend of old, how, exactly, does one do that?'

'Well it'll be easy for you. Everyone always falls in love with you.' Too true, I thought.

'That was when were kids, Hans. Those guys at school just worked themselves up into a frenzy. It's a whole different ball-game now.'

'Nothing's different, babes.' Hannah turned around and jumped off the Wall to crouch in front of Stella. 'You're still amazingly beautiful - more so, actually.' She held Stella's chin and tipped her face so that the glow from below purred across it. 'And clever and kind and generous.'

'I'm not sure Ollie's the kind of guy that goes after girls with those qualities. I suspect he prefers compliant air-heads.'

Beyond them, the Big House buzzed. The little white lights Chignon had hung earlier spangled prettily and candles flickered behind the panes of the orangery, now packed to the brim with flowers.

People were fair thronging about down there, a kaleidoscope of colours rotating around Issa, a statuesque fulcrum in a column of sparkling silver, like a moonlit mermaid. Dave stood beside her, his hair in a long plait and wearing a shimmery navy blue suit. He had his arm around Issa's waist and his head arrived at her shoulder. Her feet sparkled and Po, Tinky-Winky and Laa-Laa scampered around them, each wearing a patent leather collar: red, purple and yellow respectively.

Hannah stood up and looked over at them. 'There!' she shouted, pointing through the crowd at Sid and Ollie, who were chatting to a girl with bleached blonde hair and a dress slit down to her navel, displaying what appeared to be most unnaturally globe-like breasts. 'Are we ready?' She turned back to Stella. 'We're going in for the kill!' She leaped off the Wall and grabbed a pair of boots on her way down the Hill. Stella followed.

Chapter Five

The party was a merry sea of humanity on the patio. There were seemingly hundreds of bodies constantly moving about. I hardly recognised any of their faces and all of their voices merged into a hubbub so that individual words and conversations became indistinguishable. Digby flew from the roof to me and back regularly, but he was also baffled by the sheer volume of activity.

I withdrew into myself, metaphorically. It seemed I would be leaving. When? I wondered. To where? Having craved change and excitement for so long, I was surprised to find that now that I was fearful. The unknown was actually pretty terrifying.

I tried to keep my eye pinpointed on Stella in her golden gown but kept losing her in the crowd and around the back of the Big House. Early on I'd seen Sid and Ollie greet both her and Hannah, the pair of girls initially looking a little aimless, and hand them each a glass of pink champagne, received with grateful smiles. I was surprised to see Stella friendly but perhaps she had taken Hannah's advice and decided to make this enemy her friend. This quartet then roamed around the group of smaller groups, whispering to each other and sometimes rudely pointing at various guests.

Hannah had been unsubtle about her plans for Sid and was looking up at him, touching his arm, giggling and flicking her hair. Superlative flirting. I wondered where she had learned it. A book, perhaps. Or perhaps mating rituals were innate in all creatures; the most essential act powered by the chemicals of desire.

The party buzz became, to me, a lullaby and I drifted off only to be woken by an immense bang on my shell. I had just been kicked. Kicked! The pain rattled through my side and around me. For safety's sake, I stayed indoors. I had momentarily left the ground, I think, but appeared to be remaining in the upright position. There were voices near me, those of Sid and Hannah. His was low and stealthy and hers was high and coquettish. When my curiosity transformed my fear into courage, I stuck my neck out to see what was going on.

Hannah had Sid up by the Oak, although it was apparent he did not mind, and certainly was not resisting her advances. There was amusement on his face. I could see him closer than before, softly lit by the multitude of tiny lights down the Hill. The wide mouth he'd inherited from his father had a generous sensuality. His jaw and cheekbones were smoothly stunning. But it was less his looks and more his manner that was magnetising. He had a supreme self-confidence, which was powerfully attractive. He was reeling Hannah in, like I'd seen the Arnolds do with a line and a pike at the fishing lake down by the patio, a little encouragement here, a little rest there. He was baiting her, knowing he had her, knowing that it was all a matter of time. And he was absolutely choosing the timing.

'So what are we looking at, then?' Sid asked, as they stood just above me on the Hill, their backs to the Oak, facing out to the Glittering. He rubbed his hip against hers, teasingly.

'Oh, I don't know,' Hannah said. 'The view. The stars, maybe.' She leaned her head in towards his shoulder.

'Stars?' Sid asked, crinkling his mouth at its edges. 'Can't see any stars up here, Hannah. It's a bit cloudy. They're all down there, getting wrecked.' Sid turned to face her and she looked up at the buttery murmur of moon waltzing behind a wrap of writhing mists.

'The sea, then,' she said and gestured at the Glittering, pulsing away.

He said nothing and she turned and put a hand on his belt and pulled him towards her so that the tips of their noses met and their eyes were locking. Still he said nothing. She leaned in and pressed her bottom lip to his top lip just as Digby arrived back in the branches above them. Neither of them noticed him. He sat and looked at me and I at him. Then we both turned our attention back to them.

She was still holding her lips against his but he was still holding back, even as she pressed her hips against his and, on tiptoes, slipped her arms around his neck. Only then did he release her by opening her mouth with his and wrapping his arms around her waist.

For a while they appeared to be devouring each other and then, as his hands lifted up her cobalt skirt revealing the backs of her pale thighs, her hands went towards his crotch and started to fiddle with his belt. He pulled down her knickers, all flouncy layers of navy chiffon, down until they drifted about her ankles and she bent to unlace her boots and slip them and her socks off. He kissed her again and as she went to unbutton the front of his jeans, he dropped to his knees, lifted the front of her skirt and kissed her there. She leaned herself into him and, with her hands on his shoulders, arched her back so that her silky white hair hung in the air. She moaned. She grabbed the back of his neck and pulled him up. Now that she was barefoot, he was much taller, but he put a hand on each buttock and picked her up, balancing her against the trunk of the Oak.

As they kissed, she pulled his jeans down until they were around his ankles and he pinned her up against the tree. She let out another stronger, longer moan.

Then it was a rhythm, driven by a bass note thumping behind the hiatus below. A thrust, a moan, a thrust a moan a thrust a moan until, in the time it took to top up a glass, there was a short gasp from Sid and they stood, forehead to forehead, one of Hannah's legs around his waist and the other tucked between his knees. They stayed like that, for a moment, all four eyes shut, and then he extricated himself.

He tucked himself in and zipped himself up and she said, 'After that, I need to sit down,' and so she did. He sat down beside her, reluctantly. Still he said nothing, and he did not look at her.

She put her hand on his and he kissed her on her lips briefly, his eyes shut, and said, 'We should go back to the party. I'm gagging for a drink. But maybe first…' He leaned back a touch and took a tiny brown jar from a pocket in his jeans. Unscrewing the lid, he revealed a tiny spoon, heaped with white powder. He held it to his left nostril whilst holding his right closed with a forefinger, and snorted it. He passed the jar to Hannah who did the same. She then sniffed and rubbed the tip of her nose.

'Good coke,' she said. 'Where did you get it?'

'I have my sources,' he replied, pinching his nostrils together and swallowing. 'You want to buy some?'

'Are you serious?' She looked at him in surprise. 'You're a dealer?'

'Best way to get guest listed. And laid.' She winced a little. He did not flinch. 'And funds my own, not inconsiderable, it has to be said, habit.' He stood up. 'Come on. If you've got the cash, I've got the stash.'

She stood up and pulled her knickers and boots back on and followed him back down the Hill. As he walked away, she asked, 'Can I take some now and pay you tomorrow?' He stopped, put his arm around her shoulder and walked her down the rest of the Hill, back to the patio where the melee continued to sparkle.

As they rejoined the group, Sid picked up two glasses from a tray being held by a man in black. He gave one to Hannah and then went to talk to Issa. Hyacinth sat on Dave's shoulder and Issa's doglets sat at their feet, gazing up at her adoringly as she hand fed them tiny morsels of food delivered by more men in black. One of them offered Sid a choice of the delicacies lined up on his tray and Sid waved him away, knocking back his champagne in one. Hannah stood on her own for a few moments staring after Sid, abandoned, and then walked around the back of the house, searching, I assumed, for Stella, no doubt in order to boast of her conquest.

Sid tickled Hyacinth under the chin and he hopped off Dave's shoulder to investigate the tip of a spear of asparagus dropped by Laa-Laa. As his feet touched the ground, Laa-Laa barked and then, growling jealously, pulled an aquamarine feather his own length from Hyacinth's tail with a snap of his mouth. Hyacinth let out an almighty squawk and unexpectedly took flight, landing on Atlas' sphere. He was so tame I had assumed that he could not fly. I had heard that some birds had their wings clipped. Indeed, we thought the flamingos' were, but it was to turn out that they were just as lazy and unadventurous as the Family.

Sid grabbed Laa-Laa by the scruff of his fluffy white neck and dropped him, kicking him as he fell to the ground. Laa-Laa's purple collar sparkled in the fairy lights as he somersaulted over the throng's heads, shock I suspected rendering him silent, apart from a small yet audible yelp as he splashed into the fishing lake. Those who had witnessed this act of pure cruelty followed his arc, mouths agape and frozen for the moment it took Laa-Laa to resurface with a splutter and a paddle. A ripple of relief ran through the onlookers, followed immediately by the appearance of the head of a large, gleaming pike, jaw wide open as he inhaled Laa-Laa whole and then vanished with a swirl into the blackness of the water.

Issa slapped Sid hard across the face. Sid staggered on the spot slightly, for a split second looking like he might dare to return the favour, but he had the good grace to remove himself from the scene. Issa ran to the edge of the lake and looked like she was going to jump in after her lost doglet. Dave sprinted to her side and clung onto her arm.

The party was over. It took a few minutes for the horror story to be whispered through the revellers and some of them didn't immediately comprehend that, as a result of the incident, it was now time to leave, but gradually they did. Issa was sobbing into Dave's arms, the pair of them huddled on the edge of the fishing lake, its surface now eerily serene. It was blank to the crime committed within it, almost as if it were hiding it. Po and Tinky-Winky stood by, their ears flat against their heads, looking mournfully out across the water, occasionally scraping their feet and yapping, but too terrified to risk going in. Probably realising, I thought, that there was no point.

Ollie was shaking hands and air-kissing and helping people to their vehicles, saying that he hoped that everyone had had a good time and apologising for the sudden end to proceedings but thanking the guests for coming along. Hyacinth remained on the top of the sphere and said, 'May life throw you a pleasant curve'. The girls had come and sat on the zebra and alpacas' fence and were smoking and swigging from a champagne bottle. Stella was stroking Daisy's nose and I strolled down, wondering if I might be in luck for a tickle.

'Fuck me,' laughed Hannah, 'that was absolutely hilarious!'

'Hilarious?' cried Stella. 'Hannah, Sid just killed one of Issa's... babies!' Stella stopped fondling Daisy and stared disbelievingly at Hannah. Daisy butted and nuzzled her hand.

'Oh, he didn't mean to. It was that massive fish, anyway. It was like some kind of mutant. Has it been living on that old lady's gin or something? Besides, that stupid little dog shouldn't have attacked Issa's big blue bird. What is that thing, anyway? I thought they were meant to be getting rid of the menagerie, not adding to it.' She slipped off the fence and disappeared from view.

'But...' began Stella. 'But you think it was... okay, then... for Sid to kick Laa-Laa into the lake?'

'Well, no I suppose not. But I guess he's very just a very passionate type. And completely off his tits, of course. With hindsight, it was a bit inappropriate, I concede. But he wasn't to know there would be quite such an unfortunate ending. I think we all thought the dog would just get a bit wet. I guess life's pretty fragile, really. Laa-Laa's time was up and, hey, the fish got a square meal. It's nature doing her thing, right?'

Stella stared at her. 'You've changed, Hans.'

'Oh, for fuck's sake. You're like a broken record. I've grown up, Stella! Welcome to the new me. I'm here to stay and I'm going to have fun. Now, would you like a line of this?'

'Where did you get that?'

'Where do you think?'

'I haven't the faintest. Although, now I think about it, I am guessing Sid. You spent enough time fawning around him this evening. Ollie said he'd brought a load in, kept offering it to me.'

'And you kept knocking him back, did you? Shame, it's pretty good.'

'I didn't want to do anything I might regret. He's pretty full on - like his brother.'

There was a loud flapping noise as Hyacinth launched himself off the celestial sphere and said, 'Anger begins with folly and ends with regret'. He landed on the roof of the Big House where I could just make out Digby, his head under his wing, upset or dozing, I couldn't tell. Hyacinth landed beside him like a lump and slipped a little on the green copper. Graceful, Hyacinth was not. Digby popped his head out.

'Do you want one or not?' said Hannah, and I heard her sniff long and deep.

'Oh, go on then.' Stella balanced the bottle she was holding on a fence post and hopped down. There was another long sniff and a cough. A hand reached up and grabbed the bottle off the fence post and I heard a couple of fizzy glugs. 'So… what happened with you and Sid, then? We did notice the pair of you sneak off, you know.'

'He had me up against that big tree over there.' Hannah giggled.

'Had you?' Stella spluttered. 'Had you as in 'had you'?'

'Yes, he had me. Fucked me, did me, shagged me… it was kind of romantic, actually.'

'Er, how, exactly, was it romantic? You don't waste any time, do you?' Part of Stella seemed amused, but most of her not.

'You know what I say, Stellamouche.' I heard the metal lighter spin and ignite.

'You don't ask, you don't get,' replied Stella, as I smelled plain old cigarette smoke waft over the Wall.

'Spot on, babe.'

'Well, well. I hope you had the presence of mind to use something during your 'romantic' encounter. Do you think you'll see him again?'

'Who knows? He lives here, you live here. Chances are we'll bump into each other, I suppose.'

'You didn't use anything, did you?'

'No, I was quite overcome by the throes of passion.'

'Hannah.' Stella sounded quite stern. 'He's a complete slapper. You could catch something! Or worse. He's hardly the type to stand by a girl he gets up the duff. What were you thinking?'

'I was thinking, 'There's no way I'm knocking back this opportunity'. Anyway, as if I would be foolish enough to stay knocked up if was stupid enough to get knocked up in the first place. Christ, I saw what happened to my mother. Shotgun wedding and five kids later, she still barely has a life herself. Kids are so fucking selfish.'

A roll of thunder rumbled far away in the direction of the Glittering. A storm was brewing out to sea.

'Anyway, enough about me - how was Ollie? Is he in love with you yet? You have to admit, he's just as totally gorgeous as I told you he would be. Strange how he and Sid look completely alike but are really quite different. I'd have him too, given half a chance. Maybe both together…'

'Will you please just calm down? You can't have them both – that's just… greedy!'

'Oh,' said Hannah. 'Is that a little green-eyed monster I see? It's a slippery slope, Stellamouche. Before you know it you'll have lost that heart of yours. About time you did.'

'No, he's still a twat. Apparently work on the recording studio starts in a week. He apologised. Like that makes a blind bit of difference. We don't appear to have any legal entitlement to the property or so arse-face claims. It was a verbal agreement between Dad and the Arnolds. Talking of Dad, he is going to go completely mental when I tell him what's going on. I thought he held it together fairly well this morning, but this just keeps on getting worse. I'd better get busy looking for somewhere else for us to live. The animals are definitely going, though, starting tomorrow. Brian's been sold.'

Sold? I thought. Thankfully, Brian had retired to his tree house and so was not party to this new nugget of information. Who would buy Brian? I asked myself. Had I been sold, too? How much would I go for, under the hammer? Who would be my highest bidder? Which of the menagerie would turn out to be the most valuable? The thunder rolled again and the air around us felt fit to break.

'You could come and live with me for a bit? Or maybe we could get a place together.' Hannah hummed a little.

'I'm not sure your parents would like that. They've only just got rid of your brothers. And I'm a student! Even with the waitressing I can barely do more than feed and clothe myself and pay the gas bill. Besides, what about Dad? I need to find him somewhere else to live. Other than the pub.' She stopped and sighed. 'I don't want to leave. I have my own plans for here: I want to do a PHD, my grades should be good enough. My thesis will be on the Foetal Freezer. I was applying for a research grant to start work on it here. Word was they loved the idea.' Another big sigh. 'Got anymore of that gear?' asked Stella.

'Sure thing, honey. Your Dad can look after himself - you shouldn't let him hold you back. Perhaps he could live on his boat - for a while, at least?' There was some rustling and some more snarfing sniffs. 'Well, the offer's there if you need it, babe. Shame about Brian, too. I always liked the gibbon, cheeky monkey that he is. Always nicking things, like my shades, and running off with them. What's this Freezer thing about?'

'Oh, just my contribution to saving the planet, the next step in conservation. Trying to rail against the unstoppable human invasion in the event of global meltdown. A sort of disaster recovery plan, if you like - a modern-day ark. Cryogenically frozen foetuses of all the creatures, cellular records. A chance to start again. A battle in the war against extinction. I suppose I could take my ideas somewhere else… but here felt like mine. I have to try and stop this, Hans.'

'Well, let's try to apply some of your world-class logic to the situation, then. What's your next move?'

'I'm taking him surfing tomorrow.'

'Brian?'

'No, silly. Ollie.'

'Nice one. Can I come?'

'No.'

'I have to see Sid, anyway. I owe him money for this,' said Hannah.

'You owe *him* money?' Stella laughed, without humour.

I was half blinded by a fat splat of precipitation. The Sourceless sky lit up with a jagged dagger that launched itself at the Spike.

'It's raining,' said Hannah as the thunder clapped.

'No shit. To bed, then,' said Stella. And as they wandered off, I wandered in.

Chapter Six

I was very wet when the Source made Her first peep in a pathetic puff the next day. On the plus side, I was really very clean. I trekked up the Hill to my viewpoint where Digby was sat under the trails of the honeysuckle. I peered at him, hanging his little head. The demise of Laa-Laa had hit him hard. Poor Digby - he liked his life full of fun and light, not this. He was a pure pleasure seeker.

He looked up at me with a sadness in his eyes that made my stony heart break. I wondered how we could protect our friends from the pain that is life, or whether doing so would be cruelty itself, since I myself was enamoured by the occasional, and unpredictable, pins and needles of feelings, nice and nasty, that pricked at me. My Family appeared immune to them: 'our cold blood' they claimed, but I liked caring. I liked this double-edged sword. I liked there being more to life than food as fuel and perfunctory reproductive sex.

'Sid left this morning before we'd even started the chorus, you know.' I didn't know, but I was pleased. 'A car with 'Taxi' on a light box on its top took him away. Do you think he will be punished for what he did?' He looked at me, hopefully.

'I don't know, Digby.' I wanted to say 'yes'. 'I don't know if they have a system to deal with that sort of thing. Let's hope what goes around, comes around, eh?'

'You believe in that?'

I'd like to. 'Yes, Digby, I do. You should, too.'

'Ok,' he acquiesced, quietly.

I was not sure why this incident had affected him so much, although I supposed he had seen how fragile life could be; perhaps it made him fear for his own. Miraculously, I think this may have been the first time he had witnessed death occur before its time. It reminded me of when a group of Stella's schoolmates had perished at the wheel of some teenage driving. It had stunned her. I guess Digby had a soft spot for Laa-Laa, too. All of the doglets seemed to entertain him - I just found them mildly irritating. I didn't know whether there would be retribution for Laa-Laa; neither Digby nor I was in a position to avenge the death, even if we had felt compelled to seek recompense. I rather sided with Hannah's cold-hearted view on the incident, that unfortunate as it appeared, it was nature doing its thing. It was an example of the way in which cycles and systems transfer energy from creature to creature, the way in which life leaps from one body to the next, feeding and regenerating. Digby was guilty of it himself every time he scoffed a grub or a bug.

What good would it do anyway if we could punish the pike? It wouldn't bring Laa-Laa back and the pike would still not think he had done anything wrong. There was no justice to be done.

The door to the Big House opened then and, unexpectedly, it wasn't Dave, naked and performing his morning scream and stretch ritual, but Ollie on his way out. I was impressed. It was extremely early still and Stella had clearly set him a challenge. She liked to surf at Sourcerise and he was keen enough to drag himself out of bed to join her.

I was becoming rather fascinated by Ollie. The way that his music moved me, moved all of us, seemed to be an extra special gift. It was generous the way he shared it with us. It was sort of mythical. There were characters in stories that had this gift. One beckoned to me, a Finnish one. He was probably at the forefront of my mind since one of his instruments that he charmed the creatures with was a harp fashioned from the jaw of a giant pike.

Perhaps if we could make him a harp from our dastardly pike, this would satisfy Digby. That character, the son of the Maiden of the Air, I struggled to recall his name, he had spent his life searching for a wife, failing time and time again. One prospective bride had even taken things so far as to drown herself rather than wed him. As I watched him, Ollie, I mean, I hoped that history, fictional or not, was not set to repeat itself. Ollie, despite his shortcomings, deserved to be loved, I thought, whatever that may mean.

He wandered over to Stella, who was strapping her surfboards to the top of her camper van. She was wearing a second skin of black rubber, stopping just above the knees. Ollie whistled at her and she stuck her fingers up at him and giggled.

'Off to the beach,' I said.

'I know,' said Digby. 'Should I stay or should I go?' he asked, thoughtfully.

'You go,' I said. 'It's pointless us both being bored out of our tiny, little skulls. You can tell me what happens later. Who knows, the others may provide some entertainment.'

They did, as it happened, as something rather unusual occurred.

Hannah had been mooning about, sitting on the Wall, looking longingly at the Big House. At one point, she even hugged the Oak, the pole star of her sordid previous evening.

Bob arrived astoundingly early for his rounds. I had not expected to see any of the humans until the Source's zenith for the day at least, given their antics late into the night before. Bob hadn't rolled in until well after the party's abrupt halt and the rain had begun to pour.

He efficiently commandeered Hannah's assistance, sending her all over the menagerie whilst he installed a huge padlock on the feed shed and blocked out the windows. Battening the hatches, I thought.

After a while, Hannah pleaded exhaustion and wended her way to the door of the Big House to be curtly informed by a shattered looking Chignon of Sid's dawn departure. Looking somewhat dismayed, she slunk back to the Gate House. This is when the something odd started to happen.

Bob emerged from the feed shed carrying a sack and a large screwdriver. He locked his shiny new padlock behind him and wended his way up to the forest, around the back of Brian's moat to the drawbridge. The drawbridge was a large, flat piece of timber attached to a concrete block on which sat a simple wooden bench that Bob had knocked together from a couple of old railway sleepers he'd purloined from somewhere. He elicited a banana from his sack and chucked it across the moat where it bounced, once. Cupping his hands to his mouth, he mimicked Brian's hoot. Brian craned his head out around the tree house's door, scooted upside down along a rope and launched himself at the banana. He sat on the moss underneath a beech tree, ponderously peeling the fruit and watching Bob as he deftly unscrewed the drawbridge.

Bob laid the loose drawbridge across the water and strode across to Brian, sat beside him and then scooped him up and bundled him into the sack. Brian's head poked out, looking in wonderment at Bob, who now was on his feet and then, in a flash, back over the drawbridge.

With Brian in the sack under one arm and dragging the now unfettered drawbridge from the other, Bob vanished into the forest, only to pop out at the far end near the Gate House a few moments later, now laden with just the sack. He peered around the trees, ran across the drive, around the back of the trees and then legged it down the fields and hills towards the Spire, Brian clinging on, wearing the sack like a flapping nappy.

Wow, I thought. Brian's having a big adventure! And, I realised, a reprieve. He was supposed to be sold today!

I tapped my toes. Where had Bob taken Brian? I wondered. Why, I thought, had I agreed Digby could go to the beach? I needed him here! Well, *there* actually, tracking Bob and Brian.

A vehicle crept up the drive. It had a paint job like Daisy and Dolly and the Palmer's sofa. It parked outside the Big House and a little lady emerged from it, very short and built delicately, like a sparrow. She wore her hair in a cap of tight grey curls and frameless glasses that expanded her matching grey eyes. She rapped on the front door and Dave and Chignon came and shook her hand and the three of them wandered up the Hill towards Brian's island. The mob of forty-two meerkats sniggered. I stood smug and snug under the Oak and surveyed the scene. They walked all the way around the island three times, stopping to stand and stare into the copse, before Chignon sat on the bench and crossed her legs at her ankles.

'I'm sure it was here,' said Dave, gesturing to where the drawbridge had performed its function admirably for many years up until just very recently. The little lady looked perturbed. I saw a secret smile skipping about on Chignon's lips. 'Maybe, if I really concentrated I could walk across the water?' suggested Dave, who was promptly up to his waist in the moat. He became very muddy hauling himself up the bank on the other side. The little lady sat on the bench next to Chignon and they watched him soggily plod the circumference of the island. He climbed inelegantly up to the tree house and shouted 'Not in here!' at the bench. The ladies looked at each other and said many things without any words. They were in agreement with whatever it was. Dave shook each tree rudely by its trunk and then returned to the edge of the moat. And jumped in again, humiliated.

'Give us a hand, love!' he shouted at Chignon and she and the little lady pulled him up and out on the other side.

'Well,' the little lady said, wiping her hands on her neatly pressed pocketed trousers, 'that was a hundred and twenty mile round trip wasted. Perhaps we could take a look at the flamingos you mentioned as some sort of consolation. Chilean, you say? Of course, we have a flock of seventy-two already. Had half a dozen chicks hatch this spring: a bumper crop! Have you had any babies this year?' She cocked her head at Dave.

'Er… I'm not sure,' Dave replied.

'I see,' said the little lady, sternly. Dave looked sheepish.

The three of them trooped off to the silly pink birds and, shortly afterwards, the little lady departed in the zebra van, free of any feathered friends. They can't have been up to scratch, I thought to myself, a little meanly, perhaps since she had not even bothered to look at me and, although I had no desire to be sold into the unknown, I could not help feeling a little peeved at this oversight. Dave slunk defeated into the Big House. Chignon followed him, still smiling. She was most definitely amused.

The day darkened as clouds increased their pressure on the Source and the air was ready to crack again.

Stella returned. Her camper van's round lights cheerily beamed through the general greyness, her fresh pinkness smiling through the gloom. Ollie and Stella hopped out, waved amicably at each other and walked in opposite directions to their respective houses.

Where was Digby, I mused, just as he puffed back over the Wall and dropped to a stop right beside me. 'Bored?' he asked.

'At this precise moment, yes. How was it?'

'Those gulls are terrible bullies, you know. At one point I thought they weren't going to let me leave.' He seemed harassed.

'I've told you before, just stand up to them. They're scavengers. They won't do you any real harm.'

'I know, I do listen. But they are so big!'

'Poor Digby,' I sympathised. 'Perhaps you should take Hyacinth with you next time. I bet they wouldn't come near you, then.'

'Not a bad idea. Although he is a tad conspicuous.'

'Says some quite peculiar things, too. Most random.'

'Oh, that's just for show. He's quite normal really when you get to know him. He was hand reared, like me, and taught that nonsense for the humans' amusement. Quite the performer - mildly brainwashed, perhaps, but a nice enough bird. It's quite impressive that he's learned to speak their language. Although he refuses to hold a conversation with them; considers that terrible etiquette.' He hopped up into the honeysuckle.

'Well, Digby, tell me, what happened on the beach today? And then I'll tell you what happened here.'

'Actually, it was much like always. Children being mislaid, sand castles being washed away, dropped ice-creams melting in puddles on the sand.' He was still despondent. I sighed, despairingly. It was enough to trigger a remembrance of duty from the parakeet, who made a concerted effort to perk up. 'Stella and Ollie looked like they were having fun, though. But before I go into details, where is Brian? I swung by The Ship on my way home to check on Bob. I may have had a bit too much Source but it really looked like he was sat having a pint with Bob and his Shipmates. He was wearing a hat - and a tie.'

'That sounds about right,' I laughed. Lucky Brian. 'They came for him, the buyer and Dave, I mean. But he wasn't here!'

'Genius,' said Digby. 'I wonder what Bob'll do next? Although, Stella seemed to be making decent progress herself today. There was definitely some romance in the ozone on the beach, Herbert. Those two would make a lovely couple, I think.'

'Lovely looking, you mean? Because, by all accounts, she cannot stand him. She's only messing with him because he's threatening to take her home away.' I didn't mention me. No need to go on about it.

'Yes, there was some discussion on that matter,' Digby said.

A bat swept over us in the falling dusk. Light was flashing on the horizon of the Glittering again but, directly above us, the sky had opened up, a pale glowing blue. The moon was a fat crescent of paper pasted on, translucent and crinkly. 'Ollie had a go at surfing. But he really wasn't very good. Stella rather showed him up. They had a little barbeque - Stella had the key to Hannah's mother's hut – you remember I told you about it before?'

I did remember. It was a wooden shed on the beach, really, one in a long line. This one was cream on the outside, turquoise on the inside, paint peeling charmingly, little windows on the front and a porch. Inside there was an armchair upholstered in a fabric printed with rose buds and a lavender leaf coloured blanket hanging over the back. There were chipped enamelled mugs, white and ringed in navy blue, and an old cooker called Baby Belling. There was a rusty padlock on the door and grains of sand skipping across the floor.

My eyes had not seen sand close up in this life, but there were images of it in my shell, piles of it, duned high and skittering as far as the eye could see - coarse, damp sand, cloggy and firm; dry, powdery sand, dervishing in tiny tornadoes like little devils being born and borne over by the wind. In my mind's eye I saw curving, sweeping beaches, white, golden and even one of olive green. These images were all part of my history, my bloodline, the path of my DNA. And then, further back, I could see sand swirling in currents, way back now. There was sand deep under water, light flicking through the brine throwing my shadow down against the rippling patterns the water made of it.

'Herbert?' Digby dragged me back into the present.

'Yes?'

'Are you ok? You looked a little peculiar…'

'I was just remembering…' I had tried to explain these historical visions to Digby before, but he had made it clear he believed it to be indicative of an overactive imagination coping with the interest-impoverished life I led. 'So they surfed, and ate and what else?' I moved on.

'Well they talked a lot - non-stop, actually. A right pair of chatterboxes! About all sorts of things: Ollie's music – he's very ambitious, apparently about to release his debut work to an unsuspecting public. And Stella told him all about her trip. They discussed what happened last night… apparently Sid's a bit of a one. I think the girls already know that, they've said as much. But Ollie says he really is a total 'skirt-chaser'. Like a 'dog with two dicks'. Ollie says he's not the same. Although he also said he's never been in love. He came across as a very calm person, very spiritual - a philosopher, a thinker. It was him that introduced Dave to all this meditation malarkey. Oh, and Stella told him about Hannah's reinvention. She's not just lost all her excess baggage – apparently he's left her job behind the counter at the Post Office and has discovered a passion for fashion. She's been making her own jewellery and selling it! Stella was wearing some she'd made for her. It was rather nice.'

'Really? What was it like?' This was intriguing. Hannah had been a hopeless, hapless teenager. Overweight and forced to dress in tatty, shapeless t-shirts and jeans handed down by one of her many brothers, she had suffered from an endless, spiralling series of heart-breaking crushes on boys who entirely failed to notice her. She had harped on about them endlessly over the years to Stella as they sat with mugs of hot chocolate on the Wall.

She also had had absolutely no idea what she wanted to do with her life. Her sole goal was snagging some spotty boyfriend. This made me want to throttle her, frankly, had I been able to take human form. I had so few, in fact, zero, options in my world within the Wall and she couldn't even begin to see her choices. It wasn't like there was a vast list of things she was trying to choose from; she simply suffered from a void of ambition. To be fair, this was the symptom of a cause that was her almost crippling lack of self-confidence - a consequence of growing up bullied by a bunch of lads, I think. Her four older brothers were unfeasibly cruel to her, by all accounts. But now she was finding herself and her vocation - hurrah for her.

'Well,' said Digby, filling me in on Hannah's craftwork, 'here was a sort of a long string of tiny pearls and minute pink beads strung on a silvery thread. Ethereal. Stella was most taken by it. And a chunky silver ring sprinkled with stardust. Stella said that Hannah's planning to go to London to some big stores and see if they can stock it - it's flying off the shelves down here. Ollie said Sid has a friend, Violet, who is a buyer for a really big store, and she should be visiting on Saturday. There's going to be a gig that night. Ollie sang Stella one of the songs he'll play at it, tapping out the rhythm on a plate with a fork. His music has the same effect on Stella as it does on us - she goes into a trance. Her eyes burn really brightly and there's a glow all around her, an indigo glow.' I remembered the music's transmogrifying power, and the hollow loss when it had gone and the real world shifted back into view. I found myself yearning for it again. But then I heard what Digby had said.

'What do you mean – a gig?'

'They are in a band.' Digby stated.

'Who's in a band?'

'The brothers. Ollie and Sid.'

'Right,' I said. 'Both of them?' I had Ollie down as the musician and Sid down as the party animal, as Dave had described them. It seemed unfair that these humans could have multiple talents, explore multiple uses of themselves and be good at more than just one thing. It was like living several lives in just one - it was gluttonous. A richness that wracked my simple life dedicated to observation with poverty and rendered it positively dissatisfying. 'So what's it called then, this band?'

'Apollemis,' Digby leaned and whispered to me as though it was the key to Pandora's Box. So dramatic, he was. However, this did ring a chime in my knowledge hidden away and barely used, a whiff of heavenly myths circulating the globe, words and stories and wild fantasies. It was there, lurking at the back door of my mind, peeping through the jar, slipping out of view when I looked straight at it, like a star in the night sky, already dead for billions of years. It crept around my periphery.

'So, the twins' band has a gig, on Saturday. In the Ship. Sid's organised it.' Digby had bored of my unintentional silence and spilled more fact. Saturday… I wondered, when would that be? 'Ollie's asked Stella to go,' Digby gave me more. 'Told her to bring Hannah, too; says he'll introduce her to Violet.'

As he had said 'twins', the answer had begun to swim up from the deep and then it popped, gloriously, to the surface. Of course - the Greek twins, Apollo and Artemis – the band's name was a conjunction of both. Apollo was the God of music and light, playing a golden lyre. He was the driver of the Source and unable to lie. This was Ollie, I thought. His twin sister, Artemis, was the hunter and lady of the wild things and the moon. This was not Sid; it did not fit him, unless you put him in the dark side. Apollo and Artemis. Apollemis. Ollie and Sid. The Source and the Moon. Truth and chastity. I smiled.

Playing together at a gig at The Ship this Saturday.

Chapter Seven

'Is it Saturday?' was my very first conscious thought at the following watery Sourcerise. I was unable to distinguish one day from the other and some days I struggled with even the time in the day. These humans with their clocks and watches. Alarms at six, supper at seven, meet me at two. They were my clocks, although Bob the Zookeeper was not a very good one. He was highly irregular; food usually came before the Source's daily zenith, admittedly, but much could happen between the dawn chorus and the delivery of sustenance. Days were longer then shorter then colder and then it was time to Hibernate - most unnaturally, I must point out, for my species mainly evolved in the tropics.

I was noticing changes in the size of the moon now that in the past would have passed me by, as I would have taken the opportunity of darkness to waste hours in diurnal unconsciousness. I had much to be wakeful for now, however.

I thought perhaps I remembered a time here when the dawn chorus consisted of more than a parakeet din. Much as I appreciated the company of Digby, I suspected that he and his relatives were infesting the area, to the detriment of species I had vague recollections of, like the spotty thrushes, the tits, the pink-pink of the stressed out blackbirds and the Ollie-like nightingales.

Colin the grass snake slipped by, through the lazy daisies. He undulated across the surface of Brian's island's moat, where I spied Brian laid flat out on the grass.

'Oh, hello Brian! You're back. Is it Saturday do you know?' I enquired, perkily.

'I don't know. My head is addled,' he groaned. Colin sailed past him and he didn't even notice.

A crunching of pebbles announced the presence of a man in a suit carrying a briefcase walking up the drive to the Big House. He knocked on the front door.

'Hang on,' said Brian, lifting his head slightly and squinting down the Hill. 'That looks like Bob's mate Jim from The Ship. What's he doing here? Ouch.' He laid his head back down and moaned a little.

Chignon opened the door and invited the suit inside. Shortly afterwards, he left, bustled out by Dave shouting, 'Sling your hook! And tell that so-called bloody zookeeper I know what he's up to!'

'Good morning,' said Digby, landing on my shell.

'Good morning,' I echoed. 'Is it Saturday?' I asked.

'No, Herbert, it is not,' he replied solemnly, 'but it will be tomorrow!' he added jubilantly. The Source suddenly bore down on us with the force of a host of angels and, out of the corner of my eye, I saw Colin curling up like a turd on top of the Wall. He was swift, that one. 'I can't wait! My first gig!' he added.

'You're going, then?' I dolefully enquired.

'Sorry,' said Digby with a little wince. 'But someone needs to be the intrepid reporter, and well, you, you know…' He sort of waved a wing about.

'Yes,' I snapped, 'I know!' I wanted a fairy Godmother. I wanted to go the Ball. I wanted to be turned into a pumpkin – well, not a pumpkin or indeed a glass slipper, either would have been eminently useless. But I did not want to be me. I had no chance of going to the gig. I had no doubt of my firm place in Stella's affections but the likelihood of her coming to pick me up, put me in the camper van, drive me to the gig, place me on a chair in The Ship and a pint of ale in front of me was staggeringly less than slim to none. I was simply too unwieldy. Mighty frustration. And Digby was going, just because he had wings. And Brian had been out, just last night. Still, I thought, if things carried on as they were threatened to, my time may still come. Although, the chances were I would end up inside another Wall somewhere, no doubt with the continued scintillating company of the Family. Gah!

Stella appeared from nowhere, startling me from my sulk. She had her bag of books with her. Digby flew off and stood on Brian's tree house, peering down at his prone form. Stella sat down and held out a floret of broccoli for me. She watched me as I ate it, tearing bunches of teeny buds off it.

Ollie wandered up the Hill to join her, a fat rose dangling from his hand, leafy and elegant. She smiled at him, winsomely, I thought. She was ingenuous, but also rippled with ambiguity. Her heart and her head were at war, I hypothesised. He gave her the rose, simply and openly. She accepted it in the same vein.

'Thanks,' she said, putting it to her nose. 'It smells amazing!'

'I nicked it from the garden. I wanted to thank you for yesterday; I had a lot of fun.'

'You were crap!' she said with another smile.

'Yeah, I know! But I'm only a beginner. In time I may master it.'

'Indeed. Practice makes perfect they preach,' she replied. 'Anyway, it was my pleasure. But thanks!' She tapped the outside of his thigh with the head of the rose as she sat looking up at him.

'This Herbert, then?' he asked, pointing at me uncouthly. I scowled at him, a difficult facial expression for a tortoise, evidenced by the fact neither of them appeared to notice.

'Yes, this is my wonderful Herbie!' Stella replied, flicking me under my chin and looking into one of my eyes.

'He's... er... quite big!' said Ollie, very unimaginatively. He was rapidly going down in my estimation.

'Oh, he's still a baby really! Look at that one over there!' They both looked at Gramps, fast asleep, as usual. Ollie did a double take and then was distracted by Brian, who was showing off, feeling better it seemed, hanging upside-down from one foot from a rope whilst peeling a banana. Digby had gone.

'I see the monkey's back,' he said, flicking his head in Brian's direction.

'He's a gibbon,' Stella replied, laying the rose in her lap, taking her books out of her bag and piling them up on the ground.

'Did you take me to the beach as a ruse?'

'A ruse for what?' She uncapped a biro with her teeth and opened a notebook.

'You knew they were coming for the monkey.'

'Gibbon.'

'Whatever.' He sat down beside her. 'What are your plans for today?'

'Well, as you can probably tell, I am going to start with doing some college work. I need to write up my notes from the trip. And after that I thought I might do a little house hunting,' she replied. Ollie grimaced. 'And tonight, I am waitressing. You?'

'I'm not waitressing, no...' His answer made her smile. Again. There was a whole lot of smiling happening here. 'But I do need to practice for the gig tomorrow. Sid called - Rufus is definitely going to be there.'

'Wow,' Stella said. 'Exciting for you! Could be your big break, honey!' She waggled his knee. Generous to a fault, I thought, whilst wondering who

Rufus was. Digby hadn't mentioned him. Where had that parakeet gone? I needed answers. Rufus sounded influential, like he could have an impact on a life.

'Thanks, babe,' Ollie said, looking at Stella until she looked away. 'I really could do with Sid being here, actually, but he hasn't made up with Issa yet. She's saying he's banned from the house. He's hiding in Primrose Hill at Violet's. Issa's been drinking martinis since she woke up after the party. Dad's trying to keep out of her way. Says she can't ban his son from his parental home. It's all very tense.' He scratched his stubbly chin. 'Added to which, I should mention, the monkey's prospective buyers are giving him a hard time about yesterday. And an unexpected visitor from the council passed by earlier; apparently there may be an issue with some of the planning permissions.'

Stella smirked, opening a book at any old page. Ollie watched her. 'I went to buy a paper and fags this morning. In the newsagents I overheard a rumour that the monkey had been in the pub yesterday. Can't imagine the appropriate authorities would be too keen on that.' The Source blinked as an aeroplane flew past. Stella looked at him, challenge standing like a bull in her eyes. 'Don't worry - I won't be on the blower any time soon. I should warn you that Dad's on the warpath, though. Apparently he's finding your father very uncooperative. Is going to hunt him down and inform him of the error of his ways.'

'What happened to peace and harmony?'

'They found themselves in the path of ambition, saw the monster bearing down on them and hoofed it.' They both laughed. 'They may be back, though. In the mean time, you might want to have a word with your Dad.'

'And say what, exactly? Try and tell him he should 'cooperate'? Have you met my Dad?'

'Might not be a bad idea.' Stella hugged her knees and looked at the ground.

Ollie put an arm around her scrunched shoulders and said, 'I told my Dad there's no urgency for the recording studio. I can go into town and rent one there for the time being. My record label can wait. I need to get me off the ground first as an artist. Besides, he's helped me enough. I want to fund myself from here, stand on my own two feet, you know…'

'What did he say?'

Ollie removed his arm and looked out to the Glittering. 'That you'd put some kind of a spell on me.' Stella froze for a second. I thought I heard her heart thump. 'I think he was joking. Anyway, the architect and project manager are coming this afternoon - the plan's for the builders to start on Monday. I think our house will be first now. Issa's demands for her dressing rooms and his and hers bathrooms need to be met before anything if there's to be any hope of marital harmony. Dad's under the cosh after what Sid did. And boy, can she make her feelings clear.' He frowned. 'You spoke to Hannah about tomorrow night? About Violet, as well? She could be a useful contact for her.'

'Yeah, I phoned her this morning. She's looking forward to it.'

'And you?'

'Yeah, of course. Should be a good night out. Not been to many gigs. Don't get out much, as I said!' She patted the pile of books by her side. He stood up.

'I'll leave you to it, then. Have a few things to sort out before I knuckle down to practice.'

'See you tomorrow, then,' she said, smiling up at him, shielding her eyes from the Source.

'Indeed you will, my dear.' He turned and walked to the Wall, vaulted it and walked around to the back of the Big House.

Stella said, 'Right then!' and looked at the book open in her lap, flicking through some pages. She scribbled a bit in her notebook and sighed and gazed around for a while. She fidgeted and she tapped her fingers and flicked some more. As the Spike's bell chimed three times, she turned to me with a grave look on her face. This look on her face told me that this was going to be a serious conversation. Or, more accurately, confession.

It had always been frustrating being unable to respond to her verbally, but I had tried my best with meaningful winks and tilts of the head. I had prided myself on my talents as a listener, but of course this was never a talent - not even a choice. I had heaps of advice to give but it was all bottled up inside my head. I had no voice that she could hear.

I had, in the past, attempted various solutions such as painstakingly writing letters in petals pulled off buttercups that made words that I thought would help her; 'patience', 'breathe', 'calm'. But they blew away before she saw them. I had tried systems of yes and no answers – numbers of blinks, stretching and retracting my head, walking to the left or right, but she had never caught on. I had even enlisted an army of creatures to appear in strange places to try and give her guidance: a painted lady butterfly on her pillow, a nightingale singing on her windowsill at dawn, a black cat walking across her path. He was useless that cat, Rupert, I think. A complete sucker for titbits, always forgot his objective.

At this critical time, more than ever I wanted to share my wisdom and debate the direction and depths of her thoughts and feelings. And there was a slew of questions I would have liked to ask her, too. But all I was was ears. I consoled myself that, for her, it was enough that I was merely the receptacle of her innermost meanderings. Little did she know how I locked them away, each thought a treasure. On dull days, I pulled them out and marvelled upon them.

'Herbs,' she said, seriously. She held up the rose, so ripe its petals hung by a thread, close to release. She fed me them one by one. They were the deep pink of summer berries, and just as sweet.

'Herbie, I think I may be going mad. I have lost control of my brain. It's full up with him and it just keeps on filling. There's no room for anything else. Some moments I suspect my head may very well burst.' She sighed and sat cross-legged in front of me. 'I can't even study. I've been sat here for what must be hours and I have not taken a single concept in and I've written a grand total of,' she ran her index finger across the lines in her notebook, 'twenty-eight words.' She sighed. 'Crap,' she said. 'I am totally distracted.'

Wow, I thought. We definitely had an issue on our hands. Stella was almost unnaturally studious, as I said before, although this had been mildly countered by her recent dabblings in illicit substances. But still, she thrived on books, devoured knowledge. She had little time for much else. She was also extraordinarily driven. She munched what she learned, ruminated upon it and spat out startling interpretations. She made information work very hard for her. There was nothing of Hyacinth about her, nothing in the fashion of a parrot.

What drove Stella was her craving for security; a place in the world, a place of her own, and she had a billion plans on how to do it. Studying was the fuel for her fire.

She grasped a handful of petals from the rose, leaving its yellow stamen as a small, furry cushion topping the tough, thorny stem. She sprinkled them on the ground underneath my head, and placed one like a hat on top of it. A raspberry beret.

'I try and try to lasso my mind but it just keeps on scarpering, slipping my knot. It runs through every word he's ever said to me, over and over and its idea of respite is to make up future conversations instead! And boy, is that an endless exercise. It has apparently infinite variations and likes to go through a best-to-worst to probable scenario exercise. My mind has a mind of its own ha-ha!' She laughed hollowly and picked a daisy. She made a little hole in its stem with her thumbnail and threaded another one's stem through it.

'It makes these little connections, adds things up, like our likes and dislikes, where we've been, why we are here, where we want to go, traits we share and it makes calculations - uses crazy algorithms that it says equal fate.' She picked another daisy and threaded it, and another, and another.

'I don't even believe in fate. It's not very practical.' Ah yes, a good word for Stella. Practical. Another would have been 'objective'. Not unemotional, just adept at viewing from a distance. Ancient beyond her years, like me.

'And don't even get me started on my body. That, I strongly suspect, is the root cause of my mind's betrayal. Lust is to blame for this sorry state of affairs, Herbie, pure and simple. One of the mortal or deadly sins, is it?' More daisies, more stars plucked from the grass. 'I don't even think like him - as a person, I mean. He's waltzed in here all cocky and spoiled and is trampling over my life, scuppering my plans. He may be all apologetic and flirty but he has everything he wants and needs. It must be easy to be nice then.

'And what's more, I only met him the day before yesterday! If this is what people call love, they must be insane. This is like a basic instinct to mate egging the body onto the edge of reason. I don't like it. I don't know him! Not even vaguely. How can my body be making so many decisions before I've had a chance to figure out what I really think? And, most importantly, he's the one supposed to be falling for *me*. This is not going according to plan. Bugger.' She started packing her books into her bag. 'I'm going to work on some contingency. I'm going house-hunting.'

Chapter Eight

Then, finally, it was Saturday. Ollie had been practising nonstop and alone for Apollemis' evening concert all day long. The menagerie had been suspended from normal service, caught by the beat, owned by the melodies.

There had been another couple of visitors by the end of the previous day, as Ollie had predicted. Bob had intercepted them on his way out to The Ship; it was possible that Stella had passed on the information.

'Good afternoon,' Bob had said effusively, tapping the edge of a flat cap that he had appropriated from the Arnolds several years before.

'Hello there,' they had replied, with a bland lack of curiosity. They were in blue jeans, and pale t-shirts, bright and clean. One of them carried a clipboard like Chignon's. The other one was pulling a large board from the depths of the boot of the car in which they had just arrived. 'Palmer Springs -Where Hope is Eternal' the board proclaimed in bold letters.

Bob stopped. 'Friends of Dave?' he asked.

'Business acquaintances,' firmly stated the one with the clipboard. 'I'm the architect.' Pompous, I thought. It was a little bit like watching the stags rutting at Awakening; a display of posturing, bravado, unsaid one-upmanship.

'You must be chuffed with this job,' said Bob, coolly. 'Beautiful place, isn't it?'

'Stunning.' The man with the board leaned his rear against the rear of his car and agreed with him. 'You know it well?'

'I should say,' Bob confirmed. 'It's been my home for nigh on twenty-five years.'

'A fraction of its history,' said the one with the clipboard.

'Yes indeed, and a very small one at that. Take the wall over there as an example,' Bob pointed at my Wall. 'Sussex flint, that is, extracted from this very hill over three thousand years ago. Used to be a hive of activity here, a proper little community, miners and their wives and children. Men deep underground all day and all night long, chip chip chipping away. Imagine it. Riddled with shafts around here, it is. You'll bring all that back, eh?' The men looked blankly at him. 'The community?' said Bob.

'Yes,' said the man with the board. 'The key project objective is certainly to attract large numbers of consumers – people, that is - to visit this site. When it's been developed to the highest possible quality standard, of course.'

'Mines?' asked the architect with the clipboard.

'Yes,' said Bob. 'Riddled. Anyway, must be off; I have an appointment to keep!' He tipped his hat again and walked away, apparently expressionless. The two men had then gone into the Big House and, whilst they were inside, Bob had snuck back. I saw him crouched by the far side of their car, hidden by it from the house, fiddling with the tyres.

A couple of hours later, during another thundery downpour, the men had returned to their car with Dave and had noticed the two flats. Once a mistake, twice careless, I thought. Bob was making himself known. Dave, tense, fists clenched, had marched to the Gate House and battered its front door. No response was forthcoming. It was more than likely that Bob was in The Ship by now. Even if he weren't, he wasn't going to be opening the door.

The men had flapped at the stricken wheels for a bit and then a yellow rescue van arrived and pumped the tyres back up and they all drove off, leaving Dave glowering at the Gate House, the rain dripping off the tip of his nose.

I chuckled as I remembered it.

Today it was dry and riotously hot and humid. A buzz of newly hatched midges skittered over the mirror-like surface of the fishing lake.

Dave had rushed through his ritual this morning and then was straight to the door of the Gate House to pummel it some more. It remained unanswered, although I was sure that at least Stella was there. I was convinced I saw some twitches in its curtains. I was right; during one of the breaks in door battering, she had run out and had performed Bob's feed round. This was not unusual, but it was the first time since this Awakening.

There was absolutely no sign of Bob, though. Eventually Dave wore himself out and, as Ollie had begun to practice again, his music calmed him - like us - until he was sat crossed legged on the thick part of the Wall, his wrists hanging over his knees, his thumbs and forefingers forming 'O's. He emitted a low, even sound.

This serenity was shattered when the phone rang repeatedly in the Big House. Like an alarm, it kicked off a frenzy of activity. Dave leapt up and he and Ollie threw all sorts of electrical equipment in the back of the purple camper van: guitars, keyboards, boxes with knobs on and suchlike.

Digby was preparing for his mission. I gave him a pep talk.

'It's no good just watching, Digby. You have to remember absolutely everything. I need to know.' I bossed him about. I couldn't help myself; I desperately wanted to be going. Digby was good, but young. He could perhaps be carried away in the moment and lose sight of his objectives.

'Yes, Herbert. Stop fretting - all is under control. And now, I must be off!'

As he took to the air, the purple camper van fired up on the pebbly drive and scooted off down through the gate, to be followed moments later by the pink one containing the girls.

Much, much later, Digby landed back with a whoop.

'Mission accomplished!' he crowed. All you had to do was watch, I thought bitterly, and then took a grip of myself. Brian was sat at the nearest edge of his moat, expectantly. Daisy and Dolly and the alpacas crowded at their intersection of the Wall. I could see the giraffes' long necks bobbing about over their fence.

'Alrighty,' said Digby. 'May I please request complete silence while I file my report? Please save your questions until the end.' We all nodded assent.

'1800 hours: Arrive at Ship. Bob already there - has been there since yesterday afternoon. Is tipsy. Discover they have refurbished beer garden. Secure reconnaissance position in potted olive tree.'

'1810: Dave emptying van onto pavement out the front. Ollie carrying bits inside and plugging things in. Instruments not making normal melodic noises. Much counting of low numbers – one, two, three over and over. Girls in beer garden, making themselves useless drinking bottle of plonk. Conversation dull; mainly concerning nail polish.

'1835: Sid arrives. With minute brunette in platform boots in tow. Huge eyes. Teeny little nose and chin. Another guy with them: really tall, really dark skin – darker than Issa's. Incredibly cool. Girl clearly with Sid - obvious by way arms constantly laying all over each other, stroking bits. Hannah unimpressed and possibly physically sickened by sight. Sid and mates installed in corner of bar. Our girls remain outside.

'1850: Dave enters Ship. Bob shuffles rapidly outside, leaving half empty pint and whisky chaser at far end of bar. First interesting conversation of evening - it goes like this:'

During the next part of his regurgitation of the evening's action, Digby bounded around, posing as each character, saying their name before their lines and mimicking their voices. He had us spellbound.

'Bob:	"Oh, hello, Stella love. What brings you here?"
Stella:	"Hey Dad." Stands up and gives him kiss on cheek and small hug. Reels slightly at stench of whisky on his breath. "We're with the band." She smiles at Hannah who mouths back, "We're with the band!" The two girls find this very amusing. Bob looks bemused.
Bob:	"Band? What band? I thought they'd given up on that live music shite down here? Never been popular. Just gets in the way of the drinking, in my opinion…" Hiccups.
Stella:	"Oh, Dad, I did tell you. Our new neighbours' band - the boys' band?"
Bob:	"Well I hope they're better than their Dad. Found some of his crap on the jukebox in there the other night. It was bollocks." Wobbles on feet and burps.
Stella:	Arms crossed, sat down again. "You know, Dad, I've been thinking; our future lies in his hands. Money talks, and we can barely even whisper. Maybe it would be worth discussing the situation with him, see if they can help us find a solution. We should put forward our case - you know, keep your friends close and your enemies closer?" Looks pleadingly. Through window, Dave spots Bob and knocks over chair rushing out. Sid's tall mate grabs his elbow on his way past

	and he stops. They shake hands, Dave's eyes flicking to Bob outside. A chat begins.
Bob:	"Fuck 'em. They try to mess with me and I'll show them who's boss." Slurring. Noisy screech emanates from inside pub - landlord is on microphone, announces evening's live entertainment. "Right, I'm going to cut and run, I'm not sticking around for this rubbish. See you at home." Wanders off. As turns corner, grazes shoulder on wall. The girls stand up to go in. Dave appears at back door, looking around, menacingly. Skips over to the girls.
Dave:	"Stella, you gorgeous thing," sliding arm around one of her shoulders. "Where's your old man?"
Stella:	"He went home, I think. Come on, they're starting!" She takes Hannah's hand and links her arm through Dave's, who's looking over his shoulder at the back of the beer garden.

'1910 – 1940 hours: The first set. Quite a crowd has gathered. Bob and his groggy Shipmates who normally haunt the bar until the bitter end are all adrift and replaced by a bunch of kids - lots of strange coloured hair and abnormally large boots. Audience of approximately thirty-three, difficult to count from position in olive tree.

'They play the one about the dusty angels, then 'Tinsel Tonsils', followed by a cover of 'Champagne Supernova', with Sid accompanying on an ancient wooden instrument called the Hurdy Gurdy. And to finish, 'I Won't Change Me, Baby, If You Won't Change You'. Girls right at front, jigging about, Stella mesmerised by Ollie. Much cheering and clapping at end.'

'Digby. This is fantastic. Almost as good as being there ourselves!' I was impressed.

'Ssh!' said everyone else.

'During the interval,' Digby continued, not missing a beat, 'the second interesting conversation occurred. This time between Sid, who had slipped outside for a cigarette, and Hannah, who followed him.

'Hannah:	"Hey, Sid."
Sid:	"Hi." Stubs out cigarette and walks past Hannah to the door, Hannah turns and blocks the doorway.
Hannah:	"Who's the girl?"
Sid:	"You don't recognise her?" She doesn't answer. "Violet Hardy. Daughter of Rob Rooney, drummer in The Spits, and Kate Hardy, ultimate groupie. She's a model, you know." He circumvents her and escapes the scene through the door.
Stella:	"Oh, hi Sid!" says on way out, a glass in each hand. Sid grunts, returns to miniature girl, continues with stroking. "Was he friendly?"
Hannah:	"He's playing hard to get. Or something.' Her eyes flash.
Stella:	"Or maybe he already got you, babe. Who's the girl?"
Hannah:	"Some rock sprog." Spitting - not actually spitting, that would be gross; just spitting mad. "Brit brat... whatever. Fuck, Stella, he virtually ignored me, after..."
Stella:	"You're not surprised? I told you what Ollie said yesterday. And you knew anyway - the rags broadcast his womanising

	philandering ways daily... what were you expecting? Marriage?"
Hannah:	"Of course not. But maybe a little... I don't know..."
Stella:	"Look, Hans. You knew he was a slut. Of course he wants to play happy families with the rest of the rock royalty. I'm sorry, Ollie said Violet might be useful to you... but. Well, I guess Sid'd rather hang with his own than some no-names from No Town like us. But don't take it personally - don't look at it as rejection. He's not rejecting you, he doesn't even know you. He's so wrapped up in himself, there's no room for anyone else!"
Hannah:	"Yeah, I hear what you're saying. And I guess you're right; I didn't really think about the outcomes at the party... was a bit caught up in the moment! Maybe should have kept my hand on my halfpenny if I wanted a better shot..."
Stella:	"You've been talking to your Gran again, haven't you?! I don't think it'd make any difference with him, to be honest, Hans - he's just one big ball of ego. I doubt he's that into Violet, either." They peer in through window: Violet sat on his lap, nibbling on his ear. "Just probably convenient." He puts hand on her breast, squeezes it and sticks his tongue in her mouth. Hannah throws glass at floor, it smashes into a million little pieces. Stella looks at sparkles on concrete. Looks up at Hannah. "Better?"
Hannah:	Deep breath. "Yes, thanks."
Stella:	"Dignity located and intact?"
Hannah:	"Of course, sweetie. Am absolutely fabulous."

Stella:	"Shall we?"
Hannah:	'Yes, let's. I find myself in urgent need of another drink unexpectedly soon."
Stella:	"Funny, that."

'2015 – 2100 hours. Second set. 'Popatlas' to begin with, all chinky and light. Much calmness and swaying, then that one about the many colours of grass, guitar solo in that, everyone watching with open mouths. Sid's tall, dark friend actually taking notes. Then 'Abuse Muse' and then that one he played to us that first night, the soothing, healing one. It's called 'I Know' - Ollie dedicated it to Stella. And they dimmed the lights. Gig finishes.

'Everyone fired up - Tequilas all round, cheering, back slapping, exultation. All outside having cigarette.

'And now for the final interesting conversation of the evening. They are all three sheets to the wind now, a chubby girl is puking in the pot of the olive tree where I have retained station. The ashtrays are overflowing and there is quite a lot of broken glass crunching underfoot - not just Hannah's contribution. Sid and the minute brunette are entangled outside and yet conversing with Ollie, Stella stood close by, Hannah glaring and the tall, cool black guy and Dave. Is 11:13 and a bell has just been rung to tell them to go home quietly and not disturb the neighbours.

| 'Ollie: | "So Rufus, honestly, mate - what did you think?" |
| Rufus: | "Well, my old mucker, having listened to enough of your brother's bullshit hype over the years, I was prepared for disappointment...' |

Ollie:	"Oh." Blanches, Stella clutches his arm and staggers. Might be the booze, might have been shocked sympathy, not sure. Sid chuckles.
Rufus:	"But he might be onto something…" A sigh of relief does the rounds. "Your sound's very…" Tenterhooks. "… Unique. A kind of ambient dance mixed with an overlay of folky jazz, undercut by a crazy kind of rhythm…" He nods at Sid, who beams. "Your voice, Ollie, is something else too… very different from mine… but you are your father's son for sure… quite bewitching, really." He pauses, but no-one seems brave enough to say a word, all hanging on his. Rufus is obviously very important as well as looking fly. Silence continues - Rufus appears to revel in it; the impact of his judgement.
Ollie:	Nervously. "So… uh… you think we could get a deal with you then, yeah? On your label?"
Rufus:	Rubbing chin, swigging end of pint. "It's not beyond the realms of possibility. A lot of it's about exposure though, of course, and the right management," nods at Sid, distracting him slightly from minute brunette's left earlobe. "It's not all about talent, you know - to break it, to make it, you know, you need to know the right people…" Ollie nods, looks at Sid, and back at Rufus.
Sid:	"What he's saying, Olls," Sid pipes up as minute brunette slides hand down back of his trousers, "is you need me, for starters. I got us this gig and that one at the Water Rats. Admittedly that didn't go so well, but I should have

publicised it more... It was a bad night, you know, a Monday, even for the students. I kind of assumed, erroneously," minute brunette squeezes his bum and he grabs her hand through the back of his trousers, concentrates, "our name would be more of a draw. I was wrong on that, of course, everyone knows who I am... some would say not for the right reasons, I say fuck 'em and I normally do, haha!" Minute brunette retracts hand from trousers and goes to ladies'. "But you've been so reclusive, being a creative - and long may that continue. You don't need this shit, the networking, the knowing the right people, knowing the right venues. You, Ollie, need to be working - I mean writing - while I do the work of being your percussionist, your promoter, creating the hype, bagging you the deals, sorting out the gigs. Promoting our name." Soliloquy endeth. Sid looking at Ollie. Ollie looking combative and resigned all at the same time. Between the devil and the deep blue sea.

Ollie: "So, what are you thinking, Sid? What's next?"

Sid: "Well, my feeling is that although Rufus is impressed, he may need a little more persuading before he signs you - us, I mean." Rufus is stood arms crossed, stroking his chin, nodding slowly.

Sid: Looking at Rufus. "Mate, you're a superstar, no question. But right now you're still riding on two years ago and the undeniable critical and commercial success of 'Assholes and Interpretations'. Your new tour kicks off in a fortnight."

Rufus:	"Yeah, the launch of our new album, you twat."
Sid:	"Yeah, mate, you tosspot," they laugh at each other. "But I've heard it. It's slick alright - of course it is, it's yours. But in my opinion, it lacks edge." The minute brunette is back but apparently invisible. "And more than that: you've said you've chosen Amuse as your support act. Very now, yeah, very run of the mill."
Rufus:	"Brit award nominee!"
Sid:	"Exactly. When have you ever been into that shit?"
Rufus:	"It's not what you know, it's who… you know that better than anyone."
Sid:	"I'm saying think about doing something different. You haven't. As in you haven't done anything different. So ride off something different then give your fans more of the same. When your next album comes, you'll find your creative juices again, but in the meantime, don't run with the mill. The mill's due to come a cropper shortly in any case."
Rufus:	"Give your boy a chance?"
Sid:	"Yeah. Give this boy a chance. He's got the talent." Waves at Ollie. "And we have the name. We're the latest in the line of a rock legend. What's not to like?"
Rufus:	"Okay I will. I will contemplate this. Now, where's the after party?"

'And with that, my friends, they return. Any questions?'

'Where was Issa?' I asked.

'Not there, Herbert.' The big tease says nothing more to this open question.

'Well, where was she then? Why wasn't she there?' He irked me sometimes, he really did. It was demeaning, having to eke the information out of him like this.

'Hyacinth has been locked in his cage, rather like Issa has locked herself indoors. He has terrible cramp in his wings.' answered Digby. 'Moving on - are there any further questions regarding this evening's report?'

'Poor Hyacinth,' cried I. 'He knows what side his bread is buttered! Why would he fly away?'

'You and I know that Herbert, but Issa's mind is unable to extract itself from the perishing of poor Laa-Laa at the fins of that ferocious fish.'

'I think it was his mouth,' I butted in, grumpily.

'Splitting hairs, Herbert, the splitting of the hairs,' Digby replied condescendingly. 'Although, Hyacinth says that Issa seemed mightily unhappy with the general situation here; didn't want to spend her evening in a grubby old pub with a bunch of nobodies - 'civilians' I think she said. There have been lots of complaints from her about lack of light, warmth, proper shops and a salon. Issues over distance from marvellous Mecca she misses.'

'Mecca?' I asked.

'Yes, Herbert, Mecca. Mecca of Mammon, admittedly. Hyacinth said their old life was…' Digby was interrupted by the screech of tyres on the road off which the drive sprang, followed by the reappearance of the purple camper van, whipping to a halt outside the Big House, pebbles spraying from its back wheels. Ollie and Stella sat up front, laughing maniacally, and the back doors popped open and Sid, the minute brunette, Hannah, Rufus and Dave spilled out.

Chignon opened the front door, in apricot silk pyjamas and stood with her arms crossed, un-chignoned and looking cute in slippers. Sid bowled up to her and gave her a massive hug. She didn't uncross her arms. Tinky-Winky and Po sat obediently behind her.

'They're not allowed out either,' said Digby. 'Not until Issa says so. Lest there be any more accidents. Chignon's paranoid about it, since Issa is spending all day in a drunken lump. Apparently there was once a fourth one, Dipsy. The day Issa brought them home, Chignon stepped off a stepladder right onto Dipsy and that was that. Despite it being just a terrible accident, and Chignon, being mortified, having invested eons being the perfect general gofer, her employ was very close to being terminated. Needless to say, another doglet loss and she'd be out on her ear, forthwith.'

'Where you hiding the champers then, Miss Mop?' Sid asked, tickling Chignon in the ribs.

She softened a little and said, 'This way,' and held the door open, shooing them all in.

Digby flew over the roof and then hopped down the other side, as the group had passed through the house and were congregating around the pool out the back. Music was playing but Digby later reported there were no instruments, just boxes making sounds this time he said. Speakers, I told him.

He also reported on an incident in the kitchen, which I found unfathomable, but this is what he said: Issa, he told me, had been woken by the ruckus and had come downstairs, and was standing bare foot in the tiled kitchen, her head in the fridge, shovelling tiramisu into her mouth. She had a navy and white striped shirt on - and nothing else. Sid walked into the room.

'Issa,' he started.

'You murderous fucker,' she had said as she turned around. Digby had said she had chocolate smeared around her mouth and that her hair was dark at the roots and her wide eyes were pink. He described a red mark across her face that he said looked like the imprint of a wrinkle of a sheet she'd been asleep on.

'Issa, I have come to apologise. I'm really sorry for what happened, honest. I know what I did was wrong, and I know I've made you unhappy. I've been racking my pathetic little brain on how to make it up to you, but I've come up with nothing. Please tell me what I can do that could make you feel better. Anything, Issa? Dad's told me how upset you have been in the last few days. Anything you want, I'll get it for you, I'll do it for you.' She slammed the fridge door behind her and leaned her back against it.

'Anything?' she asked, crossing her arms. The next few moments I quizzed Digby on over and over, but he was insistent on this version of events.

'Absolutely anything,' he had replied. Digby said it was like a light had gone on in Sid's eyes at this point and then Issa had walked towards him and stood in front of him, far closer than was absolutely necessary.

'Rescue me,' she had said, so quietly it was virtually a whisper. They had been looking at each others' mouths, poised for a kiss. Minute brunette had thundered in at that point, her eyes rolling in her head and thrown herself at Sid, who had taken her upstairs, a backward glance and a promise, Digby had thought, thrown at Issa.

Issa had stumbled through to the rest of the group and, taking this as a sign that she was feeling better and maybe smelling reconciliation in the air, Dave pulled himself out of the pool and it was not long before I witnessed his purposeful stroll down the pebbly drive to the Gatehouse, where a light shone from one of the downstairs rooms.

Once again, the front door received a hearty hammering. Bob opened it. What was left of his hair was ruffled up, a bit like Digby's. He was wearing a blue tartan dressing gown. It was ancient, judging by the frays about all its edges.

'Oh,' said Bob. 'I thought you were Stella, forgetting her keys or something. Not that she's ever forgotten her keys, as it happens. But there's a first time for everything.'

'No, Bob, it is I, Dave, your employer and landlord. I think it's about time we had a chat, don't you? I have extended the hand of friendship in the past and yet you have been nothing but rude and, I suspect, disruptive to my plans.' Dave had his hands on his hips. It seemed he had rehearsed this moment. In the half-light of the porch, the look on Bob's face was ferocious.

'Employer, landlord and friend, indeed. And as to your plans, I have heard quite enough of them from everyone else around here - some half-baked nonsense hippy shit, from what I understand.' Bob stepped out of the doorway towards Dave, who did not take a step back but stuck his face so close to Bob's that I could no longer see his expression.

'Who the fuck do you think you are?' Dave yelled. I imagined his fiery breath rushing over Bob's face and could almost feel his resentment rising up from his acid stomach. 'I own this place, Mr so-called fucking zookeeper. Fuck it, I own YOU!'

Bob head-butted him. Dave reeled backwards off the step and stumbled onto the drive into a crouching position. It was evident that he was not a fighter. He was the geek here, the meek fuelled by a false sense of superiority. Suddenly, the wan nature of his muscles became obviously apparent against the bulldog of Bob, outlined by the porch light, his shoulders hunched for a moment like a cobra poised to spring again. Although somewhat past his best, Bob's body was a barrel and at its core was pure punch.

As Dave continued to kneel in front of him, inspecting his hand stained with the blood that poured from the split in his brow, Bob relaxed. Now he knew he was the superior, powerful one; he had won this battle. But as he turned back in and slammed the door behind him, switching the porch light off so that Dave was nothing but a crunch on the pebbles as he retreated to his lair, I was left wondering who was winning the war.

Sometime in the very early hours I was disturbed by an indignant hiss from Gramps, further down the Hill. In the moonlight, I thought that I could make out Rufus straddling his back, attempting to ride him, perhaps, but Gramps was not playing. He'd pulled himself in. No spirit.

Chapter Nine

There was an eerie silence across Bestwood the next morning, exacerbated by a mild mist that hung about, muffling the light and the sound. There was a tension about as the menagerie tapped our feet and scraped our hooves awaiting fall out, the consequences of what felt like a bomb going off the night before. Bob was late with the food. No-one had seen Stella go home. Dave had not been seen since he returned to the Big House following his altercation with Bob.

We did not know whether we were winning or losing. We did not know what winning or losing meant. The general consensus was that the worst thing that could happen was that we would all be 'put down', like Gavin the Tigress was supposed to have been and, since her, the third zebra Dorothy. Although Dorothy's passing was somewhat less dramatic both in its cause and its execution - excuse the pun. Dorothy had become so lumpy that a tearful Bob and the vet at the time, Simon - a round, pink man, smiles in his cheeks and wet in his eyes - had agreed to let her go. A syringe had appeared, and we'd seen this many times before - to calm us down, boost us up, clean us up inside if we had an abscess or some such - but this syringe was different. This syringe carried relief, escape from the pain that poor Dorothy had complained about for months; pain in her insides, her head, her joints, pain when she ate, pain when she peed. Every moment full of pain.

This syringe was a relief. A classic bittersweet moment for all of us, it was. Dorothy became pain-free but in doing so she removed herself from us, and we all adored her. When anyone was a bit moody or depressed, Dorothy was the one to crack a joke, do something silly, or start a project like make a totem pole out of the meerkats. Before her pain started, her energy was endless, boundless, bountiful. Our ideal scenario, of course, would have been to have Dorothy back and the pain gone. But I don't think – well, I guess Bob and Simon decided - that this was not an option; so we all, but none so severely as her sisters Daisy and Dolly, lost Dorothy. All three of them had been born here. Their parents were sold off many years previously. All their lives, Bob had promised them mates, that their stripy line would go on, but the Arnolds had never coughed up the goods. In hindsight, I guess they couldn't afford to.

And that was another scenario we had discussed - that we would be sold off, as it seemed Dave had intended to do with Brian. The others quaked at this. I did not, but neither did I relish the idea. The others said that they had all they wanted to stay here, that they were contented. I was not contented. Brian said he would miss Bob horribly and hoped that wherever Bob went he would go too. But I just thought that wherever they sent me would be much as it was here. I may or may not be sent away with my Family, but their accompaniment did not strike me as important either.

But like Brian, I did have one very big problem with being removed, and that was Stella. She was my everything. The thought of never seeing her again filled me with a shocking hopelessness. A pointlessness. It was almost incomprehensible. I had seen her grow up; she had been there since I was born. Of course, others had too, but that was different somehow. She was the thing that made my every day come alive. She was the one that gave my paltry existence here in the confines of the Wall some kind of meaning. In all honesty, I lived for her. And living like this, without her, filled me with terror.

As I tugged and pulled at this emotion in my head, teasing at it, unable to put it down, I was thankfully relieved by the arrival of a small white car at the Gate House. A man and a woman, both in blue uniforms and setting blue hats straight on their heads exited the car and the woman knocked on the Gate House's door, her calves sturdy in navy tights and flat, blunt lace up shoes.

'Good morning, Mr Trimble,' she said as Bob opened the door, looking very much as he had done the night before.

'Gah,' said Bob, defensive but somehow forlorn. His hangover must have been raging.

'How are you feeling this morning?' she continued.

'I have a little bit of a sore head,' he said. 'Late night, and all.' He looked up at them - not frightened, but definitely with apprehension.

'We heard.' They stood and looked at him, their arms folded.

Bob nodded. It was like the fight had gone out of him all of a sudden, faced with sobriety and the strong arm of the law. A silent cheer was coming from the menagerie, willing him on, to fight for our rights some more. Cease the change. Save us! Apart from me - I wanted to see what could happen, what was possible, what was out there. Just as long as it included Stella. And I was sure, absolutely one hundred percent, totally and utterly sure, that she would always make sure that we were together. She had promised me enough times - I'd heard her say it: she would never leave me. She would always make sure that I was with her. We would never be apart.

Bob was still not saying anything.

'Bob…' said the man in uniform. 'We received a complaint about you.'

'Well, I wonder who that was from.' He jerked his head up.

'Apparently your temper may have got the better of you last night,' the man in uniform continued.

'I was provoked. Repeatedly.' We all applauded in our minds. Even me. It was true; Dave had been an absolute horror.

'Yes, Bob, I suspect you were. And the complainant suggests that you may have been quite provoking yourself. The fact remains that we have received a complaint; that you attacked your neighbour, physically, and therefore, under the guidance of law, we are required to take you down to the station to discuss this with you further.' The policeman put his hand on Bob's shoulder.

'Jesus, Tim, I only head-butted him. He's threatening everything I stand for, in the way of everything I care for. And he's an arsehole.' Bob hung his head and wrung his hands, a picture of penitence. The whole menagerie panicked.

'We'll pretend you never said any of that,' said the woman in uniform. 'Let's go and get a nice cup of tea and have a chat about this, shall we?'

'I'll just get changed.' A few minutes later Bob was back, the frayed old dressing gown replaced by a greying shirt that had seen better days and some trousers that stopped short of his ankles. They all went and piled into the little white car which puffed out of the drive, leaving us despondent and speechless. Bob - BOB! - was in trouble with the Law over this. The injustice! The outrage! The inordinate unfairness of it all! The menagerie saw red.

As the car was pulling out through the gates, Stella appeared at the door of the Big House wearing last night's clothes. She peered at the rear end of the exiting vehicle and saw her father looking at her through the back window. He looked ashamed and he now looked frightened. He looked like he had the fear. She stood on the drive and stared after the car. Ollie appeared behind her and snaked an arm around her waist and nuzzled into her neck.

She jumped away from him.

'Ollie, the police have taken Dad away. What's going on? What's Dave - what has your Dad done?' She looked frightened too as she stood straight on to him, her hands down by her sides.

Dave wandered out behind Ollie, his left eye blackened and swollen. A scab across his eyebrow crusted with blood. 'Shit, Dad,' said Ollie. 'What the fuck have you done?'

'I was attacked, Ollie, and so I called the appropriate authorities. It's my right as a citizen to have this situation dealt with.' Dave crossed his arms.

Stella stared at him. 'You bastard. That's my father! You shopped my Dad. Unbelievable. We have nothing and you want to make a criminal out of him too?'

'He's making a criminal out of himself, babe. I will not condone violence - particularly not against my own person.' Dave nodded to himself and stuck his chin out.

'You don't even believe in the appropriate authorities do you, Dad? 'Come the revolution,' you said. 'Blatant invasions of privacy,' I quote. The government's private arm squashing the basic human freedoms and rights. 'Fuck the pigs,' you said!' Ollie grabbed his father's arm and pulled it away from his chest.

'Ollie, you know how I have changed recently. You know I know crave inner peace and seek absolute harmony in my world. That man is disruptive. He's been trying to fuck up everything I'm trying to achieve for me, for us, my family, you. Whose side are you on, anyway - your old Dad's or your new bit of crumpet, here?' He shook his hand free of Ollie's grasp and pointed at Stella. Ollie slapped his hand away. 'Lovely as she is, Ollie, she's her father's daughter and will amount to nothing, just like him. She'll be shovelling shit for the rest of her days; it's in her genes.' Stella turned and ran into the Gate House.

'Stella! Wait!' Ollie called after her but the Gate House door slammed shut.

'You've gone too far this time. That was well out of order. She is not my piece of crumpet - she's the most amazing human being I have ever met and she is worth a trillion of you, you piece of shit. What you've done is completely unacceptable. We should have been able to sort this out between ourselves! You're a hypocrite and a bully - you don't believe in peace or love, you're just one big fucking ego and I'm ashamed to be your son.' Ollie took his keys out of his trouser pocket and stalked over to his camper van jumped in and the engine screeched and it turned in a circle so fast that a spray of pebbles span out, hitting Dave across the knees. Dave's blinked and Ollie sped out of the drive and through the gates, turning left in the direction of the Spike, following the route of the car that had taken Bob away from us.

Dave came and sat on the Wall, his head in his hands. He looked at me. I was looking straight at him. I had been contemplating trying to take a chunk out of one of his thighs. I thought maybe my jaws were strong enough. Digby was twittering above my head in the Oak. The parakeets were planning a mass attack. The mob of meerkats was throwing itself at the fence, chattering. Dorothy and Daisy had their heads over the Wall and were baring their teeth ferociously. Brian was swinging from a rope like a pendulum, clearly trying to gain enough momentum to swing over the moat at which point, he was claiming, he would rip Dave limb from limb. Dave did not seem aware of the danger he was in.

'Well, I suppose someone had better feed you lot, then,' he said and stood up and wandered over the shed, which was padlocked. He rattled the door a few times and tried to peer in through the windows, cupping his hands around his head. Bob had blacked them out. 'Sarah!' he shouted. And then again, louder, 'Sarah!'

Chignon appeared at the door of the Big House, wiping her hands on a tea towel, flour smudged across her brow. 'Yes, boss?'

'We need to feed the animals.' I took a pace towards him, still intent upon my plan to eat a bit of him, vile as I was sure he must taste. 'They look hungry.'

'Yes, boss.' Sarah with the chignon smiled.

He went down the Hill into the Big House with her and not much later, during which time the rest of the menagerie, I am disappointed to say, completely forgot their anger in their anticipation of the feast they were imagining would be forthcoming from the Palmer's kitchen, reappeared with a preponderance of edible treasures comparative to our normal rations.

Brian was first. He had a whole pineapple but someone – Sarah, most likely - had removed the husk and core and sliced it into rings. In the centre of each ring sat a fat strawberry. There were two peaches, enormously fat, furry and so ripe I could smell them, a bunch of shiny red grapes and some chewy dried apricots. Dave delivered this on a silver platter that he balanced on the end of a spade across the moat, since the drawbridge was still missing in action. Any animosity Brian had been feeling was not evident in the way that he grabbed the platter and sat down with it on his lap, looking like he had won the lottery.

The meerkats received a bowl of carrots, sliced into little sticks, another of more sticks - celery, one full of bright yellow sweetcorn niblets, a plate with several slices of ham rolled into tubes and slices of salami spread out into a fan.

The flamingos received an enormous ring of prawns, their heads and tails still on. They all inspected this seafood crown and a few of them nudged a crustacean with their beaks but they were unable to eat something of this size

– they were filter feeders and so this offering was left ignored as they swung their heads about in their muddy waters. I hoped it would be removed before it went off in the rising heat.

The giraffes were left a basket of warm, brown bread rolls, all tucked up inside a red chequered napkin.

Dave looked at the zebras and alpacas and wandered up to the edge of the forest, where he pulled up large handfuls of the lush long grass that sprang up at the edge, stinging his hands on the nettles up there but not allowing this to distract him from his mission.

And finally he came to us. I was still furious with him but a combination of my curiosity as to our gifts and my unfortunate slowness prevented me from executing my planned attack. Besides, it was, I was thinking, perhaps best not to fight violence with violence. I did not want to be taken off to the police station too. This would surely upset Stella further.

He delivered us three massive white china plates. One was piled high with raspberries and blueberries, another sweet and tender baby spinach leaves and the third, chopped tomatoes mixed with a basil leaf that tasted faintly of aniseed.

Then Dave sat on the Wall, swigging a can of beer as we all – well, apart from the idiotic flamingos - feasted on the delicacies he had provided from his kitchen.

'Dave!' came a trembling shout from one of the upstairs windows of the house. 'Where the fuck has all our food gone? She says you've given it all to that stinking zoo! What the hell are we supposed to eat? Have you gone completely fucking mad?' Dave sighed, chugged back the rest of the beer, crushed the empty can in his hand, none too convincingly, and threw it over his shoulder, over the Wall, where it caught me on my head. He belched and murmured something about facing the music as he opened his front door.

Raised voices were evident. And then Issa, made up in a tight, white, very short dress, and Sid in shades bundled out and into the limo. As the limo slipped out through the gates, in trundled the camper van, with Bob in the passenger seat, looking rather worn. They stopped in front of the Gate House and Bob let them both in.

Chapter Ten

Much later, when the plates Dave and Sarah had prepared so thoughtfully for us had been emptied and all that remained was some dried up pink juices and my stomach bulged and churned with an excess of sugar, Stella came to see me. Her eyes were pink and puffy, her hair was loosely bundled up and she wore a long baggy vest.

'Herbie, this is all so weird. I feel a bit like nothing's ever happened in my life before and now everything is. Nothing's under my control; I feel completely at the whim of fate. I want to be able to make decisions, decide what to do, but nothing seems my own any more. And my ability to judge characters - something I always considered myself to be rather good at in the past - is completely off. My radar is skewed. I can't see the good from the bad anymore.

'I thought Ollie was bad. I thought he was a selfish, spoilt brat who was about to ruin my life, take everything I had worked for away from me and destroy Dad. And yes, actually, he is quite selfish in some ways, at least self-contained anyway. He's very focussed on what he wants to achieve, very single-minded and totally wrapped up in his music. But now I find that rather appealing; I like his ambition and his determination, I like the way he's pursuing his own success and trying to do it on his own terms, despite Sid's interference. Sid's the lazy one, trying to take the easy paths, hanging on Ollie's coat tails. And, goodness, Herbie, Ollie's so talented, he's some kind of genius. I mean, I don't know much about music, can't sing for buttons as you well know, but the way I feel when he is singing! It's like there's nothing else in the world when he plays. He completely and utterly absorbs me.

'And yes, he is spoilt. He's never had it tough - but is that his fault? Is it his fault when and where he was born? It would have been stupid of him not to take advantage of it. But he is generous, too, thoughtful, kind, and a little bit wise, I think. And he's just done something that's totally blown me away: he went down to the police station and saved Dad. Ok, it wasn't a life or death situation, but it's still quite extraordinary. He's sacrificed his own family for mine - for me. And, sure, he'll probably patch things up with his Dad in time, it's just a blip. But talk about making a statement!

'They had to charge my Dad apparently, because he didn't – wouldn't - deny what had happened. He said that would be dishonest and make him a liar and therefore as bad as Dave. So he admitted what he'd done and they had to accept that as an admittance of guilt. So he's been charged with common assault. Ollie argued his case and brought him home – he's gone to try and work on getting his Dad to drop the charges against him. Even if Dave does drop the charges, Dad'll still have to go to court because the police have to inform the CPS so proceedings occur whatever Dave says now, especially since Dad has admitted the 'attack'. But Ollie spent so much time talking to them about the process we could have this horrible incident over with in a matter of weeks, perhaps even days. If Ollie can persuade Dave to go to court and say that as far as he in concerned the matter is over with, the case will be thrown out. I can't imagine Dad in prison, or even with a criminal record. Underneath his bluster, he's a softie - you see that, don't you, Herbie? He drinks too much sometimes and it makes him feisty but really all he cares about is that the animals - and me, of course - are looked after and properly treated. That's what this is about, really. He's trying to protect us.

'I'm on some sort of roller coaster, Herbie. One second I hate him - Ollie I mean - the next second I think he's the most incredible human I've ever met. It's a fine line and my emotions are running amok.' She stopped and giggled to herself here, shaking her head at the high drama of it all, I thought, the excitement that has interrupted her calm, well-organised existence.

'I took a pill - an E - for the first time last night, Herbie, and it was amazing. All I wanted to do was hug everyone. The world was perfect - full of happiness and hope. For a moment I looked at him, when he was playing, and he was looking right at me and for a while I thought I was entirely and simply in love. It was… energising and enervating at the same time. It made me strong and it made me feeble… in a kind of good way. In a way that I could give myself over to someone – well, part of me anyway. It felt great!' She looked positively glum, now.

'Last night… I slept with him - in the same bed, I mean; we didn't have sex. Not that that would have been awful. I just… we talked all night. But that may have been the drugs. I had my head tucked under his, lying across his body. He was so warm and solid… and slightly furry! I could feel his heart beating and it was like a kind of miracle, being with another human and feeling so connected to them.' She smiled as we watched a V of geese fly over the top of us and heard their honking drift down as they checked their co-ordinates and flight path. 'I can't remember a lot of what we talked about now. In fact, at the time both of us kept on forgetting what we were talking about. We'd be halfway through a sentence and the rest of it would float off, like an escaped balloon, and we'd try and grasp it, try to catch the end of its string but miss, and then it would be gone. Infuriating. We laughed at the time, but it unsettled me. Losing my thoughts – I didn't like it.

'Oh, I don't know, maybe I'm building this up too much, making too much of it. It's difficult to tell what's the drugs and what's real. But it's making me nervous, it's making me tense; I want him too much. Not in the physical sense - although… that too. But I want him to be bound to me. I used to think of myself as a free spirit and that in a relationship I would want to feel free, want the other person to feel the same. But I feel like I want to belong to him - which seems so very old fashioned and against everything I dream of. Dreamed of. I'm terrified it won't work out when I don't even know what working really means. It feels like I'm his hands, like he holds all the cards, the key to my happiness, and frankly I'm hating every moment of it. It's uncomfortable – precarious… too big.' She stopped talking.

Stella, I willed her to hear me. Stella, relax; enjoy this. Let go. Live in the now - enjoy *him*. Let it be.

A now familiar strum of a guitar thrilled up the Hill. Ollie's vanilla caramel voice rolled with it. The menagerie stilled.

'And now he's calling me. This is the song, Herbie, the one he wrote for me. He says it came from nowhere the day before we met, and the instant he saw me he knew who it was for. His music swaddles me. It comforts me and secures me. It ignites me. It sets me on fire.' She stopped speaking, laid back and stared at a cloud, herring-boning across the horizon, flickering above the Glittering. 'I am unable to resist.' She whispered. 'And he makes me feel so… last night he took my hand, and all he did was gently rub, in a circle, just one fingernail on my right hand but I felt it everywhere, even in my elbows, it stunned and stiffened me.' She was breathless. And doused in pheromones; they were oozing out of her, rich and thick - so thick I could almost see them. She stood up suddenly and it was like a sort of plasma falling away from her, wisps of oily rainbows dripping onto the grass, evaporating into an intoxicating perfume into the air.

She walked, slowly down towards the Wall, a trail of scent in her wake. She put a hand on the Wall and heaved her light body over it, her confused mind holding her back. She walked down the Hill and stroked Atlas on the cheek, smearing him with invisible war paint, and kissed him firmly on the lips, leaving them phosphorescent in the dim of dusk.

The menagerie turned as one to face the music and we all swayed in time. Stella's pheromones had induced a deep sense of love in us all. We were a love collective, joined by her joy.

Rufus exited the front door and stretched and yawned, his t-shirt stretching up above his waistband revealing muscles so tight they challenged Atlas', and a faint line of hair straight down from his belly button that disappeared below his belt. He wandered up to the Wall and sat on it.

'Hello, my old muckers. Sorry about last night; thought you wouldn't mind a bit of fun.' He stopped and stared at me. I was as usual in thrall to Ollie's hypnotic tones and rhythms, and was swaying my head gently from side to side. He peered at me, and then looked around at the Family, all staring up at the balcony, none of them dancing, though, all of them still. His mouth dropped open. He looked at Daisy and Dolly and the alpacas, who were stood in a perfect line, all looking in the same direction, over at Ollie, silhouetted in the window, his top hat on, electric lights on behind him. He looked at the giraffes and the meerkats, all frozen watching the balcony in the Big House, and then he looked at Brian, hanging from a rope by just one arm, not moving, just listening.

Ollie began another song with a faster beat, and although none of us changed the direction of our gaze, I did stop swaying and start jiggling. I could hear the parakeets flapping about in the Oak above my head. Rufus stood up and walked over to me, stood in front of me. I just carried on doing what I was doing. He took a phone out his pocket and pointed it at me, frowning at me in puzzlement and humour.

'Ollie!' he shouted. 'Ollie! This tortoise is dancing to the music! In fact, this whole menagerie is musical! It's a musical menagerie! Ollie!' He shouted louder again and Ollie stopped playing and appeared out on the balcony, leaning over the railings with Stella.

'Yes, Rufus? What's up?' Just then, Rufus' phone rang, trilling just like the old phones in the Big House.

'Hang on, mate! One second. You wait there,' he said, pointing at me. I considered running off while he wasn't looking.

'What?' he said as he answered the phone. 'Sussex,' he answered abruptly. 'At the Palmer's. Saw Ollie playing a gig down here last night. Considering him for the label. What are you, my mother?' He took a pack of cigarettes from the top pocket of his shirt. 'Why, what's happened?' He laughed. 'No shit. Well that's that, then. Decision made.' He blew a smoke ring. 'No, no. No need to panic. I have an alternative right here. Yes, they'll be ready by tomorrow, just need to track Sid down. Shouldn't be too tricky. Don't worry about the publicity; we'll just surprise the audience. No doubt Amuse's shenanigans will have hit the papers already so it'll be more interesting to keep it secret. Besides, I have an idea involving a very special guest.' He stopped pacing about and crouched in front of me. He looked me right in the eye.

Chapter Eleven

'Stella!' Bob shouted. 'What the bloody hell fire are you doing with that damned tortoise of yours?'

Stella, Ollie and Rufus had retrieved Brian's drawbridge from the depths of the forest and had leaned it up against the Wall like a ramp. Stella was sat at the top of the ramp on the Wall waving a carrot around and calling to me. I'd seen them drag a crate up the Hill with them, along with a woollen blanket. Stella had been promising me a big adventure and I was trying to make my way up the ramp, but it was only just as wide as me and there was nothing to grip on.

She looked at me, and then over at Bob. Ollie and Rufus, who had just arrived at my back end to give me a shove, looked at each other.

'We're going to make him a star, Dad.' Wow, I thought; she hadn't told me this bit yet. 'He's coming to the gig in Brixton tonight; Rufus is billing him as the amazing dancing tortoise. Of course, I always knew he was extra special.' I nearly fainted. Digby squawked above my head, where moments previously he had been ribbing me about my ungraceful bulk.

'Ha!' I said to him.

'Stella, don't be so ridiculous. Where did you find that?' Bob asked, pointing at the drawbridge. Party pooper, I thought.

'In the woods, Dad. Wouldn't you have been better off locking it in your secret shed with goodness knows what else you have hidden in there?' Stella put the carrot down on the Wall and turned to face her father. Ollie and Rufus stood up too and let go of my bottom. I slithered down the ramp and braced my back claws into the grass, ready to try the climb again, seeing the

123

most exciting adventure of my life within reach and praying to Bob to let it happen, to not interfere with these most glorious plans.

'You may be right there, Stella, but there isn't room. Put it back where you found it and don't tell Dave where it is,' Bob commanded. 'Now.'

'We will when Herbie's safe in the crate and ready to come with us,' Stella countered.

'Stella, you can't take him out of here – he's an animal. This is where he belongs. Anything could happen to him! It's just… unfeasible.' Oh please, I thought, let anything happen to me, anything at all! Anything that wasn't being inside the Wall, being driven slowly into madness by the lack of anything ever happening ever.

'You took Brian to the pub the other day,' said Stella.

'That was different,' said Bob.

''Different' how, Dad? He's an animal, too, born and bred here, like Herbert. It's just Brian's your favourite. Well, Herbert's my favourite and I think the world deserves to see his talent. Would you deny them that?'

'I had to remove Brian for a few hours in order to save him – you're taking Herbert entirely for your own fun. You're going to make a gimmick of him, a spectacle. You're using him, Stella. This is wrong.'

Use me! I shouted, silently. I want to be a spectacle! I want to be famous! I want people to come and see me from miles around, like Lonesome George. Someone might even write a book about me.

'You never minded when he was little, Dad. He went everywhere with me. He went to school with me, remember? Until the teacher said she'd had enough and it wasn't fair on the other children.'

'Those were extenuating circumstances, Stella.' He huffed at her.

'Look, Dad, you know how much I love Herbie. I would never allow any harm to come to him - but he loves Ollie's music, truly he does. And I feel sorry for him, stuck in here all the time; I'm sure he'd love a night out. Brian enjoyed his day out very much didn't he? You said he did. I'll look after him. Besides, if Dave has his way, I may not have any more time with him. He might take my Herbie away from me. You have to let us enjoy the time we have left together. Please Dad, if you really can't agree then please just pretend you haven't seen us?' We all looked pleadingly at Bob. He looked at each of us in turn, especially me, and shook his head, then turned and walked back to the Gate House, closing the door firmly behind him.

'Right then,' said Rufus, rubbing his hands together. 'On the count of three!' Ollie and he pressed their hands on the bottom curve of my shell. 'One! Two! Three!'

They pushed until I was balanced on the blanket that had been laid over the top of the Wall. Between the three of them they pulled up the four corners of the blanket so I was suspended in it like a hammock, it all woolly and dark, my claws poking through in places, and they swung me into the crate. It was even darker in there but I did not mind. I was all aquiver with anticipation. I was outside of the Wall! I was going off to see something! Be part of something! I was going to be a star! I was going to be on stage! I would be a performer, an entertainer - I would have a vocation!

It was a bit of a bumpy ride as they dragged the crate down the Hill and I didn't mind that my wide flint Wall had been replaced by the wooden walls of this crate, because I was on my way into the big unknown. I was going to a gig! Digby flew past, shouting, 'Have an amazing time, Herbert! Don't forget to tell us everything when you come back! And take care!' I wondered if he would try to come too. We had heard Rufus shout the good news to Ollie about his participation the afternoon before when Rufus had hung up his phone. Ollie and Stella had been stood on the balcony and she had turned to him and given him a hug that looked as if it could easily turn into something more, even though it was broad daylight and Rufus was right there.

In fact, it was Rufus saying, 'Put him down, love; I need him to save himself for my gig tomorrow!' that put pay to that. Anyway, before all this happened, Digby had said that it was an awfully long flight for a night and also that he had been told that there were no windows at the Academy, no way to enter the hallowed halls, no porthole to peek through. We had resigned ourselves to picking up the scraps of information after the event and piecing it all together, but now it turned out that I was going! It was some sort of miracle.

They hoisted the crate into the back of the purple camper van. I stretched my head up as far as it would go and I could see that the van had wooden strips running along its ceiling. They had thoughtfully set the crate down so that I could just about see out of the back windows. The rest of the van was packed with the equipment that had been used at the gig on the Saturday, apart from a small space next to the crate. Stella jumped in holding a cushion and curled herself up there right next to me and tickled me under the chin.

'Isn't this fun, Herbie? Your big adventure!' I nodded. She laughed. Ollie shut the doors; he and Dave clambered into the front. The pink camper van loomed up behind us, captained by Hannah with Rufus in the passenger seat, beeped at us a couple of times and then our engine was started, and we were off!

I saw Digby sat on the gatepost as we went through and I settled down for the journey, watching as the scenery through the back windows changed from canopied leafy tunnels to the view out to the Glittering, punctuated by a windmill, then there were lots of small red houses, and then a long grey wall that twisted and curved, trees rising above its height and then we came to a vast road, full of cars, most of them going faster than us, and then we stopped and started and there were houses and shops and a thick scent of fried chicken in the air. Hannah and Rufus were several cars behind us as the vehicles jostled for position. The streets were swarming with humans of every shape and colour, wearing brightly coloured clothes and hats and all manner of items I had not seen before. We drove down a grubby alleyway full of bins that smelled of rotting fruit and I expected to see rats; I could sense they were in there, cleaning up, breeding, scavenging, doing their job.

'Here we are,' said Stella, leaning over the edge of the crate to look at me. I blinked at her. Hannah's face appeared, her arm around Stella's shoulders. I had a bit of a crick in my neck from the journey. The doors were opened and the crate was pulled out onto a trolley and into a doorway, behind which it was dark. It smelled old and fusty and mouldy in there and someone hit a light switch and something flickered pale, pale purple above our heads. We went down several corridors, one of the wheels on the trolley squeaking, lights flashing in strips above my head and then we stopped in a room.

It was dark and gloomy. Two florescent strip lights tried and failed to make it otherwise, one blinking like it had a tic. There were no windows and therefore no sense of day or night. It felt strange that the Source was banned from here.

'Here's your riders, lads – wife beater, vodka, pills, coke – cans of, coke – pile of, bananas and a bag of spinach for the star of tonight's show.' Rufus peered in over the edge of the crate, his features sleek and slightly oily in the dim light. I heard a clatter of heels on the floor behind me. 'Well, well, well and who do we have here, then? The not-so prodigal son and his very wicked step-mother!' Rufus said.

It was Issa and Sid, then. I could see her head leaning against the doorframe, her expression dour. I heard Hannah say she was going to watch the gig from the front and was going to get a good spot in the mosh pit, a beer and pocket a couple of those Es if no-one minded and then she was gone, her trainers squeaking down the corridor. Dave went over to his wife and kissed her as she turned her cheek away from him.

'Why haven't you been answering your phone, gorgeous?' he asked.

'I've been busy,' she replied. Dave snapped open a can of beer.

'Right, then,' said Ollie. 'How are we doing for time?'

'T-minus thirty,' replied Sid. 'We'd better get cracking; all your arsing about with that ridiculous creature has screwed our schedule. We've got some gofers though - let's get out to the van.'

Stella sat down on a chair next to the crate, her hand hanging in over the edge. 'You okay in there, Herbie?' she asked. I was fine, but I was bored of being in the crate. The journey had been exciting, whilst we had all been stuck inside a tin box of sorts, but now people were moving about and exploring and I wanted to stretch my legs. I was also - dare I admit it - a little nervous. What were they expecting of me? What if I let them down? What if - the Source forbid - I made a fool of myself? Would I put Ollie's career in tatters?

I tried to temper my worries; they just wanted me to be me, to do my thing. I was here - I was on my big adventure! There was no point ruining it by fretting about it. I was in the Brixton Academy – I had heard them talk about this place so much with so much awe and respect. I was honoured to be here; I was honoured to be a part of this.

Besides, they must let me out of the crate soon. There was little advantage in having an amazing dancing tortoise stuck inside a box, was there? No-one would see me!

Issa and Stella were talking. Stella was telling her about Ollie going down to the police station to rescue Bob, how Ollie had been trying to persuade Dave to go to Bob's court hearing and tell them that the matter was resolved and that there was no need to continue with proceedings. She was asking Issa to talk to Dave too. Issa asked if this would make Bob happy, if the case could be dropped, thrown out. Stella said no, not happy, but perhaps less unhappy. Issa said they weren't all bad, those boys, after all. Stella said that no, Ollie wasn't. Her omittance of Sid was blatant. Issa hummed a little and offered Stella a drink, a line of coke, a pill. Stella accepted them all, one after another. I heard the chink of ice, the gurgles and fizz of liquids poured, the chopping and snorting of the cocaine powder, the sniffing of the users, the glugging of their drinks.

Then Stella asked Issa if she was coming back to Bestwood. Issa said of course, she'd be coming back tonight after the gig with Sid. Said that she had just needed a break, was new to this marriage thing and had just let a couple of things get on top of her, but she would work her way through this, was sure she loved Dave, really.

'Making yourself at home then, ladies!' laughed Rufus, as he returned with the twin brothers and their father, all of them huffing a bit, no doubt from their exertions preparing for our show. They all took drinks and swallowed pills and snorted lines.

'Alright, Herbie, we're ready for you now!' said Ollie.

'Don't worry, darling; I won't be far away from you,' whispered Stella to me, and once more I was being transported down corridors.

We stopped. It was really dark here; pitch. I could hear the deep swell of the murmur of a thousand voices not far away. I could smell onions and beer and sweat. Fresh sweat and old sweat. I heard rolls of laughter and the shouts of people calling to each other over each other.

'I reckon we lift him up inside the blanket,' said Ollie. 'I don't think tipping him out's a good idea. He might end up on his back or hurting something.' I agreed.

'Please be careful!' said Stella.

'We will be honey, don't worry! You can help!' Again I was in a hammock, all my weight pressing against the bottom of the blanket, suspended in the air. And then I was on the ground, the blanket flat on the floor around me, caught on my claws. All I could see was the outline of four pairs of legs in front of me; Stella's in knee-high flat boots, Ollie's and Sid's in virtually identical pairs of jeans and Dave's in loose, flowing turquoise trousers. Another pair appeared in what appeared to be purple snakeskin.

'Looking good!' said Rufus in the snakeskin. 'Time to get this show on the road. You boys ready? You rock! I'll see you out the back afterwards.' His scaly legs vanished into the shadows, closely followed by Dave's floating past.

'Go on, my sons! May the force be with you!' he said from somewhere in the gloom behind me.

Through all the legs ahead of me I could see pale blue lights like mushrooms in a wide semicircle. Inside the curve of them, they shone off the feet and ribs of a drum kit, played up the steel strings of a guitar leaned against them and glowed on the edges of a keyboard. Ollie's and Sid's jeans turned away from me and walked towards the instruments, and I could hear clapping and whistling and some cheering from over to my right. I took a step forwards and peered around the corner and blinked.

There was an ocean of people out there. Arms were waving about like an anemone's tentacles on a reef but chaotically, without the rhythm of currents.

An immense heat came off them, along with a noise. Convection seemed to carry each of their smells to my nostrils, unaccustomed to such variety. I could smell food and drink, spices and perfumes, hormones and pheromones, sweat and alcohol. My nasal passages were being assaulted. I was rather giddy and unsteady on my feet.

A warm hand pressed onto the top curvature of my shell. I recognised the heartbeat in an instant. It was Stella, immediately calming, reassuring. I turned back to look at her. Her eyes bored into mine.

'Are you okay, my darling? Are you up to this?' I blinked, unsure exactly what I was saying. Was it assent, was it a question back at her, was I telling her about the onslaught to my mind, the sense of dissolution in my body?

'If you like,' she said, 'you could take a few steps onto the stage, towards Ollie and listen to the music. I'm sure that they would all love to see you. Hannah's out there; she's waiting for you. She'll give you a wave. And I'll be just here - I'll be here just in case you need me at any moment.' She crouched down in front of me and gave me a kiss on the top of my flat head.

The mood in the crowd changed. They were impatient. They were chanting: 'Apollemis! Apollemis! Apollemis!'

They could see Ollie and Sid in the shadows on the stage. I turned back and I could see them too. They were waiting for it to start. It was waiting for me to start. They were all waiting for me.

I took a step forward and discovered that my legs were holding me entirely correctly. So I took another and another, keeping my eyes on Ollie. As I came closer to him, the blue light below revealed that he was looking at me and smiling, his hands poised on the keyboard, his mouth hovering over the buzz of the microphone. Sid was sat at the drums, his legs spread wide and one foot tapping to nothing, but something inside his head. Sticks hung lazily from his hands and he was staring out into the ocean waving about at the front of the stage.

I looked out to it as a flood of light engulfed the stage and suddenly everything out there was dark and I was inside a bower, a balconied Romeo and Juliet tower, and then Ollie began to play.

Once he started to hit his notes, my awareness of the outside world curtained. It was much more apparent here than in the menagerie. There I had just had the sense that I was concentrating, but here it became swiftly obvious that his music entirely swallowed me up and that I had no resistance to it. As he struck the first few chords, I thought that the hall, wide as a bullfrog's mouth, had fallen into a silence, but I am not sure if that was them or me. I heard a faint 'woohoo!' that may have been Hannah, or it may have been every single human creature out there in synch. I do not know. I was sucked in and I was enthralled. I became oddly aware that I was, as Rufus had put it, dancing. Clearly I was never going to win any prizes for it; a tortoise will never be known for agility and flexibility, pace and definitely not speed. But I didn't worry about this. It was not me that was dancing; the music was dancing me. I wasn't exactly a puppet – it's not that there were strings; it's just that it owned me. It was in every part of me, in every sinew, tendon and joint. I was entirely relaxed and in total ecstasy.

I turned to face outwards to the ocean, and I could hear its waves crashing along with Ollie and Sid, the tides of voices running over me and out again. My eyes were becoming accustomed to the light I was under and the darkness out there and I started to be able to make out hands and eyes and teeth in the audience.

It went on and on and I truly never wanted it to stop. I was safe in the knowledge that Stella was behind me and I could see that Ollie, even though we were both entirely wrapped up in his music, I saw that he kept checking on me. Every now and again there would be a short pause, but I had enough ripples left from the previous melodies to sustain me through the gaps to allow me to dwell on the strangers' faces and interrogate them for friendliness, antagonism, curiosity, suspicion. Once again the music would start and it would take me with it.

At one point, there was a longer gap and Stella rushed over to me and poured compliments into my ear and I overheard a conversation between Ollie and Sid that she must have missed herself, as I saw no reaction in her to it.

'So,' said Sid. 'Pretty damn fine, your new bird.'

'She's beautiful,' Ollie answered simply.

'You remember,' said Sid, 'when we were kids, how we used to spoof each other and share the girls for fun?'

'Yes,' said Ollie. 'I remember.'

'Do you think…'

'No,' said Ollie, before Sid had even really started his sentence. 'Absolutely no chance. And if you try anything, I will not be responsible for what I do to you. You are my brother - my twin brother - but I'm not sharing this one. If you do, then…' He left the 'then' hanging.

'Okay, I get it. You're a goner. You ready to go again?' And the music started up and Stella melted off stage.

When Ollie stopped, it was far too soon for my liking; he could have gone on forever as far as I was concerned. This was another thing that was very different about the music here - in the menagerie, I heard him from a distance, couldn't truly see him. But here, everything he touched was so close to me that it was part of me.

Sid's role in this seemed merely to keep time, to provide on stage support. Ollie led and operated mainly alone, and was unaware of Sid a good deal of the time. I watched Ollie as he worked and sometimes, when a moment of consciousness pricked me, I could try and unravel how he was doing what he did. I'd watch his fingers, his mouth and his expressions. I could almost smell his breath, almost see his blood pump. I could see his sweat ball about his hairless hairline, roll down to his eyebrows, sometimes dripping off his chin. I could feel the energy, the energy that he was sharing with me and with everyone else in the vast room. He was giving us something. I wanted to try and put it in a box and give it to someone else - Digby, maybe. Or save it for a day many years from now. I was convinced that I would not see many days more enriching, enthusing, life-affirming than this; if my past was anything to go by, this memory would come in useful on a very rainy day.

But he did stop. And the ocean roared for an encore. He and Sid left the stage and I turned to go, but a spotlight shone on me and I could hear the ocean chanting, 'Tortoise! Tortoise!' and I froze - not in fright but in delight. In all honesty, I had forgotten where I was, forgotten that I was there, forgotten who I was, even. And suddenly I was the thing on stage, the thing that they were all baying for and just when this concept became a little bit too much, Ollie and Sid came back and sang once more. And when they stopped this time, Ollie introduced me to the ocean, and I blinked and it cheered and ripples ran up and down my spine, and then they turned the lights out, apart from those little blue mushrooms, and I was bereft. It was over. The most amazing night – nay, time - in my life, the most incredible adventure and it was done.

I was to be shipped back to the Wall to the Family and when I was back there - then what? My future opened up before me but like a black hole. I couldn't see any light ahead, it was all behind me. Unless - unless perhaps I had made such an impression that I would be a permanent fixture on stage with Ollie? I could not see this happening though, not really. It was not like I was contributing to the musical genius; I was just a gimmick, like Bob said. The best I could hope to be was a crowd puller. My talents were not my own and were, in fact, naught. Ollie would not want me here, stealing his limelight - not even stealing it, just distracting from it. I was merely a sideshow, a freak-show even. There was something faintly Victorian about it.

Stella called me over to the side of the stage, to the blanket. I was going to be put back in my box. I tried to hold on to what had just happened. I tried to hold on to everything that I had just done, experienced. I needed to relive every moment, burn it into my memory, into my carapace. I could share it then with every other tortoise now and in the future. No other tortoise I was sure had ever been on stage at the Brixton Academy. No other tortoise was a rock tortoise. No other tortoise was an amazing dancing tortoise. No other tortoise had my gift.

If this was what I had lived for, then this was fine. If this, so early on in my life was what I was here to teach, to experience and feel, then so be it. I had served my purpose. I had lived my fate. I could resign myself to a life of browsing plants and soaking up Sourceshine. Could I?

The hammock blanket lifted me up. It let me down. Trolleys, corridors, rushed words between Stella and Ollie.

'We'd better get him home.' Ollie sounded certain. I was sure I had heard word of an after party.

'Are you sure? What about the others? Don't you want to stay? Are you okay?' I gasped at the string of questions from Stella. I could see frown lines on her forehead when I looked up.

'Let's just go, honey. It's been a great night. But I only want to be with you.' She smiled at him and stood up. He stood opposite her, nervous. She took his hand and she put it on her waist and she placed the other on his jaw and she pulled him to her. They kissed gently on the lips, meeting once, twice, three times. Now sure, he pulled her waist to him and she wrapped her arms around his head and they were lost in each other.

Frankly, I did not know where to look. That moment was too private, so intimate. I withdrew inside myself.

The next thing I knew, we were on our way back to Bestwood. Home, some people might say - home, sweet home. Home, sour home. Home, horrid fetid home. I dozed the whole way there, alone in the back of the camper van, grasping onto myself and the impressions of my night just-passed. The low tinkling voices of Stella and Ollie reached back to me, comforting and unsettling at the same time. Had Ollie replaced me in Stella's heart? Was it right that we took up the same space? Did we even take up the same space? There were so many different things he could offer her… the relationships did not compare. But my question to myself was this; now that she loved Ollie, would she love me less? Would I be cast aside, or would she protect me and keep me safe? He was no longer a means to an end for her, I felt. He was some sort of end - or maybe a beginning.

I tried to look at it from her point of view. She was thrilled, enamoured, fascinated and adored by him - things we had once shared ourselves, of course. But a human and a tortoise can never mate, never produce offspring, and these were the basic drives every creature on the planet had inbuilt. I had no doubt that she loved me; but, as anyone knows, there are many types of love, and ours was not one that would generate a new generation. Ours could never satisfy the commonly held meaning of life. The meaning of life, it seemed, was to make life go on. Survive and reproduce oneself in one's own likeness, combined with that of one's lover.

As the familiar smells of the menagerie pervaded the night air, dark in the back of the van, I felt a deep sense of loneliness and it held the hand of hopelessness. So perhaps loneliness was not, in fact, alone, but it certainly was not in the best of company. As I ruminated and cogitated myself into a slough of despondency, Stella and Ollie left the van and slammed their doors, behind themselves and crunched away on the pebbly drive. If I could have cried I would have wept and sobbed and blubbered until my eyes fell out. Instead, I remained curled up and flicked through the encyclopaedia of memories in my shell, trying to find something to inspire me and sustain me in my despair. From ecstasy to agony. What goes up must come down. No pleasure without pain.

Voices ruptured me from my dissolution and, with a clatter, the back doors of the camper van opened. I was not alone, not forgotten - not, perhaps, unloved.

'I see your issue.' I heard Sarah's practical tones. 'How about a wheel-barrow?' I could imagine her head tilted to one side and her hands on her hips as her smart, pretty brain unravelled the conundrum of how to juggle me back inside the Wall. I did not care that I was going back there now. I was exhausted, exalted and a little bit scared. Once again, my future looked foggy. I was sure there should be light within the fog, since surely a known future is not a future at all? A future should be full of surprises, hopes, dreams and terrors to work through. A future is a promise of life. I had never understood humans' (in particular Hannah's) addiction to the soothsayers, ball gazers, psychics. I could not comprehend their need to know their future was safe, or that they would believe someone that would tell them so.

My box was dragged out of the back of the van and landed on the drive with a bit of a crunchy thump. I was hammocked again in the blanket and there was much huffing and puffing - which I found slightly offensive, since I did not believe that I weighed as an individual as much as any of them - and then I was lopsided in a wheelbarrow. My legs felt slightly tender from the knocks on the sides of the box as they had pulled me out, and now two were squashed underneath the cold, unyielding metal on my left hand side, as the other two stuck out on the right, the top edge of the wheel barrow awkwardly digging in. Still, I couldn't complain. It was an efficient mode of transport and the height of the barrow meant that it wasn't too hard for them to haul my lump up and over the Wall. Although they tried to lower me gently, that last foot was a big of a rush, and although I could not sense the speed at which the ground hurtled towards me, I knew it when we met each other. Still, what's a shell for?

Once there, and after they had left, Digby hopped about and the others were mewling for details. I was so overwhelmed with my sadnesses though that I could not bring myself to speak about my joys. And so I told them I was tired and was to sleep and that they would wait until the Source shone again and warmed my blood enough to tell my tale. With varying degrees of grumbling, they accepted this and dispersed. I pulled myself in and thought. Several hours later, a performance drew me out.

Chapter Twelve

Stella stood naked on the Wall.

Her right foot was pinning down the grass snake, Colin, who was frozen by the music, his scales iridescent in the early morning light that washed the sky. A bank of clouds glowed in pink ribbons. Ollie played and sang. She swayed from side to side. She held her arms in the air and hung her head back and her hair swang free. In her right hand she held a glass with a shallow bowl, the liquid in it spilling and fizzing.

Ollie looked up and saw her, full frontal, smiled and put the guitar down and, still singing, walked to the edge of the balcony and leaned as far forward as he could, stretching both of his arms out and sang the final words to 'I Know'.

'It's you...' He held the last note and all of my bones melted.

Silence.

Colin snapped out of his trance and bit Stella square on her big toe.

She jerked her leg up sharply and smudged the bead of blood that bloomed. Standing on just one foot, she lost her balance and slipped.

As she fell, she hit her hip, and then her left temple banged on the jagged flint of the Wall.

She lay, in a crumpled heap, inside my boundary.

She didn't move.

I went to her to look at her beautiful, sleeping face. There was a pool of blood spreading darkly across the ground beneath her head.

After a while, blue lights blurted, and they took Stella away.

PART TWO

Chapter Thirteen

Hope House

Palmer Springs

Bestwood

West Sussex

PO42 1DP

14th August 2008

Dear Stella,

It's been three days now. Three whole days since the singularly best and worst night of my life so far.

The best because it was such an awesome gig, at such a legendary venue. I've been there so many times, seen so many bands, dreamed so often of being on that stage myself. I consider it the pinnacle of my career. I never wanted to be a stadium band. For me, Brixton is everything. It's all that is cool and it was totally magic. Just how I knew it would be.

And to top it all off, you kissed me. And then you made love with me.

But then my perfect night turned into a total nightmare. My worst night ever, which has left me here, alone, waiting for you to return to me so we can pick up where we left off, finish what we started.

Dr Shah tells me that when you fell and knocked yourself unconscious your brain suffered a trauma. I like Dr Shah. I find his beard comforting. He has expressive and intelligent eyebrows. You would like him and his eyebrows too. In fact, you probably do.

He's explained to me that your body has gone into some sort of stasis in order to concentrate on fixing this trauma, the deep damage, inside your brain. He says that the drugs you had taken most probably didn't really cause or haven't even exacerbated the situation. He also says that even if I had managed to reach you and get help to you any sooner, that it's unlikely there would be any difference at all to your current condition.

None of this helps me. I still feel hideously guilty. I feel as if I've let you down. Like I have a responsibility for you. That I should have been looking after you. I was not supposed to let this happen to you. Somehow, this is my fault. If you hadn't been so off your tits, you wouldn't have fallen. You wouldn't have been off your tits if it wasn't for me and I should have caught you.

When the police came to talk to me about what happened, I wanted them to arrest me. I wanted to confess to this terrible crime that I'd committed. I told them everything but it turned out there wasn't any crime. Ok, I left out most of the stuff about what we'd been taking since the State likes to call it illegal. They just said how sorry they were, told me I was not to blame and then left me. I was angry with them, as if they had refused to allow me to purge. They abandoned me with my shame.

Of course, you know all of this already, I've confessed repeatedly to you over the past few days. Apologised endlessly. You can hear me. Or so Dr Shah says. And I do believe him, even though actually he doesn't seem that sure himself. He keeps on referring to theories and case histories. I must have been boring you stupid. Sorry. There I go again!

I don't want to not believe him for a second. He says you're in there. I know you're not far away. I can feel it. And so, I'm by your side, talking to you every minute that I'm allowed. I play you music. I read to you. Today I read you 'Charlotte's Web'. Hannah said it was your favourite when you were little girls. A tear rolled down your cheek when I got to the bit where the pig took the spider's egg sac home from the show.

Hannah's doing okay, although is still pretty obsessed with Sid and quite angry with him. I've seen this before with Sid. It's not like he really leads the girls on, but he seems to pick the ones that don't take rejection all that well, those that are easily infatuated, that take the slightest glance or off hand comment as an encouragement. Or maybe he's just bad at rejecting. He definitely is an incorrigible flirt. He really gets off on it. Anyway, she'd be angrier I'm sure if she knew the half of what's been going on…

It transpires that Sid's been shagging Sarah, you know, the housekeeper, for quite some time. Even I had no idea about this. Which is unusual since it's rare for him to be subtle or discreet, rarer even for him to not boast of his conquests and unheard of for me to not just know. One of those twin things, I guess… OK, so no biggie. He's shagging the housekeeper, porking payroll. Nothing new there then that's not gone on through the ages. And it's hardly like we're some different class, we just happen to have stumbled into a life where the money's rolled in and Sarah's staff. I totally see what he likes about her. She's refreshing. And doesn't stand for any crap, even from Dad and Issa. And boy, does she know how to get things done. She could move mountains, that one.

Sarah also has the sanest head I've ever seen on anyone's shoulders. She sees through everything. X-ray woman, I should call her! No bullshit, no bollocks. What she sees in Sid, I don't know. You think she'd know better, really, wouldn't you? Well, the thing is, and I know that I am biased, we share the same genes after all, and I know he doesn't come across well and I also know that even I, his brother, twin, best mate, band mate has had barely a good word to say about him, but he does have some depths. Deeply hidden depths, but they are there if you scratch the surface hard enough or if he decides to part the waves.

All his bravado is driven by insecurity. Behind his misogyny, his apparent need to treat women as sex objects, to play his endless games, is his actual need to validate himself. He's never felt comfortable in his own skin, Sid. I've found it difficult to understand, being so confident in my own. But in moments of weakness, okay, extreme fuckedness, he'll tell me about it. How he's always felt like he's competed with me for Dad's attention. True. How he doesn't know who he is and copies things from other people that he likes. I have seen him do this. We'll go out of an evening and he'll admire someone's jacket and then the next day we'll be out there getting the same one, or a more expensive version, if he can find one. He says he's like a pin-board of things he's coveted, a husk embellished with a magpie's glittering trinkets.

Inside, under all of that nonsense, is a little boy that just wants to be loved. Just wants to feel secure. He should have come travelling with me. No, he should have gone travelling on his own. Spent some time navel-gazing. He was the one that was lost, not me. But he wouldn't come. Said it was time for us to be ourselves by ourself for once and he was right. But the wrong twin went travelling. I learned nothing new. But I did find lots of inspiration, so it was by no means a wasted experience. I just think he would have got more out of it, grown more. He would have found himself, maybe.

Instead, however, Sid has continued to lose the sense of himself. Created layer upon layer of invention on top of himself. But Sarah, even without the benefit of a lifetime with him, right from the egg, the egg that begins in the mother's womb, without this she still sees him. And I think she loves him.

She can unpeel the badness, peep underneath the dirty skin he's made. And her instinct to nurture leads her to reach for his soul.

Sadly, though, a malevolent force stands in their way. All six foot of her. She is a giantess. Sarah is a teeny girl beside her. The giantess is superior and flawless. At least, that's how she sees herself. I see her as a monster, throwing fire, empty inside.

This monster ensnared my father and now, realising her mistake, intends to ensnare his son, my twin brother.

I am not sure what she hopes to gain by this. I doubt, actually, that she's thinking. She's responding, like a flytrap, to stimuli. Too engrossed by herself to contemplate, ponder the consequences.

Anyway, yesterday I caught them together, in the orangery. They, both of them, and, to be honest, it's not like I hadn't seen it coming. They did look suitably guilty. For fuck's sake, a son with his father's wife. It's only a matter of time before Sarah catches them, and from what little she's told me, she thinks it's The Real Thing with Sid, whatever that is! She's sane as I said, and wise and true, but you know what they say about a woman scorned. Who knows how she'll react. He's made her promises, and it's broken promises that really hurt. I doubt she's the murdering kind, but trouble, big trouble definitely lies ahead.

I can see the headlines in the redtops already. This is going to be major media hoo-hah if, probably when, this hits the press. Sarah or Hannah will blow it if they can. They won't be able to resist the rewards, even Sarah. Particularly if it seems he's been messing her about. She'll shop him; I would. The media are already going crazy over what's happened with you and your Dad's arrest. Apparently it's doing my profile no harm at all and the fans are baying for the release of our album. The one we are not even close to recording yet. This is of no consolation to me. I don't want fame or a fortune. My father's shown me the damage of both of those things. I just want to make good music. Excellent music. The best music that I can make. I don't want prying eyes, judgements cast upon me, my image snatched and stolen and printed a million times. So you must keep quiet. Sorry. Again. That's an appalling kind of joke. I can actually hear you laughing though.

On another subject, I'm concerned about your father, Stella. He doesn't seem to be coping so well, babes. I know you haven't seen much of him. I think he finds it difficult to see you so... incapacitated. He'll come round. I'll go and find him in the pub when I finish this missive. I'll try and talk to him. If you have any hints on how to handle him – please somehow let me know!

So there is a purpose to this communication. It's sort of like a diary that I'm writing to you and for you in order to record the days you seem to be away from me, so that when you return you will know where I was and what I was doing and you will have a sense of what passed here while you were away. It should fill in any gaps you might wake with.

I'm making you a promise. During this time that you are away, I will devote all of my time and every joule of energy to finding you and bringing you back.

Your Ollie. X

PS I've been feeding your tortoise for you. He had a cabbage today. Your Dad told me off afterwards for picking it. Said it was far too early. But the tortoise seemed to enjoy what he ate.

Hope House
Palmer Springs
Bestwood
West Sussex
PO42 1DP
15th August 2008

Dear Stella,

Today I think I'll document our relationship so far, since my most precious thoughts are my memories of the moments we've spent together when your vibrancy, your zest, lit me up. I replay them constantly. They are movies on a loop in my mind's eye.

So we start from the very first moment I saw you. You were sleeping like a wood nymph out on the grass. I was playing my guitar. Your beloved tortoise was not far away, watching over you as ever.

At first all I could see was your extraordinarily sexy body, stretched out, unencumbered by inhibition, in unconscious bliss. How differently unconscious you are now. Flat on your back and still, in that blank white room, tubes springing out of you, monitors flashing your life signs. You are breathing on your own and your heart has never stopped beating. All we have to do is feed you, liquid carbohydrates straight into your bloodstream. Feed you and love you and beg for your return. Every second I am with you I have hope that something, maybe me, will startle you from your dreamland, and you'll jump to your feet and straight into my arms.

There's a painting above your bed. I don't know whether I cheat by telling you here about it. I won't read you these letters. They are for when you wake.

But you could mind read me. You could be sat with me right now as I scribble. Anyway, the scientists, the doctors, they have put a painting there. I'm not going to tell you what it is. But if you come to and you have seen it, then some kind of soul exists, they will say. I am sure there is, anyway. I don't need proof. There couldn't be that much depth behind your eyes in just a few centimetres of grey matter. There's something much more lively at home in that gorgeous head of yours.

But back to when we first met. We didn't start off on the right foot, did we, my darling?! You were so cross with me. Absolutely fucking livid. Your beautiful hazelnut, chocolate, praline eyes scolded and scalded me. They were so sweet and rich and so unutterably angry and your brain was working behind them so fast and so furiously. You were combative, aggressive, so fiercely protective of your space. I don't mind admitting that you frightened me. And excited me.

After our encounter, I spent the entire rest of the afternoon thinking only of you, repeating our conversation word for word. Hating myself and my stupidity, my insensitivity. Astonished by your powerfulness, embarrassed by what must have looked like arrogant superiority. That's when I wrote my first song about you. I'd started it the day before. Almost like a premonition, it had come from nowhere and then slotted into place. I'm very sure it won't be the last song I write about you.

Then, that evening, at Issa's party, I handed you a very sincere apology with a drink and you sent me speechless with your smile. You had decided to charm me, I think, and I was a sucker for it. I noted every brush of your fingers, every time your knee hit mine, every second you looked into my eyes.

I was completely absorbed by your questions, your conversation, your laughs that sometimes ran along your surface and sometimes sprang from deep inside of you, triggering echoes in my own belly.

Hours into the evening, I realised I had virtually nothing of you, so adept you were at entertaining me. So able you were to flatter and delight me. So practised in deflecting attention from yourself. So naturally aware that everyone's world revolves about themselves, and so easily you exploited this and kept yourself hidden, private, tucked away inside of yourself.

So when Sid and Hannah went for their tryst, I tried probing deeper. You had surrounded yourself with some sort of enchanted circle; every angle I tried you blocked, locked the doors. You wouldn't talk to me about your family, your mother or your father, your childhood. You wouldn't tell me anything about you. Whether you had a boyfriend, or had ever had one. You wouldn't tell me what you wanted from your life. You didn't even tell me about Herbert, then.

All you told me, as we sat side by side watching over a crowd of people none of whom interested me in the slightest, not when you were there, pilot light to my attention, were stories about marine iguanas diving to eat algae on the ocean's floor, the testosterone fuelled rehabilitation in a sea lion's bachelor pad and the natural monogamy of albatrosses. It was an education and I hung on your every word. These were clues to you and your passions, even if you wouldn't part with your own secrets.

It was a pleasure to watch the words being formed on your lips, to see the frowns pass across your features as you emphasised your points on the destruction and threats to the world we, as you put it, think we own. It was heavenly for me to see your fury as you railed against the irresponsibility and selfish vanity of the western world. Your theories of competitive child rearing were hilarious, your seriousness enthralling. And yet you kept you from me. Your mystery was enraging.

You were so articulate, but every now and again you'd forget a word or knock one of our glasses over. You stood up and you'd been sat on your leg and it was dead and you collapsed in a heap. You had me in pieces. Your blushes were so cute.

You said you'd take me surfing and my heart soared. I knew there was a likelihood I would struggle to impress, but the opportunity of spending some time with you and sharing an experience was too good to turn down. And frankly, having witnessed how mal-coordinated you could be, I wasn't that threatened. Although I should have been!

Seeing you that next morning and finding you even more beautiful than when I'd left you the night before was a shock. I don't know how you did it in that wetsuit. I've never seen a wetsuit flatter a figure before, but you just looked sleek, like you had evolved with it.

I was so bad at surfing. I had never been much good at sport, as I told you. I wasn't all that interested in it for starters and was really terribly geeky until my late teens. Sid was excellent at sport. Like chalk and cheese we were, indeed, are. Captain of the cricket and hockey teams, he was. Trophies cluttered the shelves in his room. Dave, unfairly I think, never seemed that impressed. I guess sport wasn't much to him either. I think probably he must have been a geek like me, but he should have shown more interest in his son's achievement. Congratulated him, encouraged him, thrown him a bone.

Fuck, he was always sticking his nose into my affairs. Booking me private tuitions for guitar lessons, the piano, even the harp. I thought at one point he wouldn't rest until I had mastered every instrument ever invented on the entire planet. When he discovered I was making a lyre, I thought he was going to write to the Vatican to request that I was made some sort of saint. I almost gave up just to get him off my back, but some things are intrinsic, part of ourselves, so compelling that we cannot do without them, and have no choice but to write those words down, sing that tune, make that music.

Anyway, that's enough about me. This is about you. How you have arrived in my life and changed its course.

I desperately wanted to kiss you that whole time we were at the beach and when we said good-bye that day, but I was terrified of scaring you off, that I might blow it. I had taken your hand on the beach and you froze and stared at me and I am sure if you were less well mannered would have snatched your hand away. I couldn't fathom for a moment what you were thinking. You laughed with me and had taken me there so I would naturally assume you were interested in me, but you keep your distance. You're wary. I offer myself up and you don't take me up on it. Are you waiting until you are sure? What tests do I have to pass? Is it trust you want? To trust me, I mean? It scares me. I worry about putting a foot wrong, messing it up. I've never felt like this before, although admittedly, being in the position I am, I normally have girls throw themselves at me and their desire is so obvious only I have to decide. It's strange because when we speak, how we hang out, I feel like I could have known you forever - we're tuned to the same chord. But then you feel so breakable. Not that you are weak or fragile, just that I am walking on thin ice.

And you have this uncanny knack of being two things at once, two contrary, opposite things, I mean. Like powerful and vulnerable. Supremely self-confident and endearingly shy. Graceful and clumsy. Fearsomely wise and sweetly innocent. It's completely galling how one moment I think I have a handle on you and the next you whip it away, revealing some new element of you that completely floors me. I just can't quite work you out.

You went to work that night, waitressing, at the Dining Rooms. It was all I could do to restrain myself from going there. I tormented myself with the thoughts of all the drunk men you would serve even more drinks to; their leering at you, their propositioning you. I wanted to come and collect you and make sure that you arrived home safe, and, more importantly, alone. But I knew that this would infuriate you. Your independence would be compromised. You wouldn't find it flattering. You would find it smothering.

I distracted myself with my music. Threw myself into practising for the gig you had said you would come to the following evening. Tried not to allow myself to worry that you might not turn up. Tried to make myself as good as I could be in order to impress you. I knew by this point I had to win you.

I started to form a strategy to attain you: you were my goal and having you would be the reward for my efforts. And when I say 'having you', I don't mean in the sexual sense, although clearly that was never far from my mind, I mean connecting with you, having you acknowledge our connection, creating some kind of bond between us, exclusive, unbreakable, some kind of tether you couldn't break, wouldn't break, a rope you held the other end of through choice, because you wanted to.

First, I had to stop you leaving. In order to succeed, I needed to have you near, in my immediate proximity. You could see me live, know who I was, learn that you could trust me. You had begun to tell me how much Bestwood and the menagerie meant to you and to your father. Self-obsessed and spoiled as Dave, my father, is, deep down he is a good man. Really. I know I seem to be defending and justifying my family members, but I am telling the truth. People are complicated and people are flawed. Nobody's perfect, and Dad's been very, very badly behaved, but he works harder every day now to find the goodness inside of him, much to Issa's irritation, but more of that another day.

I expected you to be happier when I told you that you were going to be able to stay, but of course I was only returning something I had stolen. I shouldn't have expected you to be grateful. You were sweet and funny and teased me though, and touched me. I can still feel the touch of your fingers on my leg, the buzz that ran up my body, the heat that engulfed me.

You did come to the gig that night. Showing me your commitment to promise, your loyalty, a reliability that told me I could trust you. You would never be one to run to the rags. You stood by my side, reassuring, encouraging, sharing my moments of success with me. You became, in that moment, my muse. When you took my hand and squeezed it with your own, I knew I could never let go.

Wow, I've just read over what I have written tonight and what I suspected is true; I am completely smitten by you. I am nervous of you knowing all of this, the innermost workings of my heart, but when you wake up, I will tell you. I will show you.

Your Ollie x

Hope House

Palmer Springs

Bestwood

West Sussex

PO42 1DP

16th August 2008

Dear Stella,

I hoped you'd wake up today. I kissed you gently on your lips and whispered in your ear that I loved you. I wonder if you heard? I think you did and it makes me sad because the first time I said that to you I wanted to see your reaction in your eyes, I wanted to hear your response. Would you smile, laugh, brush me away or reply in an affirmation? Would you get up and run, tell me you just wanted to be friends, or invite me to kiss you, to show you what I felt, show me that you felt the same? I wanted reciprocation.

I couldn't wait any longer, though. And, as I said, I hoped you would wake. I hoped I would wake you.

So, it's nearly a week now since you went off into your altered state. I've done a lot of reading. You have one to three weeks to go until Dr Shah will start telling me you are in a Persistent Vegetative State. Much as Herbert loves the green stuff (rocket today – he is a gourmet), I'm not such a big fan of vegetables. The chances of you waking any time soon drop dramatically should you reach that particular state of being.

I want you out, Stella, I want you here with me. I can't work out if you're in a prison or if you're free, but really I don't care. I want you here with me.

I've known other girls, Stella, as I'm sure you know. I've never been as prolific as Sid, though. We like different things, I guess. He'll fuck anything that moves. Whereas, I have always wanted a little bit of interest, a connection, I don't know; something a bit more than 'her tits look great in that top and I can get my end away tonight and maybe with that one too', which is pretty much how Sid's brain operates on its low level.

So I've known a fair few girls, Stella, but none of them, not one has brought me here. Where is here?

Well, I've felt the urgent need to fuck them, sometimes within that minute, sometimes I'd like to wait for a few days. I have had them fill up my mind. But so soon I've been distracted, not by another girl, like Sid, who flits like a hummingbird from flower to flower. Usually my music reclaims me and I find there's nothing left after my lust is satiated. I don't get attached. I like them, don't get me wrong, and I respect the women I've been with for the people that they are. I just don't think about them all that much.

But you, Stella, you are something different. You are not easily had. And even if I were to have you, I think you would keep a maddening million miles between us. I would be ever reaching and you would be ever powerful. You would never make yourself known to me, never make yourself owned by me. And that is the most seriously sexy thing I have ever seen a woman do.

But I think I'm not alone in this. I think you want me too. You're just pacing yourself. You'll let me in and maybe it'll take a lifetime to get to know you, but it'll be a wonderful life.

However, you are currently in your coma and these may easily be my fantasies, who knows? You may laugh at me when you wake and run off with Sid. Or Dave!

I did see, in the tree, tonight, a small green parrot. Actually he was there last night, and if I'm not mistaken the night before too. He's a motif, a mascot, a friendly omen. The first night I thought nothing of it. The second I noticed him. And last night I thought he might be watching you, me, us. I'm not sure. He's like some kind of sentry. He doesn't sleep there. He leaves as I leave. I don't know where he goes, although I have seen some little parrots just like him that live in the big oak tree in the tortoises' enclosure.

I think maybe I will make him my little friend. A bit more company in our lonely days together. I'll need to bribe him with something, no doubt. What do parrots eat, I wonder? Fruit and nuts, I suppose. You would know. I will find something in Sarah's larder tomorrow. Let your thoughts help me find him a tasty snack!

Anyway, I have digressed. As well as about Persistent Vegetative States, I also learned something else today that might help me in my quest to save you, to bring you back from the apparently dead, to make me your hero. Conveniently, I am already mildly skilled in it, but it seems that meditation may be the key for me to reach you.

I told you a little about the year off I took before I went to university. Off I went to 'find myself', like some typical adolescent teenager. You must think me such a trustafarian… And I am, I suppose. I guess I think I'm different because my Dad's not a stuffy old banker or something and because I'm not going to be a stuffy old lawyer or something. And I suppose I think I'm making something of myself because I've told him I don't want his money, but I think we both know I've only got this far because I've plundered his resources. Sure, I've worked hard at what I've done and there's an argument to say that I have some talent, but there are not many people who are lucky enough to have the chance to focus themselves completely on the one thing that they love doing. Most people have to earn a living, pay the rent, the bills, feed themselves. Ha-ha, who am I kidding, you know all of this. Okay, you didn't have to pay rent and I'm trying to rectify that. But I've never paid rent in my life. I probably won't even have to ever pay a mortgage. Either I'll be given a house or I'll be given a contract on the strength of my name and unless I piss all the money up a wall I'll never have to worry that I can't afford the heating. I've never wondered where my next meal's coming from, only tussled with what it was that most in the world at that moment I most craved to consume, that wouldn't, of course, bother my perfect waistline.

When I was travelling, when I was eighteen, only a little bit younger than you are now, I was oblivious to this. I went to India and all I could see was spliffs on the beach. Thailand and all I wanted to know about was when the next half moon was and who had the magic mushrooms. I didn't see the beggars and I didn't see the slums. I was incredulous at how cheap everything was and yet I still haggled. Felt obligated to, even though I had riches they couldn't even dream about.

Twenty pence for a chapatti? I stuffed my face. I laughed at the cows wandering in and out of the shops in Goa, thought it was ridiculous. Had no concept of sacred.

But then I went to Tibet.

Honey, I am going to be your necromancer. Shamanism is the way to go on this one. I have to release my mind from my body and find your mind, wherever it is, or get inside your body and eke it out if that's the way it needs to happen. Modern medicine's been left far behind on this one. Although they are seeing the light. I'm going to be your healer. Honey, I'm going to rescue you.

The hospital is generous with me and lets me stay most of every day. So every minute when I am not with you I will be practising altering my own state in order to join you in yours. I may have to get some sleep every now and again, but hey, I don't think you will mind that, even though you're doing enough of it for both of us. God, I hope that's not sick. No, I think you'd probably find it quite funny. You can be quite twisted, too.

I've been wondering and wondering where you are. If you are in some kind of purgatory or if you're just floating about somewhere. It's a bit tricky when you have no faith in any particular religion, like me. And like you. Actually, at least I have some sort of belief system. A vague attachment to this kind of spirituality that Dave's gone mental for. I am probably to blame for that. I'm sorry. There I go again. Must stop apologising. Actually I think that was the first time this whole letter. When I came back from Tibet and he saw how sorted I was, how good I looked - I'd been on a major de-tox - when he heard me talk about the inner mind and stuff like that, it was like he transferred his lifetime's addictions to the pursuit of his own soul. He became addicted to the search of his perfect self. It was the birth of Hope Springs – and perhaps the death of Bestwood.

Anyway, you; the fury you have for corporate irresponsibility and competitive child rearing I learned you also have for religion. The source of all evil, you said. I thought that was a bit harsh to be honest but I got what you said about controlling the masses, management of the drones. But you wouldn't listen to my counter argument about psychopathic behaviour and the necessity of a few simple rules. You said there was only one rule: 'Do unto others as you would have done unto yourself.' Sweet, I thought, but possibly naïve. And anyway, it failed to answer the big question at the heart of all religions. The number forty-two. The meaning of it all. Is there a God? Are there Gods? Why are we here? Where did all of this come from?

Fresh back from the Galapagos, of course, you were brimming with the joys of Darwinism; full of primordial soup and banking on the survival of the fittest. And I get all of that, too. But you concur that life is a miracle. The most essential part of you is dedicated to the exploration, no, conservation of the wonders that you see: the skin of a cuttlefish rippling colours to match itself to its environment, the happy partnership between a clownfish and an anemone, the animal that is coral, making hard castles and fans in a myriad of shapes and colours... flight, speed, the algae on a sloth's fur, the vicious claws and poison in an ecosystem. You see very little, if any wonder, in humans. Ironic, given that you are such a wonderful human being yourself. But you do see so many things that amaze you that you do admit there is a God of some sorts. You claim to be a pantheist. Not an atheist or even an agnostic for you. That would be too simple. So as you explained it to me; God is all, it's universal, it's in everything, nature is God. Just like you to be so abstract.

So really what I am asking myself is, if this is what you think, how you believe, where are you now?

I figure that all religions and belief systems demand faith and if that's what it rests on, if that is the crux of it, in order to find you I must find and follow your faith.

I started with the basics: are you in heaven or are you in hell? I got thinking about hell a lot. I couldn't imagine you there really, but if, for lack of the correct faith, you are, then the accepted wisdom suggests you are either underground or in some sort of fire. This struck me as hugely unoriginal, since what do we do with the bodies of our human dead? We either bury or burn them. So those without faith succumb to eternal earth or forever fire.

Or they waft about aimlessly worrying the living, lost. I do hope if you were just wafting about that you would have found some purpose and come and shown me yourself by now.

Those with faith, whose minds or souls truly believe, obtain the afterlife they seek, choose, believe in. Potential positive afterlives seem to include some kind of ever after in Elysian fields with those that you have loved, or reincarnation as something appropriate given your behaviour in your previous life. Since you are not an atheist, you must believe in an afterlife. I interpret your altered state, as Dr Shah insists on calling it, refusing to leave his medical terms behind, as an in-between state. You are not fully alive and yet you are not dead. You are somewhere between. Purgatory seems wrong. You are stood on a bridge and although he tells me to have faith that you will turn and walk back to me, back to life, I am concerned that your very refusal to do so, so far, indicates your indecision. And therefore, the possibility that you may choose your afterlife.

I, fundamentally, my dear Stella, do not believe that there is only the body.

What afterlife, Stella, would you choose? Where is your faith? Where will I find you? Where is the pantheist in a coma?

And so, my sweet, that is the extent of my work on you today. However, I have much to update you on our home life. As I said, this is a diary for you, for when you wake, so you know what time has passed. I have seen the documentaries on the guy in a coma for thirty years who wakes and still thinks he's seventeen. I so hope you won't be in a coma for that long. That I can get you out before then. If you are, though, I will wait for you, I promise. I will always be there trying.

So, Herbert seems well. He's right by me now. I watch the sun set with him every night as I write these. I read them out to him when I'm done. You're right, it really is like he listens. It's difficult to tell, though, whether he approves or not. He doesn't give much away, your tortoise. But I enjoy tickling him under his chin. His eyes are so intense, like yours, like there are billions of universes inside them.

The conversations with your Dad aren't going so well. He's not pretending he likes me. I'm lucky to get a word out of him. I don't know what to tell you, Stella, so I'm going to be honest. Hopefully you can fix this or help me when you get out of there.

I know you always laughed about his drinking, or seemed to, write it off as a sailor's right. But this is twenty-four seven, babe. He's getting up to go to the pub and leaving when it closes. I had a word with the landlord, but he threatened to bar me. Told me I was out of order for interfering. Shouted at me whilst manhandling me that it was entirely my fault he was there. I'm sorry. Again, again I am apologising. Everything here seems to be my fault.

I will keep on trying though, honey. Tomorrow I will try and get him out of bed before the pub opens its doors and bundle him into the split-screen and get him to you. I am sure you need him and he's an idiot if he can't see how he needs you too. I will fix this. Even if I have to chain him to the radiator.

Onto the ongoing saga at home - Issa and Sid. They have not been caught yet. Well, by nobody but me. Should I tell someone? How could I? How could I not? Who would I tell? How I wish you were here. You would tell me what to do, the right thing to do. You with your wise head on your young shoulders. I think Sarah has figured out something is up. She keeps looking at me suspiciously and I find her lurking in places like she's listening. Perhaps I should talk to her about it. The thing is though, given her history with Sid, and knowing she has fallen for him too – what is it with women that they can't sleep with a guy without falling in love with them? - I continue to worry that she might freak out. Blow the lid on the whole thing. Anyway, I can hear Issa's screeching from here. I must be off, my darling, see what the problem is. More tomorrow.

Your Ollie x

Hope House

Palmer Springs

Bestwood

West Sussex

PO42 1DP

17th August 2008

Wonderful Stella,

Light of my life, how I wish you had been awake to witness today's events!

Breakthroughs, breakthroughs everywhere. Today your father went to court. And with him, mine. The hearing was the first of the day.

To my utter amazement, your Dad knocked on our door this morning and asked me to give him a lift. After what happened last night at the pub, you can imagine my surprise. He even apologised for that (stupendous!) and explained that his friends had been looking after him, but that he realised I was trying to help and had heard that I had been with you every day, all day. Apparently he bowled up to the hospital, finally, after closing, to see you so I guess some of what I was trying to say to him must have got through. Fuck knows how he got in. He was wankered when I saw him. I am slightly concerned about the lack of security, although I guess he is your Dad. And they are always quite strict with me on visiting hours.

Anyway, it seems one of the nurses, the Irish one, I think, Moira with the enormous pillow of a bosom, each of her breasts the size of your head I would estimate, relented despite his beery breath. My own head's spent quite some time buried in them recently. Purely innocently, I hasten to add. You know I'm more of a leg man! But I suppose I've needed a bit of a mother figure recently. I've shed a hundred times more tears in the last week or so than I've cried in my entire life before. I wonder where they're still coming from. My Mum was the best when we were growing up, but now she's on the other side of the world in Oz, living the life she put on hold for Sid and me, and Dave. I know she really resents his behaviour during the time they were together. And my current stepmother… well, the less said about that the better, methinks.

Anyway, I guess Moira sat your Dad down with one of her cups of camomile tea (his first time on the herbal teas, I would think – I can imagine his reaction!) and told him all about us. She must have put in a very good word for me as he said he really appreciated my looking after you and that he had found it really difficult seeing you the way you are, and with the assault charges hanging over his head too, he was finding it difficult to cope. He thanked me for sorting out your private room and cover. I sighed a bit of a sigh of relief at that, as I was worried he'd think I was showing off, muscling in or trying to show him up or something. But he just seemed very appreciative of the gesture. I said it was the least I could do and I think he tried to tell me it was not my fault, but he could not quite bring himself to say it. I'm sure that deep down he blames me for what has happened, and I do too. I tried to hold it together in front of him because, well, I don't think it's a good idea to show signs of weakness to your Dad. He takes no prisoners. Inside I just repeated my mantra so myself; 'I'm saving Stella, I'm saving Stella…'

Then he told me that when he arrived home, he had found a letter on his doormat from my father to him. In it, my father apologised sincerely for his part in the incident, regretful of the comments he had made and expressing his deep sadness for your accident and offering any help he could. Dave had not mentioned any of this to me, in fact we have barely spoken since he was so totally out of order the morning of the day it was all so right and so wrong, when I told him I was ashamed of him. It's a big house and it's easy to keep your head down. Besides, I think he has other things, namely the current wife, on his mind. Really, since your accident, I have only spoken to you and to Herbert. At home I have locked myself in my room and worked on some new material and slept. All waking hours I work my way back to you.

In court, we were to discover that being first on has its advantages. First off, there were no delays. Second, the court was fresh and keen to get on with it. When the first witness, my father, as today I am proud to call him, was called to give evidence, his first words were an admittance of fault. Despite not a word passing between them since the incident, a fault of which both of them bear guilt, I should add, he claimed, perjuriously, that all was resolved between them. I guess he was thinking of the letter he had posted the night before. So all was resolved for him, even if his apology had not been accepted as far as he knew. He stated that he had no desire to pursue the charges and regretted reporting the incident to the authorities in the first place, since he now considered it a minor and private incident. He explained briefly the circumstances, which he described as extenuating, and his opinion that the incident should have been dealt with without the input of the official forces and that he was entirely to blame for the situation turning out otherwise. He showed that the wound left by the impact of your father's head was almost entirely healed and that there was no scarring to speak of. No damage done, he said.

Then he started to speak about you. He said, 'Additionally, given that my neighbour, Bob, finds his daughter, Stella, fighting for her life following an accident that happened at our mutual home, it is my greatest wish that this situation is resolved as quickly as possible, with no further stress to Bob.' He looked over at Bob at this point. Bob looked cross and my father looked confused for a moment. But I think your father was only angry because he didn't want to draw attention to you and your situation like that, as it was bound to wound him deeply, and as I said earlier, I think your father has issues with showing weakness to other humans.

'I am not sure,' said the Judge, adjusting her wig, 'as the key witness, the person who initially brought the charges, that you are entitled to input into the process in that way. But, as luck would have it, I agree with your summation. There is no case to answer. Case dismissed.' It seemed so smooth I thought perhaps she had already been extensively briefed.

Everything was over. Dave apologised profusely for wasting everyone's time and we were out on the front steps and back to Bestwood in an instant.

The three of us were stood in the drive. Your father had been very quiet during the journey back from court. Dave had taken the driver and limo so travelled back separately, too. I wasn't sure what to say to your Dad. He looked so crumpled and defeated, despite the fact that the incident was behind him and he no longer had to worry. It was such a difficult situation, as I guess there was part of me that felt a sense of victory for him, and yet it was complicated by the knowledge that my flesh and blood had created the whole scenario, bowling into his life and rudely dismissing it. And even though my father hadn't lost the case, exactly, he had graciously bowed out, done an about turn, done the right thing, so it was more of a win-win.

I couldn't believe it was all over so fast. Not just today, I mean, but the whole thing. One of the policewomen at the court said that they had pulled some strings to have the hearing done so fast as they were worried about how your Dad was coping what with you and the accident and everything. I think she was also the one that had briefed the judge. I don't think any of them would have heard the case at all if they could have avoided it - she said as much. Your father is very well loved and respected, Stella. I think deep inside of him there is a heart of gold and we, my father and I, I mean, I am sure you already know that it's there, but we need time to find it. In fact, later today I had my first glimpse.

I think he seemed so unhappy because ultimately, although the court case was a pain and had potentially severe repercussions if Dave had followed it through like he had intended when he belonged to the red mists of rage, once it was out of the way, it was painfully obvious that it just did not matter. All that mattered to any of us anymore was you.

I almost suggested that we drop in and see you again, but I thought perhaps he needed to do this in his own time, at his own speed. I suspect he's a bit obstinate like you and that when told to do something is unlikely to it. Stubbornness; you manage to make it endearing. I wonder if it will frustrate me after thirty years or more?

So we were stood there at Bestwood, archenemies become - what? I was wondering what the etiquette for this social encounter would be when your father astonished me by inviting mine to a game of cricket. And not just any old game of cricket.

'We'll have to sail to it,' he said. 'And we'll have to be quick. The tide's out in just a couple of hours.'

'Wow, totally radical! Let's go, dude!' said Dave. 'Er… should I get out of this suit first?'

'Probably,' replied Bob, looking him up and down. My Dad looked like a businessman today. It was weird. He was sombre in a grey suit, pale blue shirt and tie. I had never seen him wear a tie before. He was a picture of respectability and responsibility today, unlike his usual garish garb. I thought he had procured the outfit especially. I felt a rush of love for my good Dad, the person he so strived to be.

We all rushed off and changed into something more appropriate for a sail and a game of cricket, and met back at the van less than five minutes later, Bob directing us down to the marina. I wasn't sure that the invitation was extended to me, but since I appeared to be the driver, I muscled in.

It felt like a boys' day out and all the animosity and tension had evaporated. For a brief moment, my sweet, even you slipped from my mind as I revelled in this newfound serenity. Strangely, the morning's events were not mentioned, but Dave and your Dad chatted quite easily about the menagerie. Bob told him about how he came to be there and told him the history of each of the animals. Dave said nothing of his plans, sensitively I thought, and when we arrived at the yacht the conversation turned easily to the mechanics of sailing.

Both my father and I are no strangers to yachting, but oddly neither of us have actually ever sailed one before. We've always hired them with crew, never paid any attention to the rigging or the instruments. Bob gave us a crash course in fenders, the strength and direction of the tides, motored us out into the estuary and instructed us to raise the main.

He explained to us how the sails were not bags but aerofoils and that the wind was not too strong today, so we would use a genoa as the headsail. He told us about reefing and storm jibs and told us about the trips he had done following the path of Darwin and the Beagle around South America, and the elements he had battled with and won. That bit brought you right back to the forefront of my mind, you're always in there, honey but for a moment I wanted to jump overboard and swim back to you, run and be back by your side. I thought of you alone, but remembered Hannah had said she would visit you today, and besides, I thought, I was being useful to you here, bringing our families together, securing your future. As much as I wanted to, I could not be in two places at once. I consoled myself by having you always in my thoughts, even when your hand was not in mine.

With both sails raised, your father let me take the wheel and showed me how to keep the boat close to the wind, staring up the mast at the arrow and the tabs. I found watching the speedometer exhilarating and whooped when I had her going over six knots! It was pretty awesome but I reckon I could run faster! There was something about powering her purely with the wind though that seemed so very natural and right. I understood your father's deep irritation with the powerboats that noisily passed, posing and bumping us with their dirty wash.

Your Dad told me you were a very good sailor, neat with knots and never nauseous. He said you hadn't had all that much time for it recently, that you'd become a bit too much of a landlubber for his liking. I suggested that I would insist you let me do more sailing when you were better. He smiled. He liked that idea. I think your Dad may be lonely, Stella. He needs you back, too.

We tacked a few times, zigzagging our way up the wind, and then your Dad gave me a pair of binoculars and pointed in the direction of Cowes. A sandbank had opened up before us and a cluster of boats was anchored around it. I could see little figures running about on the sand and pools reflecting the sun that broke through little fluffy clouds that sped across above us, their shadows darkening the water as they went.

Dave clambered across the boat, tripping on the main sheet and landing pretty much on top of me, but since he was aiming for one of his big hugs it didn't matter. He's always liked his hugs, my Dad. When he gives me one it's a bit like flicking through a photo album of the moments of our lives together.

I've never seen him so sorry, so penitent. He confessed his frustrations that his vision wasn't working out at all how intended. He even said he thinks he may have made a mistake with his marriage, with Issa. He seems to have reached a realisation that he cannot make her happy, that perhaps she will never be happy, her state of discontent is permanent. And the natural consequence of this is that she will never make him happy. He sounded like he was considering how to find a route out, and I was sorely tempted to offer him a signpost, but despite his obviously being in the wrong, I couldn't shop my brother. When, if, Dave finds out about what may or may not be going on with his son and his wife, and if he knows or even suspects I know, I believe he will forgive me. It's not my battle to fight. It's not my place to interfere.

I have been studiously avoiding Sid too. There has been lots of media attention since our big night. Lots of radio-play of what was to be our debut single, fantastic reviews in the NME and the like. Rufus is clamouring for us to finalise the material, but I have lost heart in that album. I don't want Sid's involvement. I want to go it completely alone, and the material I am working on now is too different, so raw and real in comparison that I don't want to start where we were. I want to start where I am and where I will be, hopefully with you.

Sid cannot understand this. All he can see of course is the money and the fame being offered to him and to us, but as we sailed towards Bramble Bank, my father's hair whipping around my head, his arms around my shoulders, it was you that was in my mind and the music I am creating for you now that the wind was playing in my ears.

169

As we got closer, I could hear the shouts of the players and the sound of the leather ball on the willow. It took me straight back to school, watching Sid captaining the team to yet another victory. And the absence of Dave. Bob asked him if he was a cricket fan. Not much of a sportsman, me, Dave told him. I kept quiet. Me neither, I thought, wondering how much our families were going to have in common, whether we could get along or whether this would just be the moment that we had.

But then, I thought, there was you. It was you that would bring us all together. Our shared love for you was the unbreakable bond. You and I share a lot, I think. The things that make us laugh, our passion for the unknown, our desire to be the best we can, our love of looking after each other and the things we care about.

We anchored and the noisy clattering of the chain letting itself out was all that I could hear for a few minutes, but when it stopped there was laughter and the chinking of glasses. I don't think I had heard laughter since that evening, since our drive back from Brixton, just the two of us, just the three of us, sorry, Herbert in the back of the van. I wonder what he sounds like when he laughs. I am sure he does.

For an hour, all our troubles seemed so far away. The sun shone and we watched Bob as he fast bowled on the sand, the ball's trajectory unpredictable as this was no carefully tended pitch. Some people had set up tables and chairs and had even brought red chequered tablecloths and cream crockery. They were so friendly, they invited us to join them and made no fuss about Dad, treated him as if he were a mere mortal, which I think he liked. He would have hated it in the past, thrived on the sycophantic hangers on, buzzed on the recognition, stamped his feet and bellowed, 'Do you know who I am?' when he wasn't getting the attention he felt he deserved. I don't think he wants to be himself anymore. He wants to be someone new, to rid himself of his old persona and be free to reinvent himself. He's discovered humility, the power of giving and the even peace in gratitude. He's like one of your butterflies, one of those chrysalises you have on the windowsill of your bedroom. He's reforming himself to emerge as something more beautiful, to stretch his wings.

I gnawed on a chicken drumstick, and ate quarters of pork pie dipped in mustard. Just for a little while I abandoned my yogic diet of no meat, no spice, nothing to disturb the purity of my soul. My meditations have been progressing well in the past few days, but I felt this was a celebration, so I hung up abstention for a moment. It was a celebration not so much of the success in court, but that the sense of deep change was a sign this morning, that all would be well, healing was on its way. It felt like it was telling us that if we could, if our families could help and support each other, that we could win through. It was a celebration of hope, my hope, all our hope that all would be well. We would weather the storm, and beyond the eye of it, the sun would shine down on us, warming our hearts, warming our souls.

Suffused with this feeling, I wended my way up to you tonight. I had missed you so much throughout the day, the coolness of your hand, your long eyelashes laying against your cheek. We just had a couple of hours together as the trip back from the Bramble Bank took a little while, the wind behind us and a bit squally, Dave a bit tipsy distracting Bob, we accidentally jibed and the boom leathered across the stern. I am not sure how it missed Dave's head; I think he lost his footing at a happy moment and ended up with a sore arse and not a cracked skull. Thank fuck. Two of you with head injuries would be too much. I think the coast guard would have been pretty pissed and it would have been interesting to explain it the same day as the assault charges were dropped!

When I came to see you tonight, Hannah was on her way out. She seemed distracted. I invited her up to the house but she said she was very busy but did not tell me with what. I wondered if she was avoiding Sid. A recommended course of action, I thought. She tried to ask me a few questions, but as I have told you, I've not been very good at talking lately, unless it's to you. You must be under the impression that I am a bit of a chatterbox, you can barely get a word in edgeways after all, haha, but really, to everyone else right now I must appear a mute.

I asked you what was wrong with her, but of course you couldn't tell me. I am sure she would have told you, though. And I'm sure that everything you said to her silently would have helped and been great advice. You'll wake up soon and you can tell me then and, if there's anything that needs fixing, we'll fix it. Nothing's irrevocable.

Despite my meat eating and excitement, or maybe because of it and the fresh air, my meditations tonight with you felt easy. In the half-light of dusk I thought I could feel you there, almost felt like I could hear you.

Moira caught me dropped off in the chair though and sent me home. I'll be there all day tomorrow. We'll see if by the end of it I haven't reached out and touched you.

Herbert's here now. I found some asparagus in the fridge. I'm not sure you'd approve, it's hardly local. I think it's been shipped in from Kenya or somewhere else equally unnecessary. But he seems to like it. And I'm thinking it's a treat for him. Hope for him, too, as I am sure he wants you back as dearly as your Dad and I do too.

Night night, my sweet, and sweet dreams to you.

Until tomorrow –

Your Ollie x

Hope House

Palmer Springs

Bestwood

West Sussex

PO42 1DP

18th August 2008

My Darling Stella,

At dusk tonight, the scent of the pink striped lilies I brought today (I bring you fresh flowers every morning - I am sure that you have noticed!) and the jasmine (your favourite smell, you told me once) candle that burned lighter in the increasingly enveloping dark overruled the smells of antiseptic and shit that are the essence of the hospital. This helped me not be there.

As I observed the candle's flame, slowing my heart, washing my brain, I saw that the wick had split in two at the top and that it resembled a newly sprouting plant, just emerged from its seed. Its first two baby leaves were reaching for the sun, hungry for the light that would fuel it to make more of itself.

The flame was a miniature representation of the sun itself and flickered into an orb and then I was inside it. It wasn't hot because I was no longer a body. It wasn't blinding because I no longer had eyes. It was pure light. I was pure light. I was part of it and all of it at the same time. There was music within it. White music, like the light. There were no other colours in this light, no spectrum and the music was a single note, E, but was also a melody. There was no singing and there were no instruments and I couldn't tell what direction the music was coming from, although it might have been me, although this was difficult for me to understand since I had no form, other than being part of the light. And then I stopped thinking about this as I realised I knew that I was in your state and that I was on my way to find you.

And so I started to look.

I became the wind. I buffeted out through the open window into the cooling air. I became a gale, gathering more of me behind me and for an instant scared some sheep in a field. I became a breeze and kissed the cheek of a baby asleep in a basket in a garden and I left her a raindrop as a gift. I rose up and up until I was wind at the top of our atmosphere at the edge of space and I looked down and I orbited but you weren't there. You weren't wind.

I dropped out of the wind and I was damp. I don't mean that I felt damp. I mean that I was damp, I was water. There was no light now, I was water, moisture in the ground. I had a sense of being sucked up and I was in a tower, a pale tower, made of spongy bricks, see-through, full of water, light travelling down from above. Up I went, pulled by the current, a drag behind me, being knocked by salts.

Then it was green and I became green, radiating it, being it. I was the only colour that I could see, the only colour I could remember. I could taste it and it was lightly acidic; the flavour of a young woman warmed in the sunshine.

And then I was at the tip of a leaf reaching out into a jungle and all around me I could see more of me, friends, family, as far as I could see, creeping, rushing forwards, upwards, outwards. I was like spring.

I saw a sort of face in front of me, green like me, smooth and round with yellow jaws that opened wide and huge and then, just as I desired it, I was chopped up and swallowed. I was inside. It was long and springy and green inside too and again I felt sucked into it. I couldn't see you in there, Stella, but I knew that I was on my way to you and I became part of this creature, I became a red spike on its rear end and I could feel it, me, becoming sleepy. I could feel it was preparing to rest and harden and that it was going to rebuild itself inside its shell and that's what it, I, did. It took a while but was done in a moment and we, I, was cramped up in there until we cracked the shell and unpeeled ourself, myself, from within and stood shivering, trembling in the light and the breeze. I, we, the being that I was, stretched new legs out over the carcass of our sleep and admired them and they were long and black and impossibly, thinly snappable. And on my back there was paper, paper with sensation. Stretching out and feeling light, heat, wind. Uncrumpling. Iridescent paper. Paper that took off and fluttered and caught the light that then turned it turquoise.

I thought I might find you then. I thought, yes, this is where Stella would go. This is what Stella would be. A butterfly, light and bright and beautiful, and just as the warmth of the sensation of being close to you flooded through me, I was snatched up in the beak of a bird and I was flying now, well, I was being flown, and then I was stuffed into the wide pink mouth of a chick, cheeping for me, its meal.

For a moment I faltered, so convinced I had been that you would have been a butterfly, free, flitting about, but I grabbed a tight hold on my faith, relaxed back into this process. I felt the feeling I knew I would: the transformation, the sucking into the being of this new form. I became a feather, a soft downy one on the chest of the chick. Creamy coloured and fluffy, cuddled up with more of me, trapping air around us, under us, keeping the pink skin and the bluey veins warm, keeping the pulsing life alive.

The wind rushed through us feathers as the chick plummeted down from the nest, a scratch of bark on our way, a gentle rubbery bounce as we hit the forest floor, covered in leaves in various stages of decay, some freshly, fragrantly fallen, some cloudy with mould.

Some of us fell away with the impact and floated away with the breeze or were stuck to the leaf litter that broke the fall. I looked and I felt but still I couldn't find you. I started to sing for you, I went to the bird's throat and I started to call for you.

I swelled until I was the whole bird and I shut my eyes against the light dark of the jungle and I breathed air into my lungs and I twittered and I trilled and I sang for you. My birdsong started with the same note, a high flute repeated seven times and then I ran up my range. I stood with my wings held slightly out to my sides and drew in more breath. Then I started to sing proper, high, low, different numbers of notes, evenly spaced, sometimes double.

As I stopped to take another breath I opened my eyes and realised that this breath would be my last in this form. Crouched in pouncing pose directly ahead of me was a spotted cat. Its ears were small and flattened against its head. It was perfectly still. Its huge, pale emerald eyes focussed right on me, every muscle in its body tensed just as every one of mine relaxed.

It pounced. My neck was broken in the flash of its next movement and then, as I heard the distress call of the mother bird that had taken me, the butterfly and fed me to me the baby bird, who in turn was to feed this cat, this cat ripped me to pieces and my blood poured, my guts spilled and I heard the crunch of my delicate, lovely bones.

Devoured again, I swelled, and now I filled up this cat. Its spotted pelt slunk about me. Being me, my fur was a blanket. I felt strong and warm and sated by my breakfast, so I climbed up a tree and slung myself lazily along a branch and cleaned a paw, admiring the even pattern of the spots up my leg. I put my head down and snoozed, the sunlight dappling my coat. I wondered again where you were, where this journey would take me next, how deeply mired you were in your state, this state, how long it would take me to find you.

I heard a twig snap and as I jerked my head up to see, there was a bang and I was off the branch and on the floor and my heart had stopped beating but I stayed, filling up the cat.

A pair of boots, green canvas, black rubber soles, came into view. They had camouflage trousers tucked into them. The man was wearing a jacket and a gun slung over his back. He had a knife in his hand. He picked up my body and skinned it. I had to choose. Would I go with the skin or would I stay with the flesh and the bones?

I stayed with the flesh and the bones.

A fly landed on me and then another and they swarmed. Dead, I could not flick them away. Dead, I did not want to. Their young, their maggots, burrowed through me. I had to choose. Would I stay with the flesh or would I stay with the bones?

I chose the bones.

Leaves fell, over and over and over. I was buried. Eons passed. Leaves became mud. Mud became stone. Water lay on top. Lakes. I stayed. I was carbon. Layers and layers lay above me. Pressure. I stayed. Instead of looking, I was waiting. Waiting for you to come to me. It felt like the right thing to do. I had faith.

The weight was great above me, heavy, pushing me down, pushing me into myself, squashing me.

There were tremors. There were movements above me. There was building, digging, drilling. There was the trundle of trucks full of rock. A chink of sunlight, I was in a hand. I was being brushed. I was being packed away. I was coming closer to you, Stella. I was waiting. I was being carved, I was being cut. I sparkled.

I was being set. I was inside a gold band. I was slid on a finger, the murmur of vows passed by. I felt a pulse pumping into me. I felt it stop. I was slid off the pulseless finger and covered in a salty tear. I was slid onto another pulsing finger and now I was here. And then it was now.

It was dark. Vanity made me want the light so I could sparkle again. You were there. There were two of us inside the ring. The ring was a band of gold. Your father had acquired it in the Middle East. There were two diamonds inside. I was one and you were the other. Finally, I had found you. Not so far at all from your human form, you had hidden inside your mother's ring. I began to sing to you.

I felt you move towards me until the two of us were spinning around the ring, like electrons jumping from molecule to molecule, racing around its circle. I felt us fuse together and I jumped us into your pulse.

We were swept into your bloodstream and pumped through the thick red wetness of your blood vessels, up through your hand, your arm, the light pouring in at your wrist, at the inside of your elbow where we nearly reached the surface. Up around your shoulder and down inside your chest into your heart.

I stopped us there and we filled it up and it beat harder.

'Stella?' I thought at you.

'Yes,' you thought back at me and then, 'Blink.'

I have no eyes I thought but I did it anyway and then we were in a desert on a mountain, surrounded by the oceans. Light rushed at you, your cheekbones glowed and your eyes burned amber. Wind blew silver silk around you, ribbons of it flashing about, the golden skin of your body glinting at me. I reached out a hand.

'I like it here,' you said.

'Come home with me,' I asked.

'Why?' you responded. The sky turned pink above us and around us and then lilac.

'Because I love you.' You just looked at me. 'Because I need you,' I pleaded.

'But here I am free.'

'But here you are not with me. Don't you love me?'

'I don't know,' you said. 'I am with you now.'

'But I can't stay here, we can't be together here, forever?'

'Didn't you see?' you said. 'We are here. We are here forever. We are forever. Everything is forever.'

'Come home with me.' I tried again.

'Will I be free?' you asked.

'Of course,' I said, 'but I will love you.'

'What is love?' you asked. 'An illusion?'

'Is this an illusion?'

'No, this is real.'

'Then love must be real, too, it's love that brought me here. Love that helped me find you.'

'Love is ownership. Love is a trap. Love is selfish.'

'It doesn't have to be that way. Come home with me.'

'Maybe.'

'Which way is it?' You pointed over my shoulder and I turned and saw a canyon open up before me. A thin gold bridge, not much wider than my foot, ran across it. It looked a mile long. The canyon looked ten miles deep. At its bottom was the ocean, wild and choppy. I could see the manes of the wild horses running through it.

I turned back to you and I held out a hand. 'Come with me?' You shook your head.

'I will choose. You must trust me to choose which freedom I want. You must not look until you are on the other side.' I stared at you, then turned my back to you and began my walk home.

Foot in front of foot, in front of foot, looking straight ahead, keeping my balance against the wind. The bridge was cold under my soles but mercifully dry. I walked and walked with the sound of silence around me, behind me. I did not look down.

Finally, I put a foot out and I could feel the warm sand underneath my toes but I couldn't hear you and so I turned to face you, hoping to catch you as you joined me on the other side.

You were there, I held out my hand. You shook your head and I understood I had broken my promise. You dived off the bridge and somersaulted in the air as you went down towards the water ten miles away. It took a lifetime in my mind but as you hit the water churning below, the air around me snapped, and the floor was cold on my cheek.

It was dark and there was an incessant beeping. A door slammed into a wall, harsh white light invaded my eyelids. I opened my eyes and saw feet attached to the footsteps I heard thundering into the room. Voices lots of voices, someone looking into my unseeing eyes. People swarming all over you. I was put in a chair. You were rolled away somewhere.

Later, someone came and said sorry. Gone. Massive brain haemorrhage. Not coming back. Time I went home. Alone.

I'm sorry, Stella, I am so, so very sorry.

All my love, always my love, Ollie. X

Stellamouche! Stellamouche! Will you do the fandango?!

Dear God, Stella, where have you gone?

Ollie told me about the letters he's been writing you and inspired me to write one of my own. Fanfare! Here it is!!! Possibly, like, my first letter EVER! Wowsers.

Now for the serious stuff. Hope you're ready! Why don't ya take a seat over here, my lovely… Take a load off… I'll make you a nice cup of tea. Scratch that, here's a voddie and coke, my love!

In all the years I've known you, I never once thought it would end like this - so soon. I truly thought we'd be little old ladies together, competing over who had the cutest, cleverest grandchildren. Maybe even great-grandchildren, if I got my act together. Maybe even more than that if we achieved our mutual stated goal of immortality haha. What happened to that, eh?

You lied to me. You told me we'd live in some kind of commune and race our wheelchairs around the grounds, beating the bald guys with the paunches and wobbly necks and high fiving like crazies. You said we could be rude to anyone whenever we felt like it and you promised me we could queue-jump. You even agreed to my plans for a green rinse. Lime, I had planned. You were sticking with lavender. BORING! But, we would have looked great together.

I know we had that chat when we were seventeen and both of us were still learning to drive when Will Kibble managed to roll his clapped out VW Polo into the field just outside Northchapel, taking himself and four of our classmates out in one fell swoop. The chat where, after the memorial service for Will, Suzie, Chris, May and Emily - er, I think! How very disrespectful to the departed I am. I cannot even remember their names - anyway, the chat where we talked about how we would want to be remembered. In the event of our department. As it were. I think I mean departure. Our popping of the clogs, kicking of the bucket, whatever phrase you prefer, my dear, is what I'm trying to get to.

But, Stella, I thought it was just a game. I thought it was just an idle fantasy. Something to amuse ourselves with. Something to help us work through the situation. Group hug, you know?

I had no idea that I would be lying on the grass here now, today, this minute, presently, where I've lain with you so many times before, grown up with you, indeed - on this very hill, staring out to the same old sea, without you and having to remember what you said that day, dredging up the finer details of what we are now going to have to treat as your last wishes. How damn inconsiderate of you!

I wonder if you would change anything that you said then if you had a chance now. It's been a few years. A lot's happened. Well, a lot happened in the last couple of weeks.

There was a poem. You kept murmuring it over and over for days on end. I've never been a super fan of poetry, as you well know. It's all a bit, yawn, too serious for me. I am much more of a devoted disciple of candy-coated pop, as you are aware. Much more relevant to modern life, as I've argued against you many a time. Plus, you can dance to it.

Honestly, Stella, there were points where I thought I might strangle you just to make you stop reciting. One night, I remember looking at a pillow, thinking... haha only joking, you know I would never ever hurt you.

But, Will and the others' car accident hit you really hard. Personally, I don't think I ever really got my head around it. Don't really understand it now. It seems like an article in the local paper or something. One minute here, one minute gone. Wilted flowers in rain-stained cellophane tied lopsided to a tree.

I'd been escaped from school for a year when it happened. I hadn't seen any of that lot since my glorious sigh of relief when I walked out of that place forever. They were all in sixth form with you though, so you did know them better, which might account for some of it, I suppose. I do remember they were the good guys, as in they weren't the bad guys. They were never cruel or mean to me, never called me fat or took the piss out of my hideous clothes, but to me they were just shadows in a past that I had wanted to close a door on. Really, by then I had well and truly slammed it shut. Five stone lighter and a platinum blonde with a talent for rolling fuck off Camberwell Carrots and scoring amphetamines at four in the morning. I doubt they would have recognised me if they had seen me, to be honest. Blondes do have more fun, it turns out. Especially thin ones.

But that poem. Jesus-mother-of-the-son-of-God, Stellamouche, I heard that bloody poem so many bloody times it's no wonder I got it in the end. It was by that old guy, the one who wrote about the Garden of Eden. Except he was quite young, you claim, when he wrote this.

I asked you, tactlessly, I see now, one night, perhaps having tired of your incessant intonations of his words, why Stella, I said, are you so upset when already you have lost so much when you lost your Mum? And then selfishly, why don't I feel this like you do?

Perhaps, you said, perhaps because it reminds me of losing my Mum. But more because it reminds me of me. We've lost our peers, you said, it could have been you or me, Hans. Could have been both of us. You sipped our hot chocolate as you sat on the wall.

At least we'd be together, I suppose, I said.

Small consolation, you said, and even managed this weird, tiny yelp of a laugh. I leaned my head on your shoulder. Why don't I feel it like you, Stella? I asked.

Because you've moved on already. You accept it and you've chosen to pursue your way and not spend any more of your time on it. I, you said, I'm still thinking about it. Still trying to learn from it, figure out what it means.

What if it means nothing? I asked you.

I remember a bit of it now, actually, the poem I mean… it went something like…

'What could the muse that Orpheus bore,

The muse, for her enchanting son

Whom universal nature did lament,

When by the route that made the hideous roar,

His gory face down the stream was sent,

Down the swift hubris to the lesbian shore.'

I think maybe it was the lesbian bit that grabbed my attention. Not that I am a lesbian, as you well know, and I hasten to add in the spirit of political correctness that it would not, of course, be a problem if I were. I did snog Shelley Hunter last summer one time at band camp. Haha, no it was just down the George, one fateful rainy evening. I can't believe I haven't told you that before but I don't think it counts for anything anyway – we were bored, I was drunk. We'd taken some pills. She and I have never mentioned it since and it never went anywhere further. Don't know where you were. Studying I should think, my be-spectacled one.

Anyway, it seemed kind of wrong that sort of naughtiness going on hundreds of years ago. Like hearing your parents getting it on, on a Sunday morning. When I expounded my theory to you, you did a passable imitation of my Gran, saying, you young 'uns, you think you invented sex. How do you think you are here? And proceeded to read me another poem that you claimed was over four hundred years old and that contained the word 'dildo'. Shocked to my very core, I said, you filthy bitch! My, how we laughed. And laughed until our insides hurt.

Blimey, Stella, you've only gone and left me. Who's going to make me laugh until my insides hurt now? It's like losing my right arm. I am still calling you. I've turned into a bit of a stalker, listening to your voicemail over and over. You would be pleased, I think, that I had transferred my affections to you, thus saving the embarrassment of some poor, hapless lad.

Change, change, change, Stellamouche, it seems it's the only constant. What in the world am I supposed to do without you? I've lost my right arm. And my left. And both my legs. Cripes, Stellamouche, I am limbless without you, in limbo.

I am angry, I am sad, I am in a permanent state of disbelief. I'll wake up in a minute and your smiling, laughing face will be in mine and you'll poke me in my ribs and tickle me, just like you have all these years. Always there to lift my spirits, wipe away the tears, talk some sort of semi-sense into me.

But this is a very long dream. It's been going on for days and days and days. I've stumbled through each of them, not allowing myself to believe that

I would find myself here. I refuse to believe that I am here. It's only at night that I've had relief from this dream. Blank nights, they have been, blotted out, me being blotto. Totally caned on anything I can lay my hands on really. Not fussy. Just getting off my head in whatever way possible. Self-medicating, you would say. Just for now. Slippery slope, you say. Yeah, I concur, an image of your Dad springing into my mind... your erstwhile boyfriend on the other hand, that Ollie. Totally mystifying, he is. Off the stuff completely. And I mean everything. He's on a major de-tox. Has been since you banged your head. Funny, isn't it, how we all deal with things in different ways?

Shock, shock, shock. No awe. Just total and utter shock and a staggering disbelief. It's all just so very, very wrong. You're too young, too beautiful, too clever to have been taken away. I can't compute. Computer says no.

Ollie fares no better than I in this respect, even if he's off the Class A's, B's, C's, alcohol, caffeine, fags and dairy. Jesus, Stellamouche, the guy is like, totally, devastated. Seriously, he barely speaks. Every time he opens his mouth he cries again. He's wept an ocean or more. He's doing nothing but sit in his room, just like when you were still here, in body at least, all he did was sit in your room, staring at you, talking to you, singing to you. I hope you could hear him. He was adamant that you could. If you did, then you will know how hopelessly devoted to you he had become. Still is, actually. You deserve nothing less, of course. Makes me a bit sick, to be honest. With jealousy, you understand. I want that for me. And I know you'd tell me I deserve it too, but I never shared your faith in myself, was never as supremely self-confident as you... are. Cannot say 'were'. You are, you are, you are. You will always be.

I know that you'll tell me that this is the reason I find myself in the romantic scrapes that I do. Wise Stella. Wise beyond your years. Where do you get your wisdom from? You have to love yourself, honey, you'll say. What's to love? I'll ask. You'll sigh, give me a hug and tell me 'everything'.

Why can't they see what you see? I'll ask. Because you don't show them what you show me. And because they are not good enough for you, not good enough to see.

Deep despair. Bereft. Hopeless, I am without you, Stellamouche. Who will ever love me like you do? Who will ever love me like Ollie loves you? Why can't I love myself like you tell me to? Like you do.

Oh Stellamouche, it's been hell without you. You were right about Sid. Dear God, what a total shit he turned out to be. Yes, I know you said it from the start, so there's no 'turning out' for you. That little rendezvous has really been messing with my head. How I have needed you, how I still need you. Talk about pick someone up and drop them. I know you think I threw myself at him, but I think he more led me on. He's a crazy flirt, always texting me lewd, rude, crude and sexy things and then he turns up with another girl, or ignores me. I know you think he has no respect for me, but I don't think that guy respects anybody (am thinking that makes no sense in terms of reasoning really but agh whatever, I'm trying to work this out). I think you'll say he respects himself least of all. It doesn't stop me yearning for him, jumping every time my phone beeps, hoping he's reaching out to me. Disappointed when it's some old yokel I've known since '89.

I fucked a couple of other guys to try and make me feel better and it did for a little bit, a very teeny little bit. Proved that I was desirable and distracted me, I suppose. Poked Sid, unawares, in the eye. But none of those poor idiots (okay, four of them) inspire anything in me that could be described as more than insipid, so other than a few moments of forget, and a tinge of regret, I have nothing to show for my adventures.

I'm starting to feel a little cheap now, Stella, and I can see your disapproving look. For a while back there it was fun to become visible, more than visible. I transformed myself; geek to chic. The thing is, it wasn't that chic, really. Thin, with make up, ooh the glamour, and good clothes boosted my ratings with the opposite sex, but still didn't get me any closer to getting a boyfriend. A Relationship. With a Big R.

You manage to be geek and chic all at once. The geek will inherit the earth, you say. Nothing wrong with being smart, you'd rap me on the knuckles, when I ribbed you about being top of the class again. You managed to be cool too, though. Teenage boys couldn't rattle you and you helped me not be rattled by them either. Well, I should qualify that. You tried to help me not show them how much they rattled me.

Rich, gorgeous twenty-something son-of-Rock-God boys are an entirely different kettle of fish though, my darling. What the fuck is a kettle of fish? Anyway, they are all cocky now they've got some notches on their bedpost. They've learned to play games. The Game. And they prefer their little games to any kind of sincerity.

Laughing at their conquests, comparing notes, balancing scorecards.

My brothers were the worst. At least they have stopped ripping the piss out of me now. Even they admit I look good. 'Little sis is hot, now,' one of them said the other day. That's good but it's not enough though, Stella. Nothing's ever enough. I want to be loved. Why does everyone want to be loved? It's so wearing, tiring, downright bloody tedious, in fact.

It's like a division in society. The loved and the non-loved. With boyfriend or woefully without. Those who are currently mating and those who are the non-mating. The married and the unmarried. Those with children, those childfree. You can count on your children's love if your husband's runs out.

Boy, it gets complicated, Stella. Why are we programmed to target and take down someone we can want and we can trust to want us for the rest of our lives? It's mission impossible, Stella. I am already exhausted. Jeez, I may not even be like a quarter of the way through yet. This state of affairs stretched out yonder. What am I supposed to do for the next sixty odd years? I can't keep this up! I'm going to roll a fat one and think on it.

It's a little while later, my dear, the fat one is well and truly alight.

How could you leave me? I have so many questions and I need a super massive black hole hug.

Oh My God, I feel totally and utterly alone.

But then I think of Ollie, or your Dad. Oh Stella, how could you do this to your Dad? As if losing your Mum was not enough. He looks shell-shocked now. But I don't know how, if, he will survive this. He cannot love you more than I do, that's just ain't possible and I don't believe in the superior ties of flesh and blood. We are all flesh and blood. We are all one. Universal nature, right? All spawned from the same single-celled amoeba type wotsit a million, trillion years ago. So you told me. All linked. I've always loved you more deeply and simply than I love my own family, but maybe, I will concede, he loves you as much as I do. He can have an equal share.

If there's any way for you to come back, you should, Stellamouche. Without you, your father will surely die. He'll drink himself into an early grave or worse. And Ollie, he seems to be hanging by a thread, too. Oh, who am I kidding? You can't raise people from the dead - the big book lied. The resurrection of Stella. Some story that would be. And I am laying some kind of guilt trip on you, anyway. If you came back, it would have to be for yourself.

OMG, I said dead, back there.

Weirdly, this brings some sort of strength to me. I am not dead. There. I said it again. Dead, dead, dead. I spit in the face of deadliness. I am a brave girl. I am a live girl. If only you were alive too. Maybe it will be easier if I think of you as not being alive, rather than being dead, I mean.

Stellamouche, Stellamouche, where do you do the fandango? Oh my sweet best friend forabsolutelyfuckingever, I owe you so much, so many things, what can I give back to you now? I feel in debt to you in so many ways, and I can hear you now, telling me all the things I bring to you. Laughter, you say. You say no-one makes you laugh like I do. I never thought I was funny, just more than a little bit stupid. You say I make you feel safe, protected, secure. You know I'll always fight your corner, tooth and nail. True, true, true. There was nothing I could do to save you though, was there? I hope you don't think I have let you down.

Actually, actually, actually haha I am so, very dare you, angry with you – very cross indeed, Miss Trimble - because, and remember, I do love you, Stellamouche, BUT (that's a big one, okay?!) I feel like, wait for it, you chose to leave. There. I said it. I feel like you had a choice. And you chose, well, not me, I guess. Not Ollie, not your Dad. What could possibly be more, better than us? I am offended, Stellamouche. I am, I really am, and I am rejected.

I feel more at sea than when I realised you had a thing, and I mean a real thing, not a stupid crush like I go through every day of the week for some wanker or other, I mean the Real Thing, for Ollie. I never thought that a guy would come between us, we always said that we would never let that happen. We came up with a phrase one day, do you remember? The boys had 'mates before muff', which grossed both of us out but I think we came up with something else... 'mates before men', 'friend before fucks', 'pals before penis'… whatever it was, I can't remember it so it must have been Pathetic. With a capital 'P'.

Anyway, I know he didn't really, Ollie, I mean, but you were distracted by him, you can't deny that. I couldn't have the whole of you anymore. He had some of you. A big part of you.

He thinks you left him. Why would he think that? Why would you do that? Stella, he's such a great guy. Polar opposite to his tosser of a twin. Why, oh why, Stellamouche, did you let me go there? You couldn't stop me, you say. Like a steamroller, you tell me. Live and learn. Learn by your mistakes. Make your own mistakes. I hear you, honey.

That first day we met was not long after your mother died, well, months later, really, but everything's relative. I swear your cheeks still wore the tracks of your tears, like battle scars. But your beautiful brown eyes came to life as I got to know you, as the pain, well, it didn't exactly go away, it just became more… manageable, you would say.

I saw your tortoise first, the inestimable Herbie. Big word for me, huh? You taught me them all, my little tyrannosaurus. But I remember that game. The adorable Herbert, the beautiful Herbert, the charming Herbert, the delectable Herbert, the enchanting Herbert, the fabulous Herbert, the great Herbert, HUGE Herbert and, your favourite, the inestimable Herbert. Invaluable, no price too high for his head, the place he took in your heart so big. But it turned out you had room for more. You found room for me. Is love a bottomless pit? A golden goose? Is love infinite?

A tortoise. In the reading area. I had never seen such a thing before. I was fresh in from the grim north, the twang still in my voice, long gone now, thankfully, since so unsexy. I am proper estuary English now, you'd like to point out. It's something I've worked long and hard for. You Miss Doolittle, double Doolittle, elocution and animals, never let go of your enunciation (another long word, I thank you!) - the way your mother taught you to speak. Your father has always been more relaxed on the subject. Hoary old seaman that he is, and Anglo Saxon in his idiolect.

He was stood (the tortoise, not your father), blinking. You were sat cross-legged in your school uniform, your hair the shut curtains for your sad face, a book open on your lap, watching him. All the other kids were crowded around the radiator, opening mini bottles of milk, piercing sharp pale blue straws through their foil tops.

It was not long after Christmas. We'd had Christmas Day at my lovely Gran's in Sheffield. So far away, my Gran. And as you know, losing her marbles. Her wisdom retreating with her age, she's becoming more like a child. Needy and so far away. Too far away.

Anyway, a fish out of water I was, gasping at the edge of the pond, trying to flip myself in, when I spotted another of my kind, you. Another loner. Another rejected by the shoal, swimming alone. Splash! I went over to you.

What's her name? I asked. I don't know why I thought your tortoise would be a female. Some kind of hope of sisterhood, perhaps.

He's a he, you told me. Although you admitted later you could not possibly know, as he was far too young to be able to tell. But you were right. You had a fifty-fifty chance, I suppose. And that poor tortoise, he had many gender inspections ahead of him in the years to come and he tolerated every one. Bless Herbert.

The thing is, you managed to say it so I didn't feel rebuffed, rejected or corrected. The fact that you even responded felt like an invitation. Come on into my world, I heard.

What's his name? I asked.

Herbert, you said, and by answering, you proffered me a hand and invited me to sit down with you. And I did. You did not recoil. I took this to be a Good Sign. I considered asking why. Why his name was Herbert, I mean. I looked it up recently, the name. It means 'Illustrious Warrior'. I'm sorry, Herbie, but I'm not sure I can reconcile the meaning of your name with the creature I know. I knew. We'll come to that.

Anyway, perhaps I am unfair, perhaps there are hidden depths. Perhaps Herbie was a dark horse. He had a very impressive shield, it is true, but appeared a little light on actual weaponry, which one might assume essential for a warrior.

I say 'was' because, and Ollie's told me he has brought you up to date, hopefully you're listening to at least one of us anyway. But, Herbie's gone too. We don't have a body, so he may be roaming free. And despite the search parties, he remains at large. I have printed 'Wanted' posters and pinned them to every tree in the neighbourhood. Actually, I haven't. But only because everyone here has heard anyway. Everyone's got an eye out.

I think I've been obsessing about it a bit too much actually, actually, actually since the other day, well, er night turning into morning, to be a little more exact, I was lying on the Wittering, still fucked off my face on E after another entertaining night with Andy the fireman – you remember him? No? Anyway, I had a dream, I think, a vision maybe, of him on the beach and he was surrounded by some kind of halo like he was an angel or something. Anyway, thankfully I passed out again almost immediately before the whole thing got too weird. Thing is, the more I look back on it, the more real that it becomes. Maybe I am thinking about it too much.

Anyway, I digress, although I can't believe in all the years that have passed that I've have never asked this very basic question of you. Miss Trimble, you have escaped once again from my inquisition! I guess it will remain an eternal mystery. But one last try, I have the Ouija board ready, why, oh why, did you call your tortoise Herbert? Christ, I hope you aren't really there, I don't have a board ready at all. That might really anger your spirit or something. Let's keep it an unanswerable. That's fine. We should all be able to live with the fact that, even in these days with the internet available from virtually anywhere, that there are some things we may just never know. Give it up! I say. Move on. Let it go.

Although, I should probably confess that I asked your Dad the other day. He looked at me like I was insane - his usual look for me, I have to admit, and told me he had no idea. Maybe he knew once and has forgotten / washed it away in a tsunami of rum. A piece of history lost in the sands of time. Locked deep in the depths of Davy's locker.

Anyway, I digressed again. Actually, you always have had a fondness for my digressions, if not my transgressions. You love the way that three days later we pick up the threads of a conversation we had dropped, both of us knowing instantly exactly what we are talking about. Our great minds, so alike, you say. Your great mind, I reply, I'm sprinting to keep up. Not true, you say, you underestimate yourself. Where does your faith in me come from?

I owe it to you to honour your faith. I'm going to make something of myself, Stellamouche, make you proud of me. I'm going to live up to your expectations.

From little acorns you say, and I have an oak seedling. Violet, you remember that girl Sid dumped me for (I know we weren't really together, but I had high hopes and actually he's not with her either, but this is a whole other massive can of worms) at the gig at the George? Well, clouds do have silver linings and it turns out she was quite taken with my creations, as modelled by you, you beautiful creature. She rang me, SHE rang ME can you believe it? The other day. I am sure that Ollie or Dave had something to do with it. She's pretty fucked off with Sid, too. Said all sorts of stuff about him and Issa. Now I know he's sex on legs but really, Issa? She's a Goddess. But anyway, she – Violet - has suggested, and this is just a suggestion at this stage, I should emphasise, but Stellamouche, she's a buyer at Liberty and is suggesting they stock my stuff! Awesome. How I wish you were here to help me sell myself. You are the perfect model for my 'creations'. Actually, most of what I make is made with you in mind.

Additionally, Dave - where to start with Dave? I don't know how much Ollie has told you. As I said, all change, Stella! Dave, it turns out, is not on the dark side, after all. Not any more, anyway. He's changed! The plans for Palmer Springs are being rewritten. The future is under review. He asked me to consult for him. Do what? I asked right back at him.

Advise me, he told me.

But I know nothing, I laughed at him.

You do, he insisted.

Alright then, tell me what I know! I said, wetting myself.

People. This place. You are drawn to beautiful things. You are part of the Bestwood family, he said. And, bless me, I began to cry. Once I started, I thought I would never stop. And he just held me, Stella, he didn't try to feel me up or anything! Am not falling in love with him or anything, he's an old man, for fuck's sake, I was just was surprised that he wasn't being a complete perv, is all.

Anyway, I have digressed again for several paragraphs now, and personally, I blame the big cahuna a while back for that. But, in summary,

Stellamouche, something in my life is coming together, I think, as everything else falls apart. I'll hold onto this as the towers crumble around me, it's rubble raining down on me like some kind of wretched Rapunzel, and hopefully, I'll rise above it all, your memory clutched in my paw.

Your memory. My memories of you. Our moments together. Moments of being, as you like to describe them. Magic moments, I think of them, like little mouthfuls of delicious chocolate. I have felt guilty, like I have taken you for granted sometimes over the years that have gone by. I haven't really, I have always truly loved and embraced our friendship but now that you are gone and I long for so much more, knowing there is a big pile of future alone, I want even more in our past to compensate for what I am going to miss. You have cheated me.

Our past is so rich though. I admit, there is an ulterior motive for this exercise. I am hoping I'll find the words to say goodbye to you, formally, ceremoniously, at your funeral. Funeral seems the wrong word. Wake is a weird word. Sleep would be better, more fitting, wouldn't it? Wake is the opposite. Is that intentional, do you think? Sometimes I think it would be nice to sleep as you did. But I would want to wake at the end. And become something new. Like one of your chrysalises. Reinvention. You chose a deeper sleep, though.

It's not long now until we burn your remains to a crisp, something I find completely unpalatable and yet I am without alternatives. After we've done that, in accordance with your wishes, discussed when we were seventeen, we'll have a party on the beach, punctuated with flowers and cake.

What do I tell those people, though Stellamouche? I don't want to share you. You are all mine, in my eyes, mind, heart. You want me to be funny. Our memories belong to us, to me, and are intimate, private and I want to treasure them alone. This is so selfish, I know. I know!

I should make a list of things I am willing to make public, things that sum up the essence of you, things that try to do justice to the wonder that is you. And you want me to be funny? Blimey, Madam, it's a bit of an ask! It's worse than being the best man at a wedding, I'm positive of that.

Anyway, here goes:

1. When I was looking for boys, you were looking for caterpillars. Actually, you still spend more time looking for those creepy, crawly creatures than boys. It's a good strategy though, judging by the man you bagged. I might try it, too. I'm not touching them though. The caterpillars, I mean, not the boys, clearly!

2. You like Britney Spears. Now, we all like Britney. It's just most of us keep it quiet. Most of us don't drive about with her full blast out of our camper van windows and then go home to read The Origin of the Species or the ramblings of some random poet stuck in bed with his lover, cursing the rising of the sun in the sixteenth century. It's like you've never heard the word 'embarrassing'.

3. You are an Obsessive Recycler. Not just loo rolls and tin foil. To the extent of children. Too many on the planet, you say, so much waste (I think you mean their futures). No spawning for you. You're just grabbing someone else's leftovers. So 'celeb'.

4. You're so left wing you fell out the other end of the Universe. No prisons. No locking up. Treatment at the source.

5.   Five tequila shots and the boob-tube-as-a-belt whilst retching over the sink incident. No - too humiliating. That's between you and me.

6.   The dildo poetry. No. Do not want to cause heart attack in funeral audience.

The day after tomorrow. I'd be nervous if I didn't feel so honoured. If I could make it any other way then I would. But I can't. I can accept my shortcomings, too readily, you say. But now, I will stretch my wings, I'm going to learn how to fly. Haha, I do love the cheese. But seriously, honey, you're the best friend I'll ever know. Everything I do, I'll do it for you. I'm sorry, I just can't help myself. But your stamp will be everywhere. You will live on. Your memory will never fade. We'll be little old ladies together. You'll be my imaginary friend.

To the very best friend a girl could ever hope for. I love you, Stella. See you on the other side.

Hans xxxxxx

Hope House

Palmer Springs

Bestwood

West Sussex

PO42 1DP

23rd August 2009

My dearest, darling Stella,

And so then, this is goodbye. Today was your funeral. I continue to cry when I write this. I haven't stopped since I woke up. Against all the odds I think we did a good job today. We managed to pull it together between us all.

I hope you liked it, I hope we did it the way that you wanted us to. Thank goodness you had Hannah, as there are not many girls your age who would have left any sort of record of what they wanted from their own funeral. Hannah said it had been some time, since the car accident that cost you five of your schoolmates two years ago, that you had had this conversation. She wasn't entirely sure which were your choices and which were hers, but she did her best.

It has surprised me that Hannah is made of steel. She doesn't look it, doesn't act it. You know this, of course. You are her best friend. Were her best friend. I am not sure when I will be able to think, write, talk of you in the past tense. I suppose when I accept my reality of what has happened. That could take the rest of this lifetime. The lifetime I thought that I would spend with you.

You were cremated yesterday, in accordance with your wishes 'not to take up too much room and to be recycled most efficiently' said Hannah, a fond smile upon her face as I continued to blub uncontrollably. No service, just family and close friends wearing flowers in every colour around our neck, heads, behind our ears, in our button holes, any place we could put them, but clothed in black.

Your father, sober, returned to collect your ashes, your ground up bones, this afternoon. We had taken the urn from your house, the one your mother had inherited, the white crystal one with the figures revelling and dancing and drinking wine around it to contain you. A Grecian urn, he told me, portraying Bacchus he said, citing him as one of his heroes.

I drove us there. We didn't speak. This seems a repetitive scenario with me and your Dad. Neither of us I think could trust ourselves to open our mouths without bawling. The tears streamed down your father's face as he sat beside me, you balanced on his lap, in a jar, just dust.

Then Hannah and I went to the beach early. We laid picnic blankets up at East Head. The estate was remarkably helpful, very sympathetic. They remembered you. With fondness, as we all do. Me, much more than fondness.

Everyone there wore white, as you requested. We played Eva Cassidy's 'Songbird' like you wanted. Hannah talked about you. She made it through the whole speech without shedding a tear. You would have been so proud. She even made us laugh, because that's what, she said, you had asked her to do. She said that you had considered the options of being made into a firework, crushed into a diamond (I think only I saw any irony in that) or even fired into the outer atmosphere to orbit. She sobbed uncontrollably for half an hour afterwards, though. I held her throughout like I knew you would have done. Her mascara ruined my shirt. I wore it like a battle scar, even though it was just a pale shadow of the grief that ruins me.

I couldn't speak but I did sing you a song. Actually, I sang you two. The one I wrote for you that bagged me the gig in Brixton and another I wrote for you especially for your special day. I hope you heard it, wherever you are now.

Then everyone had cake. All the guests had brought one that they'd made themselves, just like you had asked. There was a classic Victoria sponge, a lemon drizzle cake, chocolate fudge cake, carrot cake, brownies, coffee and walnut cake, a banoffee pie, scones and a tarte au citron. They were laid out on the blankets, some in foil, some in tins and some displayed on stands. It was beautiful, Stella, and I took so many pictures. My sad beautiful day that I will treasure and hate for the rest of my life. So much love and so much sadness and disappointment all bound up together.

The one thing we failed to do was bring Herbert. I'm sorry, honey, but when your father heard you had gone and died on us, he lost it and smashed up the menagerie. Took a mallet to the part of the wall where you fell and bumped your head. Ripped up fences, took gates off their hinges and threw junk into the monkey's moat to fill it up. All of the animals, bar one, returned to their open enclosures after an initial foray. And, yes, that one was your beloved Herbert. Maybe he's looking for you.

None of us were there when this all happened, and when we came back and found your dad in a crumpled heap, and his shed a smoking pile, Herbert was gone. Perhaps, you should have called him Flash. We've been looking, we'll still keep looking, honey I promise.

I did something you didn't ask for, which was some Chinese lanterns. We sprinkled most of your ashes on the sand, like you asked. Actually, you looked a lot like sand yourself. We were worried about treading on you, I think some of your guests may have found the thought of getting you stuck to their feet a little macabre, so you mainly went up in the dunes. I am sure you'll blow around as you please though, much like you did in your life, my sweet.

And some of you we sprinkled in the lanterns. We had twenty-one of them; one for each of your years and one for the birthday that you're missing next month. I think I'll still celebrate it though, wherever I am.

The lanterns were fantastic. We waited until it was as dark as it could be, there were quite a few stars out and there were some fishing boats with lights on bobbing about near Cowes.

We lit them and released them all at once – quite an operation really, considering each one needs at least two pairs of hands. There were a lot of people there, Stella. You are well known for someone who describes themselves as 'pretty much a hermit'. And I don't think they were all hangers on, sweetheart before you say it, or celeb spotters. They were people whose lives you had genuinely touched.

The lanterns bundled into the sky, all of them cream and half a metre or more tall, made of waxy paper glowing as they rose, buffeted by the currents. With each of them, we sent a wish. My wish was that what happened between us, what I feel is real and that I will be granted the wisdom to understand how to find you again, and this time with the knowledge of how to make it last forever.

In the meantime though, I am leaving. My family has fragmented. Again. I should be used to this by now. Stability is not a feature of my life. Issa has run off with Sid. He's already describing her as a trial and says he's not sure what he's got himself into. Sarah is silently distraught and yet accepting his phone calls requesting advice. Dad, however, does not seem in the mood for forgiveness on this one. Sid and Issa are out of his world. He's thrown himself into Project Palmer Springs. Convinced that hope is eternal. He and your Dad are now the very best of friends thanks to the trials of the past few weeks. He's decided that a menagerie is the very thing that the centre of creativity needs for inspiration and has appointed your father accordingly, and passed him the deeds to the Gate House, which he found in a mouldy old trunk in a back bedroom. Along with a very large improvement budget. I hope he doesn't drown in it. I don't get the feeling he will, though, honey. He's turned a corner, I think, or sunk so low that the only way is up. He's been mending the damages he caused, making improvements, making plans for extensions and acquisitions with Dave. He seems settled here. Bestwood continues to provide him with some sort of solace.

I, on the other hand, am abandoning ship. I can't be here without you. Once Herbert is found, I'll be off. Sid is furious as I knocked back that record deal offered to us and am refusing to record any more material with him. I don't want to work with him anymore. I don't want to work at all at the moment. I want to heal and I want to do that far away. I want to produce something more meaningful, more worthy of your memory, and I'll need space and time to help me with that.

All that remains now is for me to say goodbye, and to thank you for being you. And to remind you, that I do hope that we will be together again. If you feel for me at all, please look for me like I look for you.

Eternally your Ollie x

PART THREE
Chapter Fourteen

Bob was back early. The Source was in no way prepared for setting just yet. She was still blazing. Bob stumbled about as if he was in a stupor. He most probably was. After all, he had spent every day since Stella's accident addled by alcohol; even more so than usual, I mean. I was angry with him, since I knew from Ollie's letters, read to me when each one was finished, and also from Digby's daily reports, that he had been neglecting his daughter, his only child, his only family; at the exact time when she needed him the very most.

His eyes were sightless as he walked past the Wall towards the feed shed. An automaton, he garnered a bunch of keys from his trouser pocket and twisted one of them into the padlock until it popped open. He wrenched the door open so hard that it wobbled on its bearings. Stress strained across his shoulders and I saw tension tauten up his neck. I was struck by a notion that his issue was not that of inebriation after all. Something entirely different suffused him. Anger, perhaps. He turned to look at me as he stepped through the door, but there was no fury in his face. It was entirely engulfed by misery.

My heart stopped beating. One, two, three it missed as I wrestled with my thought, trying to dampen it down, throttle it, but unstoppable, insistent, it scrambled out and stood before me. It towered over me, monstrously. Truth. I knew the meaning of Bob's look. Wilfully, my heart began to beat again.

She was gone. Bob's eyes were empty. He was lost. She was lost. Stella was gone. The colour leached out of the world. Like him, I could not see. I was empty, too.

Rattling and banging clattered from the innards of the shed and various implements leaped from the open doorway like wild creatures escaping joyously from captivity. A shovel, a rusty rake, a small green watering can. This last bounced down the Hill until it hit the meerkats' fence and then it lay there, motionless, as if it had knocked itself unconscious.

Stooping, Bob re-emerged from the shed, carrying a sledgehammer. It swung loosely from his hand as innocently as if it were a croquet mallet. He advanced towards me. I started to turn to run but I swiftly realised the pointlessness of this course of action. I could never outrun a human. I wondered briefly what proportion of my fellow creatures I could outrun - perhaps a sloth or almost definitely a snail. A very small proportion, I concluded, if any.

Fight or flight, I thought, as the adrenalin surged from my kidneys to celebrate jubilantly in my blood. My heart beat so loud that over its thumping I could barely hear the pulses it rushed through my ears in gushing waves.

I steeled myself for the end of me. Stella was gone, anyway. What was the point of anything anymore? Bob reached the Wall. He arrived at the exact point where Stella's fall had knocked the domino that led to this next domino's toppling, this next one being the imminent, bloody destruction of me, and he roared. He opened his mouth as wide as it could go and he let it all out. It reminded me in a way of Dave's morning screams, but this was somehow more real. It was guttural and it was poisonous.

I heard an answering roar in the forest behind me. An echo, you might think, but no, it was Gavin the tigress, or the ghost of her - I was sure of it. The tiger was reflecting her master's, her love's pain. Pain seemed like dominoes for a moment. Love makes pain contagious. You hurt therefore I hurt. We all fall down.

I was ready. I had already conquered the summit of my existence. Since then I had lost my one true love and I could move on to the next realm, whatever that should prove to be. Bob raised the sledgehammer above his head. He was too far away from me though for it to reach me. Was he going to throw it at me? His eyes were shut. His face was scrunched up, wrinkles wrinkling wrinkles.

He brought the sledgehammer down with an almighty crack on the top edge of the Wall. I felt it lurch and scream whilst I did not move a muscle. Of course, I thought. It had been silly of me, really, to countenance such an attack. Bob would never hurt any of us in the menagerie. He never would, he never could. His fury would be at the inanimate alone.

Shards of flint broken up by the blow sprayed into the air, raining their little chips down on me. The sledgehammer was raised and lowered, over and over, again and again, and the Wall was pummelled until it lay in a heap. Smashed, broken - like Bob. Like me.

It was not enough, though. His hunger for destruction had not been sated, was not abated. He'd only just begun. It was like he was trying to exorcise himself of the destruction within by directing it outwards. He was trying to rub his agony, the breaking up of himself, away, to transfer it elsewhere. He wanted to rid himself, to out his bad humour.

He hared down to the mob of meerkats, his feet beating on the ground, his voice a battle cry. The meerkats shot down their burrows in terror. But as Bob began to rip up their fence with his bare hands, they each popped their heads out, one by one, and then their bodies and they watched him, chirruping quietly to each other. The roots of the fence had been torn from the ground, their metal twists gripping clods of sod and clumps of grass.

I advanced to the gap in the Wall. The Family were far behind me, way up the Hill, ignoring Bob's madness: sleeping, browsing, nothing. Certainly not following.

I gingerly placed my front leg on the pile of rubble that had been this bit of the Wall, expecting - what? I do not know - an alarm to sound or an electric shock to violently repulse me, perhaps.

Bob sprinted up to Brian's island and, in a fantastic leap, mastered the moat. Brian ran to meet him, his small brown eyes full of concern and absolutely no fear and Bob waded waist-high back through the moat with his gibbon hanging about his neck and he sat him down by Atlas. Brian sat there, watching Bob, fretting and fidgeting. He'd caught the pain, too. Another domino.

As I became bolder and put another foot on the rubble, which shifted and flattened underneath my weight, Bob retrieved the sledgehammer from where he had left it leaning up against Atlas' mount and tenderly stroked Brian's head as he walked by. He marched back up the Hill, past a motionless me, apparently camouflaged by the pile of flint, judging by the lack of notice he gave, and he piled his weapon into the fence around the alpacas and Daisy and Dolly, smashing the timbers to smithereens.

I had reached the peak of the pile of dead Wall now. The only way was down, and out. I considered my options. Right or left. Left would take me to the newly wrecked fence, another gap to slip through. But, I thought, at the back, there was more fence. I would be trapped in there. There were no Herbert-sized gaps as far I knew. To the right, there was a lot of Wall. But then, if I followed the Wall as it passed alongside Brian's island's moat, there was open forest.

Again, I heard Gavin's roar, responding to Bob's pain. The meerkats were shuddering, but they were slowly creeping out of their enclosure, their noses twitching, their paws on ground they had always seen but never felt. They were tentative, some bolder than others. They were fanning out. They were free.

I was free. The sensation consumed me. I had been phenomenally bored for much of my life. I had had an enormous adventure when I went to the gig. I had resigned myself to a fate of nothing more of any particular interest, but now, I thought, I had a taste for it - a taste for adventure! I had thought I was to die at the hands of Bob and his sledgehammer, but now I was free and still alive. Everything was wide open ahead; a future. I had a future. And it could be anything. I could be an explorer! I could be intrepid.

I accelerated now, I almost ran, around the outside edge of the Wall. I kept my eyes focussed ahead of me, trying to ignore the sounds of the drama unfolding in my wake. The splintering of wood, the furious quacking of flamingos, the chittering of meerkats chased me as I chased myself away. I could hear Daisy and Dolly galloping about behind me, whinnying, but I did not look back.

I had seen the light. I had spied opportunity. There was nothing to keep me here. I could make my own adventures. I was starting now. I had become, I had made myself, the master of my own destiny.

Outside of the Wall was much like on the inside, it turned out, when I paused ever so briefly to look. It was mostly grass and daisies, although the grass here was long and lush and unbrowsed. It looked quite delicious but I ignored it, kept looking ahead, onwards. As I rounded the bottom section of the Wall and began to make an ascent up the Hill, a little out of breath now, but I was not going to slow down, I could see the forest up ahead. Some ferns feathered around the edge and behind them the clutter of trunks became so dense it looked as dark as a Sourceless, star-free night deep inside.

Behind me, the menagerie was an out of control, and somewhat out of tune, orchestra, every animal running about and chattering at the top of their voices. In the forest I could hear Gavin growling. I advanced towards her. I was not scared of her. Why would I be? She was only a ghost. And even if she were not, my shell would keep me safe. My shell would protect me. Tigers did not eat tortoises, did they? I wondered if they had ever had the opportunity. Geographically, this seemed unlikely. But would they if they were given the chance?

This concern was not enough to slow me down in any way whatsoever. I was at my full pelt. I imagine you would have been quite surprised if you could have seen me. I had soaked up a lot of Sourceshine that day and I was in optimum condition, even though I had not been eating so well since Stella fell, despite Ollie's entreatments and encouragements, but nonetheless, I had plenty of energy in reserve.

I crashed into the bracken and I stopped. I took a breath. I was hidden, out of sight, but I was not far away. I might not be out of mind, even if Bob was out of his at the moment. I could still be found. Quite easily, I would think. I began to move forward again when I heard an explosion in the distance behind me. My curiosity nearly led me to turn around to look, but, I thought, this is the sort of distraction I need. This is what is required to divert anyone who care's attention. Time will make space, and space constitutes my freedom.

I started to pick my way through the forest, twigs cracking underneath me as I went. I wondered if I was leaving an obvious trail behind me, whether a tracker would be able to hunt me down. I carried on. Moss caught in my claws, clogging them up. They were too long, what with me having been trapped inside the Wall for too long, for my ever, nearly.

Digby! I suddenly and fractiously thought. It came out of nowhere and hit me right between my eyes. I didn't say goodbye to Digby. No doubt he was still monitoring the happening up at the hospital, ready to relate to me on his return tonight. I don't want to know, I thought. I could die without knowing what happened in Stella's final moments. It's enough, too much, indeed to know that she has gone. He'll find me. I'm sure he'll find me. He'll understand what I am doing and why. And if he didn't, there would surely be some woodland or field creatures that I would see on my way that could take a message back to him. What would I say? What could I say to Digby?

I thrust forwards through the forest, squeezing between the trunks of two silver birch trees, their papery bark scraping off in ribbons as my shell pushed through. Onwards.

Digby could come with me! I swiftly identified a flaw in this plan. I did not know where I was going. And he would probably want to know. All about the details, was Digby. At the moment I was just a fugitive. I was putting myself in hiding. I know! I thought. I'll head for the Glittering. And when I arrive there I will... live in a beach hut! Or something. I would cross that bridge when I came to it. This was enough of a plan for the moment. Get me to the Glittering.

All of a sudden, something was very much in my way. It had not been there but a moment previously. It was very warm and very large and very hairy. And it was growling. It was orange and stripy and had a massive head. In no way did this creature resemble a ghost.

I yanked myself inside quick-sharp, emitting a hiss that was matched by the cat as my lungs expelled all of my air in order to accommodate the rest of me. I froze.

An enormous paw batted me on my back. I shuddered under the impact. I did not dare to breathe.

I could hear the stealthy crunching of forest floor as the cat, Gavin, not a ghost, padded about me, circling. A huge claw nicked a scale on one of my back legs. She'd hooked it in through one of my holes. I squeezed myself in even tighter.

'Do I know you?' she purred, her hot breath puffing in through the hole for my head. I contemplated my answer. This whole scenario was blocking my escape. She was slowing me down. Worse than that, she might be hungry. It might be less of a slow and more of a permanent full stop. What exactly had she been eating out here all this time? It had been years, all of mine, and she had not appeared malnourished in that fragment of a moment I had had a look at her. Her fur was vibrant, its tips sparkling as the Source dappled down through the leafy canopy.

It was pretty in the forest, I thought, not dark or dingy as it had appeared from the outside. The Source shone through in shafts, catching motes of dust and pinhead-sized flies in the calm air in here, showcasing the weeny caterpillars dangling from the branches on their dainty silken threads.

'Answer me!' She batted me again, harder this time. A warning shot across my bows.

'No,' I replied, words mumbling from within myself. 'I was born the day you…' I was petering out, unsure as to the etiquette of referring directly to a conversational partner's execution, their scheduled demise, in fact.

'I, what?' she growled. 'Come out of there,' she instructed, in a slightly gentler tone.

No way, I thought. I am not ready to be devoured. I had fooled myself that I was ready for the sledgehammer. But now, now I knew I was choosing life, I was choosing adventure, I was choosing freedom and a future. Life for me could go on. Stella would want this for me. I knew she would.

'Come out of there...' Gavin breathily purred at me. Her breath didn't smell awful. It was a little meaty perhaps for my tastes, deer or possibly a lot of rabbit, I suspected, but it was in no way rotten. This cat was very definitely alive.

I made a brave decision to face my fear. Courage, I thought, is not lack of fear but the conviction in the goal beyond the thing that stands scarily in the way; in this case, the goal being my freedom. I braced myself. 'Are you going to eat me?'

'Oh,' she said, sounding surprised. 'You are edible?'

Hmm, I pondered upon this. Cats are playful, curious and downright clever. This one was an example of one of the most effective predators on the planet. She was a killing machine. Her species' success was not through brute force alone. They had cunning and they had tactics. Who was the cleverest, though; the tiger or the tortoise? Could I talk my way out of this one? Think my way out? I tapped into my shell. No precedents or examples of this sort of situation were available. I was on my own. I was trying to decide whether she was playing dumb, calling my bluff, when she said, 'What do you taste like?'

Gah! I thought. I am not coming out. However, I can't stay here forever; they'll find me, scupper my plan. They'll take me and put me back inside the Wall. Although, how has Gavin managed to live so long in the forest, undetected? Perhaps I could do that, too. I could just stay here, ignoring her until she became bored of me, then live in the forest. Not much of an adventure that, though. Besides, I had my suspicions that there were certain zookeepers who were precisely aware of Gavin's whereabouts and simply chose to ignore it. More than that, on second thoughts, they positively championed the situation to the extent of making it a very well kept secret for a somewhat extended period of time.

'Alright,' she said. 'That was mean. I am well aware that I must frighten you. This is all to the good. I have a reputation to uphold, after all. I have to be honest with you, though, you don't look like much of a meal to me. I don't think there's probably that much of you in there underneath that ridiculous shell and leathery skin. And you are revoltingly cold. Besides, I have already eaten today.' She made a noise that indicated she had smacked her lips at the ample sufficiency and deliciousness of her last gastronomic showdown.

Indignantly, I emerged in a rush and stood on my tiptoes. 'How rude!' I exclaimed. Oops, I thought, that may have been a trap. But she was laid down in front of me, her huge head resting on her enormous front paws. She blinked. I felt an affection for her and, unwittingly, blinked back.

'Where are you going, anyway?' she enquired, her ears, edged and tufted in black, twitching at me like satellites.

'I'm going to find the rest of my life,' I said. 'I thought it had all been taken away from me.' I stopped.

'I see,' she said, and licked the top of her right paw thoughtfully with several rasps. 'You know, there was a time when I thought the rest of my life had been taken away from me. To be fair, it was because I had taken the rest of someone's life away from them.' Just listen, I thought. She looked at me;

her eyes were yellow, the backs of them reflecting light like the underside of a seashell does. This reminded me of my mission. Patience, I instructed myself. 'The thing is,' she continued, 'I was put on this planet to take lives away. I can't live without the feeling of a pulse expiring between my jaws - that's what I was built for. I couldn't live on grass even if I tried. It makes me throw up, actually. Fur balls, you see.' She sort of grimaced at me, a little like she was embarrassed about the situation. The tiger was sheepish.

'Go on,' I said. She's not going to eat me, I thought.

'I do sometimes think though, that maybe I was wrong that particular time. I had no intention of eating her. It was a moment of madness, perhaps. Once I had done it I saw I shouldn't have done. But by then, it was too late.' She looked sad.

'Why did you do it?' I asked gently, like she was laid out on my couch.

'I have asked myself that question often as the time has passed since...' She waved a paw at me. 'What are you, anyway? And what would I call you?'

'I am a tortoise, and my name is Herbert.'

'Well then, Herbert, let me tell you about a strange thing that these humans like to call biology. My instinct to kill, to survive, is equalled by my instinct to mate. And the instinct to mate holds hands with the instinct to love. It's a drive. The drive to live is inseparable from that to reproduce. It's all survival. Our bodies have been finely tuned to this over millions, billions even, of years and our minds are merely an organ in our bodies. Those foolish, romantic humans think that love is exclusive to them, that they are of a higher order and that we mere animals are too simple to exhibit such complex emotions. They want to believe that love is spiritual, ethereal, magic, but love is built into all of our brains. It's simply the manifestation of the drive to reproduce, the drive to survive - a simple sequence of events to breed successfully: attraction, devotion and attachment for mating, breeding and rearing the young. At its core all it is are synapses and chemicals.' I wondered if I would ever fall in love in this way. I wondered if the love I felt for Stella was driven from this part in me. Mating was not a part of what I felt for Stella, but then surely Gavin had not felt the mating instinct for Bob.

'Love, though,' I said, voicing my thoughts as they formed within my brain, 'it's not all about sex, it's not all driven by reproduction. There are many kinds of love. The Greeks had many words for love. Each a different kind.' I thought upon this. The tiger did, too.

'Can anyone love without jealousy, though?' she asked.

I considered this and then, feeling wise, I answered; 'There are some who would say that if your love was true then it would be given unconditionally and then you would want your loved one to have everything that they wanted, everything that would make them happy, regardless of your own self. You would want so much for them that it would be to the detriment of your own desires and needs. In altruism, you would find your rewards.' It was a hypocritical answer, I realised as I spoke, since for those who I felt love for the most, Stella and Digby, I had felt jealousy of their interactions with others and with the world; jealous when Stella bestowed her affections upon others that she loved, jealous when Digby had exercised his freedoms, those that I did not then have.

'Can you survive that way, though? I couldn't. Or at least I didn't. And when I heard her screaming at him, like a fish-wife, telling him he had to choose, that he wasted too much time with me, he, the only source of affection and comfort I had… so far from my home… I was homeless really, although, bless him, he had tried. But I was caged, I couldn't roam, I couldn't hunt. I wasn't me.' She rested her chin on her paws, morose. 'Was my alternative, some kind of suicide?'

'You took a mother away from her only child,' I stated, gently, as I did not wish to regenerate her wrath, but, at the same time, I felt it needed to be said.

'Yes I did,' she concurred. 'But every life I take is a parent, a child, a lover, a brother… All blood is linked somehow to something. Even you and I, Herbert, we share many characteristics, and if we went back far enough we would share an ancestor. Our backbones, you see. And more than that - life. All life is linked. We are family, in a very dim and distant way. And every, well, most lives are loved, whether it's a rabbit, a deer or indeed a human. It is not right to make a hierarchy of life forms; each is equally important, equally loved. What I did wrong was to kill not for sustenance, but for fury. Even now, I am not convinced I killed to survive.'

'Did you think he might rid himself of you somehow?' The other side of the story advocated itself to me. Although I had been the bearer of Stella's loss for so many years, I saw the loneliness in Gavin's eyes and although I could not support her actions, I conceived their purpose.

'Yes,' she replied looking straight at me. 'I was also afraid,' she confessed.

'Was it fear then, or fury, that killed Beryl?' I asked.

'Both,' she answered after some contemplation. 'And both of them, both fear and fury, were the children of my love. Love can be unappeasably cruel.' She perked an ear up. Far behind me I could hear some snapping of twigs and a fair amount of whinnying. 'Time to round up the troops,' she said. 'It sounds like Bob might need a hand with those zebras. I've always thought they looked like a square meal myself, underneath those stripes. Perhaps if one should wander in here accidentally… they are getting on a bit. Could it be considered a cull?' She stood up and her tail twitched from side to side.

She leaned down and looked at me, right in my face. 'It was lovely to meet you, Herbert. I do hope you have fun with your future.' She stood, sniffed the air and without another word, off she slunk through the trees.

Press on! I said to myself and, as I crashed through the undergrowth, I thought that this encounter had been less of an inconvenient delay and more an enrichment of my travels. What a meeting, what an escape!

Thundering on and on through the apparently infinite forest, bit by bit the light escaped from the day until the dark devoured me and much as I was driven on and did not want to stop, I felt that I had put a considerable distance between myself and the menagerie. The lack of light would conceal me most effectively and I was sure that I must be near to the edge of the forest by now. I had been going for hours. I would be able to see more clearly in the morning. Besides, the excitement had taken it out of me. All that adrenalin had left me a bit flat and I required a nap to rejuvenate. I was also cold and knew that a shot of the Source would spark me up again.

A small and very unexpected pang of something like homesickness nibbled at me. For a moment it occurred to me that I might have been wrong, that Stella may not be dead. If the choice that we would never see each other again would reveal itself to be mine and not hers then this would be a mistake. I would choose Stella over my freedom, my adventure. Perhaps, given the success of our last outing, she would take me on adventures again, not of my choosing, admittedly, but adventures nonetheless. I could always turn back, I thought, through my exhaustion. I could find my way back, I was sure of it. I could find my way back… home. Home didn't seem the right word.

As I drifted off to sleep, I was aware of tiny little eyes that sparkled brightly and the sound of little paws scurrying through the undergrowth. I fretted about what tomorrow would bring and was exulted by the realisation that, whatever it was, it was likely to be a surprise.

Chapter Fifteen

A familiar squawk startled me into consciousness the next morning and for a moment I thought I was back within the Wall. My memory had not had a chance to assure me that the previous day had occurred; for a moment I didn't know where I was. And then it kicked in and with it I was fully awake and cognisant.

The Source was not yet risen, although a creeping pale blue light announced Her imminent arrival. Familiar She was, the Source. Happily, I thought, wherever I was, She would always rise and set. This was a comfort to me, rather like lovers on either side of the world observe the moon, knowing their heart so far away sees the same satellite, joining them despite the many thousands of miles between their bodies and their yearning hands and lips.

I saw Digby pecking at loose leaves. Beyond him, I could see the edge of the trees and the vista opening out generously and in avid welcome. My sense of being on the edge, finally, last night, was right. I was closer than I had thought. It was a fine way to wake up and an encouragement for my day of travails ahead. I yawned and a twig cracked under my foot as I stretched out.

'Herbert!' Digby started. 'What in the name of the Source are you doing out here in the forest? You've missed all manner of activity in the menagerie! I missed much of it myself...' He hopped over to me, looking awfully serious. 'Herbert, I have something terrible to share with you, bad news, news I fear will affect you very deeply, but that you must know. Herbert, I have to tell you what happened...'

'I know. Digby, I know already,' I interrupted, blocking his words. It was rude, but it was necessary. My brusqueness rendered him silent for a moment.

It was true then, I thought. There was nothing to hold me back now, nothing to declare, nought to keep me. Digby had not really struggled to find me. He would always be able to find me; he had such a gift - flight, wings, the ability to travel virtually anywhere he wanted and at such speed. It had taken me a whole day to reach this place and yet he had located me in a timeframe better counted in minutes. He could follow me; he would be my companion.

'How? How do you know? You were gone before we returned. It's taken me most of the night to find you.' Okay, so maybe I had done a better job at hiding than I thought. But he still found me.

'I saw it in Bob's eyes,' I replied.

'Ah, yes,' he said. 'Bob - your captor, your keeper and also the agent of your release. Are you wild now?'

'Digby,' I said, 'I have always been wild.'

'Born into captivity though, Herbert. Will you know how to survive?'

'I eat, I sleep, I urinate,' I replied simply. 'What more is there to survival?'

'What if you eat the wrong thing?' he asked.

'I won't.' His lack of faith in me I was finding less than edifying. 'I have my family's entire history of knowledge available to me, remember, Digby.'

'As well you know, I have never truly been convinced about how that works,' he answered. I rolled my eyes at his ignorant cynicism. 'Anyway,' he continued, 'how many of your relatives have strolled free on the dangerous plains of the British countryside, eh, Herbert? How many have witnessed the wide and varied dangers that hunt across the meadows?'

'Digby,' I stopped him right there. 'We are both fully aware that Sussex hardly constitutes a jungle. Moreover, what is it you endeavour to achieve with this line of enquiry? Why do you not embrace the concept of my freedom in the manner that one would expect of a true and dear friend? You should be pleased for me and for what I have found.'

'A friend also cares for his friends' safety.' He peered at me. 'You know, Herbert, you are the only one who has left the lodgings provided for him. The gap remains in the Wall and yet none of the rest of the Family investigate it, let alone regard it as an opportunity for exploration. The meerkats had a run around but as soon as the Source set they returned to their burrows and this morning were to be found clattering their food bowls, clamouring for their breakfast. Daisy and Dolly apparently had a scare at the edge of the forest yesterday and have been cowering in the furthest corner of their field ever since. Brian clings to Bob much as Bob clings to him. The flamingos, it seems, have been free to go forever and simply choose to stay. And the giraffes and the alpacas barely twitched a hair when their doors were opened. I think the giraffes were frightened at the sight of the feed shed on fire. They, in fact, never left their den, even after Bob had razed their fencing to the ground.' I laughed. 'You though, Herbert, you can't even be seen from the menagerie. You are not a part of it anymore. What are you a part of now?'

'Do I need to be a part of anything?' I asked. 'Can't I just be a part of myself? Must I be defined by the Family that ties me by our most recent blood, or by the company that I keep, whether of my own choosing or not? Can I not just contain myself within myself?'

'That, Herbert, is the path to loneliness,' Digby demurred.

'I disagree,' I began to refute, not sure where I was going, not sure if this was an insult to one who had been a very great friend to me. 'I can be my own company - that way I'll never be alone. By being entirely reliant upon myself, I will never have to trust anyone else, never risk losing anyone. Never having to trust anyone else means that no-one can ever hurt me.' I was onto something here, quite proud of myself.

'But what if you need something?'

'Then I will obtain it for me.'

'Would it not be easier if you asked for help?'

"Many hands make light work' or 'Too many cooks spoil the broth' - which is it, Digby? Is either right? Can two contradictory statements both be true? Besides, my dear, you appear to be taking this rather personally.' I was fully awake now and a pleasure as it usually was to see Digby, I rather felt it was time to be getting on.

'Herbert, I worry for you. It's a big world out here. I fly much of it often. All my life I have found you within the Wall. It's a little strange for me to see you out here, in my world.'

'Is that it?' Immediately I was rather cross with him. 'You are upset that I'm in your space? You don't wish to share this with me? You want to keep it all for yourself.' I started to head for the light peeping about at the edge of the trees and I knocked into him as I stomped past. He looked aghast.

'Where are you going?' he asked. I considered my response at some length. I felt that it was not his business. He was exhibiting excessive selfishness for a so-called friend. However, that he remained to me - a friend, and despite my protestations to the contrary, I clung to a concept that a friend could be useful. I would not burn my bridges.

'The Glittering,' I told him.

'Do you want me to show you the way?'

'I will find my own way. You may follow if you wish.'

Chapter Seventeen

I could see it! As I left the forest behind me, the Glittering beckoned from the horizon. The Source flickered across Her brother's eternally regenerative waves. To my right, the Spike loomed above the treetops that flounced in the morning breeze. I was much closer to it now and it was much bigger. I could make out patterns in its stone decorating the base of its circumference. I could see light through its arches. On the ground ahead of me there were daisies, almost tall enough to reach my chin, and buttercups and the pale purple of ladies' smock all dancing along with the dry feathery heads of the grass flowers.

I was at the top of a vast field on a steep incline. It was fenced, but with a bit of a squeeze and a scrape I was under it and in. A black bull stood steaming at the bottom end. After my experience with the tigress, he did not worry me. I headed straight for him and reached him in a while. When I finally arrived at him, he removed himself from my path. He had watched me the whole way and now he stared at me, his hot, wet exhalations exuding from his nostrils, cooling to condensation in the colder morning air.

I arrived at a cattle grid. I had heard of these but had not borne witness to their magic before. It was manufactured of a series of metal poles laid in lines with gaps running between them. These poles were spattered with congealed mud and the dew stuck to them like drops of perspiration. This made them slippery and I must have looked a sight, but I battled my way across and onto a furrowed muddy track through a hedge that opened onto a field of lavender.

The conquering of the cattle grid had evidently taken a fair while, as by the time I arrived in the next field, the air had been dried out by the Source and I was hit by the clean, sleepy fragrance of the herbs and a gentle busy buzz of a thousand splendid bees. The field was entirely purple. Someone had thoughtfully planted the lavender in lines and I was able to follow one down the hill. I was hungry now and as I walked I would nip a flower head every now and again. I peered at one closely; it was constructed of tiny trumpets that all lined up in perfect geometry. At the top, it was peaked in a cap of four bigger trumpets that feathered out at equal angles.

The next field was of cabbages, a foodstuff I was very sure about and so I spent some time there, stuffing myself silly. Although I was used to my food mostly being chopped and therefore ripping the leaves apart was a relatively lengthy process, I was convinced that it was worth the expenditure of effort and the time, as fuel was essential to me reaching my goal of the Glittering, which continued to shimmer away in my line of sight. There were more Ups between it and me, many hurdles to leap yet. It occurred to me that soon I would be too low down to observe it. I hoped that I could keep my aim steady. This journey had an urgency to it for me that demanded a route as the crow flew. I did not want to wander off, digress from my travels. I had a very specific goal - that of the Glittering.

As I watched it, choppy and rough today, the waves spittling and the boats rigged tight with single white sails to duel against a fierce wind, a crowd of green birds, the parakeets, set off from the beach. As they passed high over my head, one of them peeled off to the Spike, where I saw it met by an immensely fast thing. There was a mid-air collision and a puff. Just one grey-brown bird retreated to the Spike; the other had vanished into thin air, imploded, perhaps, by the impact, to nothing.

A long time later, having worked my way through several more fields, one full of corn on the cob, sleeved in green velvet, high and top heavy, another stuffed with constructions covered in tight plastic sheeting, I ate a huge discarded tomato I had found, its skin split, disgustingly, deliciously ripe. A bright green feather, soft and warm, drifted down and sidled about on the breezes in front of me and landed on the chalky ground of the fallow field in which I stood.

I regarded this feather and contemplated it at great length. I did not know how it had found me or what it was trying to tell me. I ran through several thousand options, most of them involving Digby, since it was his colour. I became lost in it. I could see the pale vein from where the fluffiness sprang. I saw its points, its shape, its universal pattern. It became imprinted on my brain, a neurological tattoo.

I was disturbed from my meditation by a rumble behind me. A tractor had driven in at the top of the field, its paint a dull orange, its wheels up to its armpits and deeply trod. Its engine chugged its way down towards me. I was exposed; the grass was not particularly long here. I was poking out. Moments before I had been enjoying the rays of the Source caressing the curve of my shell; now, though, I could appreciate that She was more than likely lighting me up like a beacon. If I moved would I draw more attention to myself? I calculated. If I did not, then would the driver of the tractor think, perhaps, that I was a newly arrived boulder? I chose the latter option, tucking my head and limbs away in order to be more convincing.

As it was, the tractor's trajectory changed and I heard it chug its way out of the field from the other bottom corner, showing me the next step on my path, as well as pulling me from my feather-induced dread-driven fantasies.

I followed the brambles along the bottom of the field, still with the odd cream, pink-tinged petal and fair bursting with fruit, some of which looked almost ready for consumption: fat, shiny and black. Most were still tight and small and green. The wind began to raise itself into a frenzy. The sky had clouded over and was whipping about; I could smell rain in the air. Beyond the brambles, I could hear a regular swish swish of air as vehicles sped their way along a road.

At the field's corner where the tractor had exited, a gate was open wide, leading onto a pockmarked piece of road. Chunks of tarmac lay about and the holes themselves were filled with a thin layer of dank smelling gunge. Ahead, every now again, with no discernable pattern, a flash of shiny colour sped past in either direction, causing the air to rush past and clap behind. They each had their own pitch, and they were entirely unpredictable. I realised I was very visible, particularly should one of them choose to stop nearby.

It was raining now, rivulets running down the warm creases in my shell, latently sucking out the heat I had painstakingly collected from the Source so far that day. The road began to give off a smell of grease and oil and the cars and lorries added the sounds of water hitting their bodies and the spray from their wheels to their noise as they passed, on their own adventures, perhaps. Or merely to or from work, to visit a friend or a relative. Most of them probably were on some sort of menial business in comparison to my own lofty ambitions.

However, none of this pondering was moving my case forward, since what I needed to do was cross this road. I moved off the path onto the side verge and down into a ditch, full of the leftovers of arum lilies. I remembered how their cream waxy trumpets cluttered together like a crowd of bishops. Now these clustered with berries; summer was waning. It was damp in the ditch and, were the rain to continue as it threatened, it could possibly become a stream. Water did not bother me in the same way that it put the fear into some of my more distant, but still tortoise, relatives. My homeland could be humid and lush and so I had evolved to be fairly waterproof. I carried no concerns for shell rot.

But I did have grave concerns about crossing the road. It was common knowledge that such a feat was one that required extreme caution, a certain amount of intelligence and some significant speed. I had the first two in spades but was somewhat lacking in the last. I tried to imagine how long it would take me to cross the road and then compared this to the frequency of the vehicles haring past. An issue was that sometimes five or even six would swish past at once, in convoy, but then there would be a large gap. And they were coming from both directions. It was all very unpredictable.

Not only could one very conceivably hit me, and I was not arrogant enough to believe for a second that my shell would protect me from something of a car's weight at the velocity at which these were travelling, let alone a lorry, but I also realised that I would be seen and would not have any time to hide. I thought perhaps I could follow the ditch along the side of the road and hope to find a tunnel, but this was rather a long shot, I felt, and I had no idea how far this ditch extended. Besides, I could easily lose my bearings and the Glittering was just out of sight now. On the other side of the road, another forest grew and it obscured my view of the coastline. I couldn't see the water roads through it, although I was sure I was still pointing in the right direction. I was convinced I had not lost my bearings; I was still targeting the point of my freedom. The Glittering was in front of me, I just knew it. With a pang, I wished for Digby to appear beside me, like a genie; my navigator, my friend, my companion, but I remained alone.

I could not identify any course of action other than to sit and wait it out. I knew that the humans had certain times of day when they all liked to move around. Hopefully, this was one of them and when night fell I theorised that they would tuck themselves up at home or in the pub and I would find the traffic irregular still but spaced apart with a sufficiency that would allow me time to reach the other side and continue on my quest.

Twilight came and went and with it the temperature slumped. The rain had desisted but its remnants gurgled away in the ditch, running off the hills and through the ground. The cars and other assorted vehicles became less frequent and I imagined myself walking across the stretch of tarmac between each gap. I knew that in the middle of the road there was a double white line, a track in between which I had seen knobbles spaced apart. As the darkness drew in about me, I started to make my way back out of the ditch. It was steep and I was careful since, were I to upend myself here, there were no guarantees that I would be flipped over. I could starve to death upside down; it would be rather a sad end to my grand plan.

I peeped over the edge of the ditch and compared what I could see with what I had been remembering for hours now, visualising. There was the double white line. I heard the sound of an engine to my left and the lights appeared suddenly and blindingly around a tight corner. The vehicle flashed past me, the air pulling and then smacking behind it, making me judder. Its red rear lights, glowing like embers, sped around another corner to my right, out of view. There was no man-made lighting out here and the moon was clouded over, but I had seen the knobbles in the road light up as they received the beams from the car's headlights - cat's eyes.

I waited and waited but nothing else came. Every time I thought perhaps it was time to make a dash for it, I convinced myself that I could hear another one coming. I thought that logic demanded I wait until another one passed and then immediately afterwards would be the best time to go. However, I also considered the mathematics of probability and that it could be as likely that two or more vehicles could pass in quick succession. This was going to be a gamble. I was feeling lucky.

'Greetings, Herbert.' A voice emanated from the top of the ditch behind me, low and hoarse and instantly recognisable as that of Roger the Gregarious Badger. 'The grapevine had conveyed to me news of your scandalous escape. I wondered if I might stumble upon you. I have to admit that I had not thought you would have made such progress. You are a long way from home.'

'Hello, Roger, old chap. You know, I don't believe I have a home, as such. I think that I am my home.' Wearily I wondered if I was to have a repetition of the conversation with Digby.

'Yes, I suppose you never were awfully content at Bestwood. Perhaps you will find somewhere that suits you better to be your home. Or perhaps you will wander the world making it all your home.' His answer refreshed me. I remembered how he had told me once that some badgers preferred to live in a clan whereas others were more solitary, almost nomadic, moving from home to home, place to place. He had said that he fell into the latter group. I felt a kinship with him. I remembered that at the time, the idea had appealed to me greatly, but that I had put it away, being contained indefinitely by the Wall at the time.

'Digby said that you are on your way to the sea,' he continued.

'Yes,' I said. 'I'm currently challenged by this road, though.' This last comment was drowned out by a lorry thundering by. Its brake lights lit up the moths fluttering helplessly in its wake as it veered sharply around the corner. Now? I thought. I pulled myself up onto the bank of the ditch and out I stretched a leg onto the road.

'What are you doing? Herbert, are you mad?'

'Never been saner!' I replied, picking up some speed now, despite the stiffness that the cold had induced in my limbs. A car hurtled around the corner to my left. Instinct made me react by withdrawing into my shell, despite my earlier recognition that this would not advantage me at a point of impact. I heard Roger yelp behind me. The car flew past, flicking loose particles of gravel at me that pinged off my shell.

Mathematically, I thought, that has not changed my odds one iota, although there is both an emotional argument to say that it should be a while now before the next one comes along, and also one that says I should not be so lucky next time. I stopped rolling dice in my head and proceeded as fast as I was capable.

'Oh my life,' Roger was shouting behind me. 'You are either very brave or very stupid. These roads take no prisoners, you know! No-one walks away from this battlefield alive! Go! Herbert go!' I was halfway there now. I straddled the double white lines. This was possibly the most dangerous point; no fifty-fifty chances here. As I took another step forward, I heard the unmistakable tumultuous grumble of a very large engine on a lot of wheels to my right. Once more, my instincts betrayed me and I sucked into myself; my version of flight, I suppose. I had no fight setting. The lights from the lorry burned through the cavities in my shell so brightly that I could see the pink veins in my eyelids coursing over them like some kind of map.

A sonorous horn blew right over me and there was a skidding sound behind me as the wind raced there, a hair's breadth away. I heard Roger yelp again and a small, almost imperceptible thump. Then it was gone, leaving behind an acrid smell of burning rubber.

Be lucky, I thought to myself, and, scared out of my wits, virtually scampered the last few feet, driven by fear and the elation of having come so close to my end and having escaped once more.

The verge on the other side was shrouded in cow parsley, its thick ribbed stems gave off a bitter fragrance in the wet and they lazily dripped on me as I buried myself into them and regained my breath. I turned around.

'I made it!' I yelled. 'Roger! I made it!' There was only silence on the opposite side. I squinted out into the darkness. Lights popped up to my right and glared along the tarmac. There was a shadow, a motionless lump over there and tyre tracks leading onto the grass that was ripped up, leaving a muddy wound. Roger's thick hair looked matted and his striped face rested on the ground. He looked rather like he was sleeping. He snapped out of view for a second as the car passed directly in front of me and then the red rear lights were not enough for me to clearly make him out anymore.

Was it wrong of me not to go back? How could I? And even if I had, what could I have done? Perhaps I could have comforted him in his last moments, although what I had seen led me to believe that those had already gone. It seemed improbable that I would make it back over - there'd been two near misses this way; I was convinced I would be third time unlucky. I replayed the moments with the lorry. I felt sure that it had swerved to avoid me and in doing so had removed Roger from his mortal coil. He had probably thought he was safe, not being on the road. He had probably frozen, watching me, fearful of my fate. I had won the toss of a coin.

I felt guilty, but I was not the lorry. And the lorry wasn't really to blame, either; he was just going about his business. I had not asked Roger to come here, had not suggested he wait and watch my progress. I had not put him in the lorry's path. He had made those choices himself. They weren't bad choices, necessarily, it was just that chance had tolled.

All this death, I pondered, new lives in the menagerie, their little dog eaten by a pike, Issa's wretchedness and hate of Bestwood as a consequence, although maybe she would have despised the place anyway. She would have felt as trapped as I had. Digby too had been struck by that little dog's death. I had not been bothered. I had seen it as the natural order of life. I had been more affected by the death of a woman I had never met, Stella's mother, Beryl, because of the pain Stella had felt and the love it created in her for me. Gavin was right. Every life means something to someone, somewhere. Stella's death had ripped my heart out and that of Ollie and her father. Roger's death, the horror that had just occurred right in front of me, left me feeling grateful it wasn't me. And that thought was making me feel guilty, disrespectful somehow.

It wasn't that I didn't like Roger, I did, but he wasn't a big part of my life and I didn't think I was going to miss him. Who knew where he was now, the essence of him, I mean. Who was going to miss him, like I missed Stella? We don't know what happens after death and I would have liked to have been able to say that I could still feel her presence, but I couldn't. She had gone. Maybe I would have felt her if I had been back at Bestwood, back where I knew her. Perhaps she was there in a sort of spirit, or perhaps just the memories of her there would create a sense of her presence. It would not be enough, though. I was going to miss her voice, her laughter, her warm touch, her wisdom, watching her grow.

She wasn't going to grow anymore and this thought hurt me more than anything else. It was the end of her line and this seemed so wrong, so against the natural order of things. I would, most likely, always have outlived her, but

I would have been able to cope with her absence better if I had seen her live her whole life, not seen her removed from so much promise when she was only just standing on the threshold of it.

Death is natural, I thought. There is nothing in life more certain to happen. We cannot guarantee even the things that seem like basics; falling in love, mating, breeding. If we survive and procreate then in some sense we have succeeded in our role here. We have reproduced. We have survived. So had Stella failed? What had she left behind? Could there be anything positive in her departure? I couldn't think of a single thing. Death for Stella was unnatural. It spat in the face of the order of things, the way life should be. This was the tragedy; this is why I would never make sense of it, even if I spent every minute of the rest of my life trying to unravel it, trying to make a meaning of it.

I turned back again on where I had come from and pointed myself forwards in the direction in which I aimed - past behind, future ahead. I nuzzled through the thick stems of the cow parsley, dislodging droplets of rain and tiny white petals that clung to my shell, suckered to it by the damp. Behind it was a hedge, a thick hawthorn one, its branches spiky, its haws not yet turned and ripened for the autumn, still green and dodging about behind the leaves. This hedge was thicker than I had imagined from the other side and I did not believe I would be able to barge my way through it.

I would have to look for a gate or a gap, some kind of hole. I was hidden from the road now, which was just as well since the birds in the hedgerow sang in a unison that indicated the Source was on Her rise.

I tossed a coin in my head and turned right, beating my way through the foliage. It occurred to me that it might look quite strange from outside of the tunnel I was building myself, in that the plants were swinging about for no reason. I amused and distracted myself with this thought until I arrived at a point where a hawthorn bush had died, wizened and unnaturally bare, leaving a convenient gap for me low down in the hedge between the trunks of two more successful plants. The trunks were far enough apart for me to squeeze through and the thorns on the plants snapped off on my horny shell. The barbed wire that I had not observed in the low light of the advancing dawn did not snap off, however. No, indeed; as I pushed my way through the gap, its barbs lodged themselves in me and scraped thin channels in my shell, which is surprisingly sensitive, since, despite having the appearance of armour, is in fact packed with nerve endings. I considered beating a retreat but judged the damage to be occurring at the upper echelons of me, and therefore estimated the pain would shortly ease off. Besides, what was achievement without some scars to show for one's trials? No pain, no gain, I had heard.

It did end quite quickly, well at least the making of the pain did. The channels scored into my body, an outward extension of my vertebrae essentially, continued to throb. Each throb was a reminder of every obstacle I had climbed, every challenge I had seen down so far, spurring me on somehow, like a warrior.

As I advanced into another wide, open space, the sensation underneath my feet reminded me of being in the ditch once more. It was squelchy. The mud was loose as if it very rarely experienced being dry. The plants in here were different, too. There was less grass and more clumps of thin, hollow reeds, stiff and upright. As the sky to my left was flooded with lilac light, glassy puddles winked at me. A number of pheasants were dotted about, ambling and flicking their long brown tails, nodding their red, wattled heads at one another.

I double-took. One of the pheasants was bright turquoise, a hue entirely out of place here. He stuck out like a sore thumb. The other pheasants did not seem unduly concerned about him and as I stared at him and observed the yellow rings around his eyes, I recognised him not to be a pheasant at all but, to my surprise, Hyacinth.

He spotted me and took to the air to fly the few feet between us and land clumsily before me.

'What ho!' he squawked. I was taken aback by the friendly tone of his greeting, since we had never had much to do with each other, but I did recall Digby purporting that he was a nice enough chap.

'What a pleasure! And a surprise!' I exclaimed.

'Yes, indeed,' Hyacinth replied. 'Much changes up at the Big House. Issa has gone, but she elected to leave me behind. The master of the house came across her pleasuring his son and his displeasure of this turn of events was such that she was unceremoniously ejected. Lucky for me, such was her indifference to my existence, following her initial excitement upon the receipt of me as a gift, that she, without a second thought, left me behind. Dave and Bob, generous souls they are, let me have the run of the place, content as they are that I will return. In fact, I have found Dave a fascinating conversationalist. He thinks he teeters on the brink of insanity but I have found breaking my vow of silence with the humankind rather rewarding.' I began to regret not speaking more to Hyacinth sooner; he was rather interesting, after all. Still, I had not had much opportunity whilst Issa had had him locked up indoors in a cage.

I was, of course, aware of the carryings-on between the wife and Sid, the philandering, womanising twin, but felt a rush of satisfaction that action had been taken to right some wrongs. Monogamy I questioned, but fidelity was surely merely a matter of good manners.

'That is good news,' I said. 'There is much to explore out here, as I have found.'

'I know!' he replied. 'Of course, it is not the jungle I am used to and I feel a little obvious, don't really blend in as I am sure you can see, but I am big enough for no-one to bother me here. The same, unfortunately, cannot be said for Digby.' I pushed the little green feather that had lain before me out of my mind and hoped he would not continue in the vein that I suspected he would. 'He was rather upset the last time I saw him, said that you two had had a bit of a row. Some say that when he was taken, he was looking for you; coming to find you to make the journey with you, to do what he could to ensure your safety. Unfortunately, the search drew him a little too close to the Spike.'

'He was always terrified of those peregrines,' I mumbled, feeling a loneliness I had not expected. Stella was gone; now Digby, too. Another part of me went pop.

'Yes, of course he was rather in awe of them - enamoured, some might describe it as. I think, although this is small comfort to us who knew and loved him, that he might feel it was an honourable death.' He tipped his head to one side rather like Digby often did whilst having a thought. 'Anyway,' he continued, sensible to my inability to comment on the matter, since all I wanted was this not to have happened, to have my friend back, here with me now, to tell him I was sorry for the argument we had had, to continue together on my journey with some jolliness. 'I suspect Digby would want you to know what had happened, since it was not his intention to leave you to adventure on your own. Circumstances somewhat beyond his control, you see.' I saw. Poor Digby did not stand a chance. 'He told me you were on your way to the sea, that you call the Glittering?'

'Yes,' I confirmed.

'Good work, then,' he said. 'The next field leads right down to it. You can almost smell it, can certainly hear the gulls from here.' I listened carefully and, yes, their eerie cries reached my ears. As if to entice me, one popped up above the cluster of oak trees that flanked the bottom edge of the marshland. 'You know,' said Hyacinth, 'more than anything, Digby was thrilled for you.'

Chapter Eighteen

I sloshed my way through the marsh. I liked Hyacinth, I did, but now was not the time to be making new friends; there would be time for that in the future. I had not known Digby long, but he had become a good friend instantly and I was sure I would meet characters like him again and hopefully they would be able to hang about a bit longer. I was on my journey now and I would likely make new friends along the way, or at its destination, my destiny, wherever and whatever that may be.

The marsh smelled faintly of rotten eggs. The water was frequently surfaced with creamy foam and bubbles lifted from the silt as I clambered through the little pools. Mud and decaying fibres of reeds and other vegetation stuck to my legs and underside.

I thought again about everything that had happened since the day the Palmers had arrived, shaking up everything that I knew. In my mind, a great sequence of events unfolded, dominoes laying against each other, triggering each others' downfall. There had been a lot of downfalls, beginning with the Arnolds'. Behind me there was some great tragedy, a concatenation of disastrous events, these untimely, unjustified deaths, some of which affected me more deeply than others. Truth is stranger than fiction, I thought. It seemed as if history was repeating itself, that I had witnessed a story retold. I was reminded of a story of a musician whose music touched the animals, tamed them. His love, his nymph, was taken from him by a snake. He went on a journey to find her, to save her; he opened locked doors to retrieve her. There was the tragedy of his failure and the rest of his life to be spent without his one true love.

I had no doubt that Ollie would not fall again. Not in the same way, anyway. The first cut is the deepest and to die in the full bloom of youth is to be eternally young. He and Stella barely knew each other. She hadn't had a chance to bore him, nag him, to show him her faults that would be there as they are in any creature. None of us are perfect; all of us are flawed. Some are better than others, depending on the value scale you subscribe to at any particular time. Does success beat happiness? Do good looks beat cleverness? What combination of qualities make a superior being? What beings are the fittest? Which will survive?

The sense of going over old ground, ancient stories, plots and tales having their own immortality overran me again. The Golden Age of Greece, came to me. The master storytellers. The Renaissance, thousands of years after then, hundreds of years before now, way before the birth of Bestwood, retold the stories in their glory, spreading their entertainment and truth to the masses.

The Golden Age of Greece, I thought, the image of Atlas, forever frozen in Bestwood's grounds, fixed to endure the heaven's openings as they railed against him; the world he would never see, never explore, firmly adhered to his ample shoulders. I hoped that I was on my own Odyssey, that Atlas bound somehow would show me my way.

I remembered Stella, one afternoon, reading to me, stoned and impassioned, epiphanies sparking in her brain as the evolutionary truths she studied locked like a jigsaw in her mind, eclipsing the banal idea of a single entity creating this small world we know in this huge universe. The absurdity of creationism, that theory that her mother implanted in her, and out of respect for her dead parent she had tried to believe although every part of her being denied its truth, possessed utter clarity as nonsense. That day she had let it go.

She had described how if you somehow concertinaed, squashed even the elapsed time that life has existed on this planet, some mind-boggling nearly four billion years since a bombardment of meteorites sparked the beginning of being into the primordial soup, into just a single one, just three hundred and sixty-five days, then my forebears, the earliest reptiles appeared around the start of December. And so began the steady creep of the tortoise.

The ancestors of man, however, didn't wake up until about six in the morning on New Year's Eve, the very last day of the year. The Golden Age of Greece, she said, whose stories and ambitions weighed so heavily on me now, that time, so significant to the humans, and dare I admit it, to all of us creatures since it was a great step forward in terms of what they term civilisation, although there are many who would see it as the dawn of destruction; The Golden Age of Greece, that was just thirty seconds before midnight.

Everything was so recent. Everything felt strangely near. I felt like everything revolved, orbited around me. I felt like I saw the truth. I felt like I was just in the first chapter of my story, my journey and that eons lay ahead of me, like sparkling treasures in my path, waiting to be discovered. It spurred me on.

As I approached the oak trees, tremendous in size, their roots gnarly and vast, their canopies thick, dark green with clusters of acorns ready to ripen to feed the squirrels during the slim months, I saw a mirror of water and a huge bank of dunes covered in a pale green grass that wafted in the wind.

The sky had turned from lilac to a pale lemon yellow now, and I advanced past the shaded, mossy area around the trees onto a field, the grass low and shorn, and went on towards the water.

Now I could smell the ozone in the air, and the faint odour of seaweed lying out on the beach. The grass faded away into marsh again but the marsh this time was salty, and instead of pheasants there were plovers flashing about, skipping at the water line, and a group of white herons, still as statues. I plodded through the marsh, samphire growing in little rubber spikes, springing up at me as I moved over them. Their miniature towers thinned out and damp sand mapped itself out between their shoots. I stopped to observe a small purple flower and on it there was a bug, sleeping, I thought. It was black, with red patches on its wings. It was mercurial and flamboyant and I recognised it to be a moth, a moth that liked the daytime. A little freak in nature. An exception to a rule. I warmed to him.

At the edge of the marsh, there was a sprinkling of little crabs, dead - death again - meaningless, their meaning being part of the cycle, their translucent corpses feeding microbes, rotting away to apparently nothing, their energy being endlessly recycled, finite, never dwindling, a changing constant.

Then there was just sand beneath my feet and I crossed a path between the dunes and the marsh, perpendicular to tracks left the day before, dogs' paws, bicycle tyres, gulls' feet. I crunched over a carpet of seashells, speckled pink and their pearliness shining through their dampness from the tide gone out or the dew, I was not sure.

I looked to the right and the water spread out. A small estuary flowed beyond the turn of the dunes. Small sailing boats sat patiently on the mud, waiting for the water to come and float them again, to bring them back to life.

I headed up into the dunes, the sand was dry and powdery here and I slipped, just the coarseness of the grasses giving me grip. The gulls were swirling about my head, crying in the morning. I stopped for a breath, near a ragwort, tall with deep green fronded leaves and topped with a yellow head of flowers, smiling at me, egging me on. It housed the larvae of the red and black day moth I had seen. Its children were flamboyant too, dressed in yellow and black stripes, steadily stripping the plant for their future of flying.

Onwards, upwards I clambered and as I reached the pinnacle of the dune, the Source peeped Her head out and cast my shadow long and over to my right, where it rippled in the grasses. There was a breeze up here coming off the water, which was there, right there, everything before me.

The tide was at its lowest and the water was far out. Sand glistened and beckoned me in the very early morning Source. The Glittering was flat as a millpond, the curve where it ended, or where it began, just a very small wave, a lap. I went to meet it.

Over to the right, I could see a stretch of land beyond a spit that raised itself like a whale's spine. The land silhouetted trees as though it was made of paper it had so little depth. Beyond that, more directly ahead, there was, I thought, more land, but it was shrouded in mist like some kind of Avalon. I wondered if I would make more sense of it if I managed to be nearer.

I shuffled down the slope, skidding and sliding, coming to a stop in the shingle at the base of the dunes.

I looked to my left and saw the beach houses standing sentry in the dawn, its light illuminating their muted colours, making them glow like the sky, the sand, the water. I was no longer interested in the beach houses. I could hear the mysterious lands across the water beckoning me now. They were where I was headed.

I looked to my right and my shadow was three times the height of me in its length, exaggerating my dome as if it were reflected in a fairground mirror.

I laughed at the thought of me looking like that and stopped when, beyond it, I saw the burned out black embers of a bonfire. Around it, two piles of clothes, humans I surmised, lolled in slumber. Clothing and blankets swaddled them but a mass of blonde curls, knotted and matted in the coastal breezes, caught my eye and recognition.

A gull shrieked as a current of air gamely whipped it from its path in a new direction, two bright blue eyes opened up and a hand swept the locks out of her line of vision.

Hannah, I breathed. I was undone. So close to completing this mission, so close to beginning my new chapter. But, with the merest shake of her head, her eyes closed again and I moved on, letting the sandman bring her her dreams.

As I walked, the sand changed from a dry powder that the early morning breeze puffed over me, layering on top of the marsh mud I had collected. I felt it gathering in the wrinkles of my neck. Then it became spongy so that I left deep tread marks as I moved forward. I was not worried about leaving a trail now. Not only had I reached my goal, the tide was surely on its way in and would cover my tracks. An oak leaf, unseasonably brown and dry and far away from home, like me, was stuck to the sand.

Nearer the water's edge, the sand became deeply and roundly pitted, like I imagined the surface of the moon might be. Seaweeds, flat green glossy sheets, loosely folded, and sprays of red featheriness, lay about languorously. Seawater hung about in the holes and I tried to pick a path through the maze to the water's edge, but soon decided to trample through the waters and up and down the sides of the landscape. Tiny fish flashed about in the pools and worms had left their casts like miniature sand castles. There were the carcasses of razor clams, and charcoal coloured mussels, and creamy brown whelks and cockles. Tiny crabs floated and scuttled about here. It teemed with life.

Finally, I reached the place where the water stroked the shore. The rest of my life swam about in front of my eyes. I waded right in.

Find out more about Helen and her writing at www.helenjbeal.com.

You can add Herbert as a friend at www.facebook.com/herbert.trimble